FOREIGN
SEED

"*Foreign Seed*, with its subtle, subterranean *Heart of Darkness* rumblings, is one of the most satisfying novels I've read in a long time. I got completely and gratefully lost in its rich setting and memorable characters. You will, too."

—RICHARD RUSSO, AUTHOR OF *SOMEBODY'S FOOL*

"*Foreign Seed* is an ambitious novel about a cautious man. It's 1918 and Samuel Sokobin, the new American vice-consul in Nanking, China, lives in a stressful milieu of casual anti-Semitism from his colleagues and his own ignorance of the Chinese world. In order to succeed, he tries to subvert his Jewish identity and present a bland, anonymous self. Then Sobokin is assigned to find an explorer who has drowned the Yangtze River—or perhaps has been murdered. Alsup handles the fascinating complications of *Foreign Seed* beautifully, pulling the reader through Sobokin's fears to his triumphant growth."

—LAURA FURMAN, AUTHOR AND FORMER SERIES EDITOR OF THE O. HENRY PRIZE STORIES

"In Allison Alsup's stunning debut novel, *Foreign Seed*, American Vice Consul Samual Sokobin's search for a missing explorer forces him to come to terms with the probable death of his brother, an MIA WWI fighter pilot. Sokobin ultimately finds comfort and wisdom in the most unlikely places and fortitude in his abandoned Jewish faith. With soul, grace, and psychological savvy,

Alsup infuses hope into this tale of uncertainty and grief. *Foreign Seed* is an elegantly constructed novel of our time, one that will stay with me for a long while."

—MICHELLE BRAFMAN, AUTHOR OF *WASHING THE DEAD* AND *SWIMMING WITH GHOSTS*

"Alsup has produced the perfect book. It is beautifully written. The characters are maddeningly interesting. She explores issues of the time with a persistent whisper. And it revolves around the man who sent the Meyer lemon to America. The barest thread of a connection anchors the entire book in her astonishing imagination. It was a delicious read that I did not want to end."

—LIZ WILLIAMS, AUTHOR OF *NANA'S CREOLE ITALIAN TABLE*, *LIFT YOUR SPIRITS*, AND *NEW ORLEANS: A FOOD BIOGRAPHY*, AND *TIP OF THE TONGUE* PODCAST

"Allison Alsup's deftly propulsive debut illustrates the profound, rippling impact of even the smallest gestures and revelations—and how empathy transcends language and customs. What begins as a missing person's case shifts into a moving journey of one man's reckoning with grief, loss, and personal fallibility. Evocative and elegiac, *Foreign Seed* casts a spell of quiet wonderment."

—CHIN-SUN LEE, AUTHOR OF *UPCOUNTRY*

"In a narrative that relies less on the facts of the historical events that inspired the author than it does on the perennial human quest to stay longest with our most unanswerable questions, Allison Alsup creates the story of one man's reckoning with history and himself. Alsup's Sokobin embarks on a sojourn that is rooted in his physical movement up the Yangtze River, though it is the way that journey forces him to traverse his own psyche that takes over. A read that will deliver a satisfying resolution for fans of fast-paced historical fiction."

—RU FREEMAN, AUTHOR OF *BON COURAGE: ESSAYS ON INHERITANCE, CITIZENSHIP, AND A CREATIVE LIFE*

FOREIGN SEED

FOREIGN SEED

A NOVEL

ALLISON ALSUP

KEYLIGHT
BOOKS
AN IMPRINT
OF TURNER
PUBLISHING

KEYLIGHT BOOKS
AN IMPRINT OF TURNER PUBLISHING COMPANY
Nashville, Tennessee
www.turnerpublishing.com

Foreign Seed

Cover and book design by William Ruoto
Map by Alexis Seabrook

Library of Congress Cataloging-in-Publication Data
Names: Alsup, Allison, 1970- author.
Title: Foreign seed / Allison Alsup.
Description: First edition. | Nashville, Tennessee : Keylight Books, an
  imprint of Turner Publishing Comapny, [2024]
Identifiers: LCCN 2022055504 (print) | LCCN 2022055505 (ebook) |
ISBN
  9781684429967 (hardcover) | ISBN 9781684429974 (paperback) | ISBN
  9781684429981 (epub)
Subjects: LCSH: Americans—China—Fiction. |
  China—History—1912-1938--Fiction. | LCGFT: Thrillers (Fiction) |
  Historical fiction. | Novels.
Classification: LCC PS3601.L697 F67 2024 (print) | LCC PS3601.L697
  (ebook) | DDC 813/.6—dc23/eng/20230210
LC record available at https://lccn.loc.gov/2022055504
LC ebook record available at https://lccn.loc.gov/2022055505

Printed in Canada

With loving gratitude to my parents:
my mother, who taught me to grow gardens,
and my father, who pushed me to climb mountains.

A NOTE FROM THE AUTHOR

THIS NOVEL IS SET DURING COLONIAL-ERA CHINA. As such, it contains views and terms reflective of that time and which some readers may rightfully find offensive. While I have done my best to limit such triggering references, to totally eradicate them from this work would misrepresent the era. More importantly, their exclusion would be to whitewash the experiences of those who not only endured daily discrimination but who thrived despite it.

Et maintenant, au cœur de la nuit, comme un veilleur, il découvre que la nuit montre l'homme: ces appels, ces lumières, cette inquiétude. Cette simple étoile dans l'ombre: l'isolement d'une maison. L'une s'éteint: c'est une maison qui se ferme sur son amour.
    —from *Vol de nuit (Night Flight)*, Antoine de Saint-Exupéry, 1931.

And now, in the heart of the night, like a watchman, he discovers that the night shows mankind: its calls, its lights, its worries. This single star in the shadow: the isolation of a house. One of them goes out: a house that closes itself on its love.

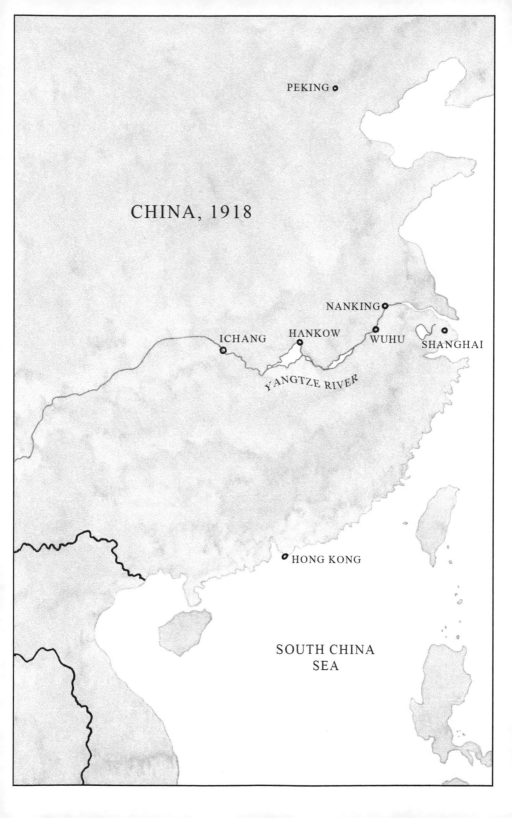

PART I

CHAPTER 1

Nanking, China
Thursday, June 5, 1918

By the time Sokobin receives the Consul General's wire, the American explorer has been missing some four days, and the affair is already well muddled. From what Sokobin can gather, Frank Meyer, forty-two, was last seen aboard the SS *Feng Yang Maru*, just before midnight on June 1. According to the passenger manifest, Meyer and his Chinese boy boarded the steamer with the intention of disembarking at Shanghai. But the following morning, the captain declared Meyer missing, most likely having gone overboard late the night before near the industrial city of Wuhu—some two hundred miles from the coast and sixty miles from Vice-Consul Sokobin's office in Nanking. The SS *Feng Yang Maru* docked in Shanghai yesterday, where the American staff has been at work inspecting the ship and interviewing the crew; the dossier is to arrive sometime tomorrow.

In the interim Sokobin is to make preparations to head upriver to Wuhu where, as the nearest American officer of rank, he is to organize the search for Meyer. Or what remains of him. *Spare no effort in ascertaining Mr. Meyer's whereabouts*, the Consul General's message concludes. *Leave no stone unturned.*

Sokobin stares at the paper, willing the words to evaporate. There's no saying how long the search will take, if he can even find Meyer at all. After four days, the missing man could be anywhere. The river is vast, and a body in the water leaves no trail, no trace, save itself. Nor is Sokobin particularly keen on the idea of coming up empty-handed on his first major file as vice-consul. Failure straight out of the gate. Sokobin rereads the lengthy wire, looking for any concession to the obvious—that the missing man has drowned in the Yangtze—but finds none. As if after years of trekking through China's backwaters, the rough-and-tumble explorer has somehow managed to lose himself aboard a steamship.

Of course, there's a chance, albeit small, Meyer is still alive. After seven years in-country, Sokobin has gleaned that not every American who disappears wishes to be found. China readily obliges the man intent on losing himself in any number of ways: gambling, opium, alcohol, salacious prostitutes, violent entanglements. Sokobin was privy to a dozen such cases while posted to Shanghai. Usually, the missing man turned up within a few days, still very much alive and stinking of whiskey and with all the explanation needed etched across his unshaven face.

If Sokobin is lucky, Meyer will prove one of these. But it's a stretch. Meyer disappeared from a passenger boat, not some back-alley den or brothel. And having once met the man, Sokobin would hardly count him among the ranks of the reckless or dissolute. Meyer's reputation as a rugged explorer of the remote Chinese interior precedes him, and his expeditions on behalf of the United States Department of Agriculture have been notable enough to make the international papers. Sokobin has seen the photographs: Meyer in lean profile, one boot perched on a snow-capped mountaintop or fording a rushing river while a crew of porters trails behind. Not exactly the type to throw years of hard-earned research away on easy temptation or vice. No, Sokobin thinks, had Meyer been given to excessive risk, he would have certainly met his end falling off a cliff or at the blade of bandits years ago. Indeed, only an exceptionally aware and calculating man could have lasted this long in China's backwaters.

Rather Sokobin's instincts are already whispering that it's the rarer, trickier kind of case at work here, the slippery sort that never gets closed, only shuffled down the stack and eventually stuffed in the file cabinet. The sort of case whose causes no one, not even the missing themselves, could ever put a name to. Sokobin has been witness to a few such cases, and while he's never considered himself the morbid or superstitious type, he knows this to be true: men hope to outrun all sorts of dark beasts when they come East, only to wake one day and find their monsters still scuttling about the dank holds of their minds.

He lifts the scrimshaw paperweight at the edge of his desk, adding the Consul General's wire to the pile, and runs his fingers over the polished ivory. A tic, he knows, but the simple act helps sort his thoughts. Despite the heat, the paperweight somehow always manages to remain cool to the touch. Its etched top depicts a typical Chinese pastoral: a sampan floating past a tree-topped cliff and a cluster of V-shaped slits meant to imply a flock of birds. His college mentor, Everton, gave him the scrimshaw as a graduation gift years ago. Sokobin can still hear the professor's dry Connecticut clip slicing the classroom's stale air, the sharp tap of his chalk on the slate.

Mark my words, gentlemen. China is very old and full of ghosts.

Sokobin reaches for his handkerchief, pressing it to his forehead. The Meyer case is only a few minutes old; even so, he can already feel it pushing down on his shoulders. He thinks of the package of Chesterfields waiting in his bottom desk drawer but pushes away the thought. *No*, he thinks. *Not yet.*

The fan groans overhead, stirring the damp air and making the Consul's cable flutter like a trapped moth beneath the scrimshaw. Among the stack are the week's memoranda from Peking and Shanghai. Of late, the news is rarely good: missionaries kidnapped, mail boats captured, scattered skirmishes between more military factions than anyone can keep track of. And in the past few days, intelligence of yet another province plotting to break away. At times it's hard to know who's in charge of the country—

the Republicans in Peking or the local rebel warlords. It's been six years since the Dragon Throne toppled nearly overnight, and yet nothing solid has surfaced to fill the imperial void. So far, Nanking to the coast at Shanghai has held firm, but further inland, the seams are badly frayed. Bit by bit, the country is rupturing. Chaos. Civil war. Sokobin sees them coming. If only Britain and the States weren't entrenched in the conflict in Europe, the West might help to restore some order. But as of now, there's nothing to spare, save a few American gunships. From where Sokobin sits, it looks like China's one shot at democracy may have expired before it even began.

And now Meyer.

He swivels toward the room's singular window, only to remember that the secretary, Miss Petrie, has already closed the curtains against the afternoon sun. The heavy fabric glows orange. Summer is close, hovering. Despite the heat, he tugs open the drapes and squints into the glare. Beyond the glass, the Yangtze stretches into turbid infinity. The river. One way or another, everything here seems to come back to it.

He tracks a steamer inching across the panes. The boat's stacks send up a thick black cloud, and again he thinks of the cigarettes waiting in the bottom drawer. The smoking is a recent development—one that's already found a much firmer hold than Sokobin would care to admit—and he tells himself to hold off, if only to prove he can. So far, he's avoided indulging in front of the staff. Not that Miss Petrie or Mr. Windham, the junior clerk, would take issue. And the senior clerk, Mr. Brundage, must inhale a dozen cigarettes a day. Even so, Sokobin doesn't like sharing the act. The Chesterfields are private, a ritual for him alone.

He can feel himself delaying on Meyer, the self-doubt creeping in. But there's no getting around a direct order from the Consul General. If Sokobin's going to get himself upriver to Wuhu by tomorrow night, he needs to set things in motion now. He considers logistics, most pressingly the need for an interpreter. His own Mandarin is passable when it comes to official functions; the myriad local dialects, however, continue to elude him. Assuming Meyer doesn't turn up by tomorrow evening, he'll need help with hiring a crew to comb the water. Sokobin pushes the image away before it can take shape.

He swivels back toward his desk, calling for the junior clerk through the open doorway. Windham quickly appears, his shirtsleeves rolled and cheeks flush. A lock of strawberry blond hair has come loose from the slicked fold and spirals over his smooth brow. The clerk originally hails from farm country, somewhere in Indiana or Illinois. Sokobin can never remember which.

"Sir?"

"You haven't received word from any of the patrol stations about someone pulling a white body from the river?"

"No, sir."

"Well, send dispatches to all the patrol stations between here and Wuhu just to be sure. Otherwise, it looks like I'll need to head up there tomorrow evening."

"It this about the wire that just came in?"

"Yes. Frank Meyer, the explorer. He's with Agriculture."

"I've heard the name, sir."

Sokobin nods. "It seems he went missing from a steamer a few days ago."

"Missing, sir? From a steamer?"

Sokobin knows what the clerk is thinking because he's been thinking the same thing from the moment he read the Consul General's cable. Meyer is dead, sunk into the river's depths, never to be found. But Sokobin isn't a clerk anymore. He's a man of rank; the official line is his to tow.

"That's correct, Mr. Windham. Missing until proven other-wise."

"Understood, sir." Windham pushes back the errant lock of hair. It's no use, and within seconds, the long curl has slipped down again.

"I'll need an interpreter—neither of the last two." Sokobin has had his fill of the Mandarins' pomp and fuss. There's no telling what he'll meet with upriver. What he needs is a modern man: calm, smart, forward-thinking. Provided one can be found.

Windham purses his lips. "I believe there's only one other approved interpreter on the list, sir. A Mr. Lin."

"Do you know him?"

"No, sir. But his CV should be in the files."

"Bring it here then. He can't be any worse than the others. Meanwhile, see if he's available."

"Will do, sir. How long should I tell him you expect to be gone?"

Sokobin exhales. Of course, there's no way to know. "A few days, maybe more. Explain that I'm waiting on the dossier to come from the Shanghai office tomorrow afternoon. We'll be leaving soon after it arrives, assuming Meyer doesn't surface before then." Sokobin cringes at the word choice. Sloppy.

"By train or boat?"

"Ferry. The last run, I expect. Reserve a pair of tickets, if you would."

"Yes, sir. Anything else?"

Sokobin runs his fingers over the scrimshaw. He's debating whether or not to contact Arthur Chase, his old classmate from college, now in Wuhu and working for Standard Oil of New York. Sokobin isn't sure he wants to drag Chase into the Meyer affair. In truth, he isn't sure he wants to see Chase at all. The last time they met with one another was four or five months ago—before Sokobin's transfer to Nanking in March. Still Arthur knows that stretch of river. And his house will be far more comfortable than any hotel.

"Sir?"

Windham taps his fingers against the threshold, not impatiently, Sokobin knows, only anxious to please. The clerk is terribly young, no more than twenty, with skin the color of an unbaked biscuit. Sokobin considers that he and Chase would have been no older when they first met in Everton's class. Somehow it seems impossible they were ever so new.

"Yes, one more item," Sokobin says. "Wire my friend Arthur Chase. See if he can put us up a few nights. Miss Petrie has the address. That's all for now, thank you."

Windham withdraws. Sokobin runs his fingers over the paperweight, its tiny sampan forever adrift. It's been nearly three years since Everton passed, dropped by a stroke while raking leaves from his lawn. If not for Chase, the years at university, even Manhattan itself, would seem little more than a dream.

Once more his eyes fall to the bottom drawer. He pictures the cigarettes within, the blue envelopes from his brother resting beneath. He can generally last until late afternoon, sometimes even until the office closes, before lighting up. But not today, not with the Meyer dossier waiting to land on his desk. He's about to reach for the handle of the drawer when he hears a cough. Windham is back in the doorway, his blue eyes blinking, his too long, rose-gold hair flopping down.

"Sorry to disturb, sir, but it's the messenger boy again with another wire."

"A second cable?"

"Yes, sir. It's dated earlier."

"Earlier?" Sokobin hears the exasperation in his own voice. "Why not just bring it with the first one?"

Windham nervously shifts between his feet, prompting the floorboards to groan. Sokobin is well aware that the clerk's right leg is several inches shorter than his left and that he must wear a specially outfitted shoe to make up the difference. If not for the leg, Windham would likely be rotting in some Picardy hellhole this very moment. The trenches are full of wide-eyed farm boys who've had to trade their pitchforks for rifles. And worse. *This putrid war*, Sokobin thinks, suddenly unable to tamp down the anger. *This putrid, Godforsaken war.*

"Well?"

"I can't say, sir. You should know the wire is dated from several days ago."

"Several days?" Sokobin breathes in, telling himself that the fault isn't his clerk's. "Never mind. Send him in."

The rumpled message is short—an attempt to notify the vice-consul's office of Meyer's disappearance as the SS *Feng Yang Maru* passed Nanking on its way to the coast. The sender is Inwood, the steamboat's captain, and on the list of those to be interviewed by the Shanghai Consulate today. Sokobin guesses from the name that Inwood is like a lot of Yangtze sailors, an old British sea dog who's hired himself out to the highest bidder. Sokobin reads the June 2 time stamp with considerable frustration. Had he received Inwood's wire on time, he could have anticipated the Consul General's cable and launched the search for Meyer from Nanking himself. As it is, Sokobin's lost some seventy-two hours he could have been out searching for the missing man.

When he presses the uniformed deliverer why it's taken three days to bring a message marked URGENT, the boy avoids his eye and stumbles about in broken English. It was the *other* boy, Sokobin pieces together, who failed to bring the wire. Still new and very young, this other one was too afraid to press the bell of the town's number one American.

Sokobin dismisses the deliverer and adds the telegram to the growing stack. He wipes his forehead, only to find his handkerchief hopelessly twisted with sweat. He tells himself it's just a bout of nerves, the thought of undertaking an important case alone. In Shanghai, before his promotion, there'd always been a team handling such matters. And he knew the city, at least as well as an American ever could. But he's only been in Nanking a matter of months. Upriver remains an even greater mystery. With the exception of Arthur's house in Wuhu, that deep in the interior might as well be uncharted territory.

"Sir?"

He looks up. Inexplicably the junior clerk is still in the doorway, seesawing between his uneven legs. Sokobin waits for Windham to speak, but the young man's lips remain shut, his usual grin replaced with a sober expression that looks far beyond his years.

"Is there something you wish to say, Mr. Windham?"

"Yes, sir. I was just wondering. I mean, this business with the missing man."

"What about it?"

"What I mean is . . . well, will you be all right going upriver, sir?"

If Sokobin's lungs weren't crying for a cigarette, he'd find the youth's fear touching. The truth is, he's grown quite fond of the junior clerk these past months. Nanking is Windham's first foreign post. Sokobin still remembers the keen ache of loneliness he felt during his initial months at university—and this with only a move from Newark to Manhattan. But Sokobin's patience has begun to slip with the sweat now sliding down his cheek. The missing man. The impending trip upriver. The late wire. It's all ambushed him and left him feeling on edge. At this point, what he wants more than anything is to shut the door and fill himself with smoke.

"No need to worry yourself on that front, Mr. Windham," he manages. "We haven't received any reports of fighting around Wuhu. Now if you don't mind, I have much to consider before heading out tomorrow."

"I didn't exactly mean that, sir."

Sokobin grips the arms of his chair. "Out with it, Mr. Windham."

"I was wondering if a missing persons case might not prove..." Windham clears his throat. "Difficult, sir. Considering all that's happened."

"All that's happened?"

At last Windham stills his restless feet and pushes back his hair. Concern briefly ripples across the clerk's forehead, and for a moment Sokobin sees the older man Windham will one day become. The thought nearly breaks his heart.

"I meant with your brother, sir."

Sokobin searches Windham's face, but the earnestness he finds there is unbearable, and he drops his eyes to the paperweight. In the blurry air, the small boat appears to move. "My personal affairs have nothing to do with this office or Mr. Meyer's case. I'm certain that I and the interpreter will manage."

"Of course, sir. I didn't mean to imply you wouldn't—"

"That will be all," Sokobin says, cutting him off. He can't have the clerk looking at him another minute. He knows it's irrational, but at times he swears Windham can read his thoughts. "Save emergencies, no more interruptions for the rest of the afternoon. Understood?"

"Yes, sir."

"Close the door behind you then."

The lock clicks, muffling the sound of Miss Petrie's typewriter. Sokobin stares at the brown slab as if assuring himself of the door's continued stillness. He sheds his jacket and pulls at his tie, hoping for some relief from the heat. When it doesn't come, he unbuttons his shirt collar and places it atop the fluttering stack of papers. He runs his palm over the scrimshaw's cool surface, willing his heart to slow, but it's no use. Windham's words continue to hang in the swollen air.

Considering all that's happened.

He tugs open the bottom drawer. The Chesterfields are there, exactly where Sokobin left them on the blue envelopes. He presses his finger to his own name spelled out in sepia ink across the topmost envelope, then shuts the drawer before the temptation to reach for his brother's letters can overtake him. He flicks open his lighter and draws down the searing air. Unlike the rest of his colleagues, he's avoided buying a silver case to house the cigarettes. Too permanent, he supposes, too flashy. Besides he's come to like the feel of the innovative packaging, its slick waterproofed coating. Chesterfield, his brother's brand. A cigarette for soldiers, for war.

As far as he knows, Ethan hadn't smoked before joining up. And yet each of the three letters in Sokobin's desk drawer is pierced by tiny burn holes where ash clearly dropped onto the onionskin. The Chesterfields were all the rage with the other flyers, his brother wrote from his base in France. Every airman got them as part of his rations. *A few drags and my fingers feel ready for the Boches.* It's how Sokobin still likes to picture Ethan: a bundle of muscle and sinew, his drawers loose and dog tags clinking as he rises from his cot. Sliding one firm leg after the other into a thick jumpsuit, making a side-lipped wisecrack, and laughing with the others as they snap flints. Ethan's clean, wide palms reaching for a leather trench coat and cap on the hook. A Chesterfield between his lips flashing orange against dawn's cool blue.

Sokobin inhales deeply, holding down the smoke, containing it. He shuts his eyes, willing the images to come. Eventually they do. Streaks of fire across the night sky. The strafed wing. White plumes streaming from the engine as the small plane hurtles like a bright meteor toward the black-colored sea. For a moment, it isn't Ethan in the cockpit, but Sokobin himself. He keeps the cigarette between his lips, wanting to feel the burn of its advancing heat. Every instinct tells him to break free from the cockpit, to push up and out into the wide darkness. But gravity's hold is too strong. He's pinned to the spinning dashboard, barely able to breathe, unable to tell up from down, the throttle shoved hard against his chest like a knife shaft. He waits for the inevitable: the nosedive, the spiraling free fall toward the water below. Fatal surrender. He hears the scream of the engine, only to realize the cry is his own.

Sokobin opens his eyes; within moments, the plane and dark sea are lost to the clip clop of the ceiling fan above. Other sounds seep through the door. The faint strike of Miss Petrie's typewriter keys, the slap of a file drawer. Voices. Mr. Brundage's Southern drawl. Laughter—its cruel irony.

The ash on his cigarette is curling, threatening to fall. A cracked teacup has been standing in for a tray, and he taps the Chesterfield against the rim, watching as the cinders collapse in a silent heap on the bottom. He doesn't know if the images in his head bear any resemblance to the truth or are simply the wild whims of his imagination. Nor can Sokobin say how they first came to him, only that he can't stop them from appearing. Nor does he want them to. The fact is, he knows nothing of his brother's whereabouts, if he is even still alive. It's been nearly three months since Ethan's plane failed to return from a night mission. Aside from the trio of letters in Sokobin's desk drawer and a single photograph, the images in his head are all he has of his brother's life as a soldier.

He runs his fingers over the paperweight, sees the cables and remembers. Meyer. Tomorrow he'll be headed upriver for who knows how long. He needs to get out of the office and clear his head. Take a walk, go to a teahouse, or simply go home to his rooms a few blocks away. But inertia has already set in, and he does none of these things. His legs feel heavy, his head thick with fog. Sokobin can't bear the thought of returning to the small apartment right now. He can't escape himself there with nothing or no one to distract him. And the windows don't overlook the water. The river. He can't say why, but he needs to see it.

He takes a long drag and tells himself, even as he slides out another Chesterfield from the package, that it will be his last.

AT HALF PAST FIVE, WINDHAM'S MUFFLED VOICE wishes him a good night through the door.

"Sorry to interrupt, sir, but we're about to head out for the day. Mr. Lin has sent word back that he's available. I have his résumé here."

Sokobin sees the slice of hovering shadow at the threshold. He knows the clerk is lingering on the other side, nervously shifting between his mismatched legs, and waiting for some sign of life within. The moment stretches into an eternity before Sokobin can manage the requisite response. Shame breaks across his chest like a wave. To have been finally promoted to vice-consul only to hide from his own staff like a frightened boy.

"Leave the résumé on your chair," Sokobin says. "I'll get it on my way out."

"Will do. Good night, sir."

The shadow recedes and Sokobin listens for the trio of footsteps he's come to recognize these past months: the junior clerk's loping footfalls, Mr. Brundage's heavy shuffle, the *click click* of Miss Petrie's boot heels as they file out the main door.

At last silence falls over the office. He feels hollow, his organs scooped out. Emptiness. Sokobin reaches for another cigarette. It frightens him to think of how much he craves it.

At dusk the air begins to cool, and he lifts the window sash, inviting the river's brine to drift inside. The electricity remains off, and eventually the office grows dim, almost tolerable. The sinking sun lights up the water like a channel of molten iron.

The strand below thrums with passing voices and rickshaws, the clang of cleavers. In Shanghai the docks around the consulate were swept clean of street vendors, but here in Nanking—dusty little Nanking—the smells stay thick and close: garlic, ginger, scallions, blistering chilies, frying fish, the loamy scents of tofu, mushrooms, and cabbage. He'll need to stop on his way back to his apartment—he hasn't thought to eat since receiving the Consul's cable before lunch.

By half past seven, his throat feels too flayed to continue. He dumps the ashes from the teacup into the waste bin and returns the remaining Chesterfields to the drawer. As always, the blue envelopes are there, their edges puckered with use. Three letters, the contents of which he could probably recite from memory. For weeks he'd held out hope another envelope might arrive, having been waylaid in the post or found among Ethan's effects after the fact. But none has ever appeared, and now the wish that one might seems as much a delusion as the idea that his brother might still be found.

The sun makes a brilliant last hurrah and drops below the horizon. Below his windowsill the lamp men are lifting their poles to hang lanterns along the cobbled bund. From afar, the effect is like a string of flickering pearls. Again, Everton's words sound in his head. *Mark my words, gentlemen. China is very old and full of ghosts.* At the time, Sokobin and his classmates brashly dismissed the pronouncement as romantic sentiment, as nothing more than an old man pining for the adventures of his youth. But what had any of them known of China then? Absolutely nothing. Now Sokobin wonders if his teacher's words hadn't revealed a singular, haunting truth.

He takes his jacket from the chair back, stuffing his tie and shirt collar into the pocket. There, under the scrimshaw from Everton, he catches sight of the cable from Captain Inwood and remembers. Meyer. He keeps letting himself forget. By tomorrow night, he and Lin will be far beyond the river's bend at Chase's house in Wuhu. The mere thought exhausts him.

Briefcase in hand, he casts a final glance over the disappearing river. Scattered lights from anchored boats dot the dark gleam, and he strains to make out the shadows among the roiling black waves. But of course, there's nothing, no one there, and he pulls the window down, the curtains shut.

CHAPTER 2

SOKOBIN MET MEYER ONLY ONCE, IN SHANGHAI THE year before last. It was the Fourth of July. The new consulate building had been complete only a few months at that point—the most expensive embassy in the world, they'd been told, and they were throwing a party to show it off.

The Consul General had already given his speech on the bund, the gunboat cannons fired, and the marching band dispersed. By then it was afternoon, and everyone was drinking upstairs in the large reception hall overlooking the river. The champagne had run out, and the punch turned heavy, cherry lemonade spiked with ever-increasing amounts of whiskey. Striped ribbons and carnations adorned each lapel: red for the men, white for the ladies. Sokobin himself wore a straw boater with a small flag tucked into the band. The CG had them made up custom for all the staff, but the hat didn't sit right on Sokobin's square head or his wiry hair, and he felt a bit absurd, like a failed dandy, wearing it.

The fans and windows couldn't keep up with the temperatures. Or the smells, which rose throughout the packed room like spices from a hot pan. He remembers the overbearing aftershaves of the import-export men, the slight stink of the deviled eggs and salmon paste left on the buffet. The big parties, with their incessant chatter, always drained him. The happiness felt clinging and desperate, the laughter shrill. Independence Day was the worst, even more than Christmas or Thanksgiving when piety, or at least its pretense, tempered behavior. Rather the Fourth only reminded them of how very far away they were from American soil and of the thinness of their ranks.

Especially that summer. The city hung in suspension with rumors of a Japanese invasion. No one was so naïve as to think the Chinese national army—or what was left of it—would come to the foreigners' rescue. Just days before, one of the secretaries had broken down at her typewriter, crying about starving to death in a prison camp. Sokobin had stood immobile on the edge of the carpet while the other ladies circled the sobbing woman, whispering and patting her back. He'd wanted to say something consoling, but the words had failed to appear. The terrible truth was that the scenario wasn't beyond the realm of possibility, and as he made his way across the crowded party, he had to push down the thought that this sordid end wasn't what awaited them all.

If he hadn't been up for promotion that autumn, he would have made his excuses and left early. Instead, he found himself putting on a good face and making the rounds—it was all part of the dance. He knew he was being observed, not in any way that would ever appear on his official record but one that would determine his prospects just the same. He understood his chances in the game, what was really meant when the higher-ups talked about wanting *the right type*. Having a Russian family name no one could pronounce was already a strike against him, possibly two. He wasn't from "good stock," like Arthur. As a Hebrew, there was no margin for error. And so he would do exactly as expected: mingle until the party's end and, come dark, help nudge the lingering sots out the door. At several points, he had to remind himself not to be among them. *Dignity and control at all times*, the CG had drilled into them at the pre-party meeting. Naturally, they were to avoid talk of the war in Europe, or any speculation about the United States joining the fight.

And so Sokobin was pacing himself, alternating rounds of punch with soda water, and wishing Arthur, ever the master at small talk, were there to part the waters. No matter how many drinks, no matter how tricky the conversation, Arthur Chase IV always managed to stay afloat. But Arthur wasn't there, having wired his regrets the evening before. *Sorry, pal. Pressing business in Wuhu.*

Sokobin drifted from one group to another, at times losing the thread of conversation as he searched the crowd for Meredith's face. He couldn't stop picturing the afternoons they'd spent in his room, the shadows from the shutters striping her face and neck. He recalled the imprint of her lips. The sensation was so strong, he was certain others must have seen the traces branded onto his flesh. The rest of the nurses from the mission clinic seemed to be making a point of keeping their backs to him. They'd hardly proved the sweet, tender things he'd expected. Instead, they were a steely, clannish bunch. He supposed they had to be, as unattached females, out here on their own. By this point, it had been a couple of weeks since the split, and Sokobin figured Meredith must have told them. It all seemed so tawdry now. The restaurant table, his cold, rehearsed excuses about having "to let things go in order to move forward," Meredith's blanched visage. And the coup de grâce itself: a parting slap in full view of the place. He'd been lucky no one he knew had been there to witness it.

But those had just been words. They'd changed the circumstances between them, not his heart. Despite how it had ended, despite the fact that *he'd* been the one to end it, a part of him still hoped she'd show. If Meredith had walked into the hall right then, he would have needed only a single look to know if he still had some claim to her body. He couldn't say what he'd do if she actually did. Ask her to dance? Whisper he'd been a fool and beg forgiveness? Far more likely he'd play the coward and do nothing.

But of course, Meredith didn't show. It wasn't her style; and her absence only made him desire her all the more.

CLOUDS OF CIGARETTE SMOKE GATHERED LIKE THUN-derheads against the ceiling. Sokobin wasn't yet a smoker himself, and so when the orchestra took a break, he edged past the empty stage and the tuxedoed Chinese waiters toward the open windows. As he did, he spotted the explorer perched alone on the sill and looking terribly out of place. Meyer was the only man in the room without a necktie, and his reddish beard was in serious need of a trim. Sokobin recognized him from the newspapers. By that point, Meyer's expeditions had made him a bit of a known quantity about the consulate. From time to time, the office helped out by storing his plant specimens or forwarding them on to the Department of Agriculture in DC.

Sokobin introduced himself and they shook hands. Sokobin expected some looming figure, but the explorer was only slightly taller than himself. He was quite a few years older, likely forty or close to it, Sokobin guessed from the gray flecks in Meyer's hair. However, the fitness was immediately apparent: broad shoulders, heavily muscled shanks, a gut so flat it appeared concave. Meyer's face was deeply browned, save for a small pink patch on his nose where the skin was peeling away.

"I'm finishing an expedition," Meyer explained when Sokobin asked what had brought him to Shanghai. "Packing up and writing final reports before I sail for the States. Much easier in a hotel room than in the field."

"And have you been searching for any kind of plants in particular?" Sokobin asked.

"Useful species."

"Useful?"

"Mostly things people eat. But also building materials, shade trees. I work for a small office called Foreign Seed and Plant Introduction. We're tasked with finding species for possible cultivation on U.S. soil. As you've probably deduced, I'm the man for China."

"So, in other words, you're not looking for roses," Sokobin said.

Meyer grinned. "Right. No roses."

The explorer's English was grammatically perfect, too much to ever be native. And Sokobin detected a faint accent, a Scandinavian precision that hardened the edges of his words. He recalled the papers mentioning something about Meyer immigrating to the States as an adult.

"You're a botanist then."

The explorer sipped. His punch glass appeared far too small for his thick fingers. "In my experience, botanists tend to be university men, Mr. Sokobin. They prefer their plants dead and locked behind glass doors. My official title is *Agricultural Explorer.*"

Sokobin sensed he'd trespassed. He attempted to adjust his hat to no avail. He briefly considered excusing himself, but the smoke and the thought of facing the throngs kept him rooted at the window. "I assumed a degree would be necessary in your line of work."

Meyer frowned slightly as if tasting something sour. "I take it you completed university, Mr. Sokobin."

"Yes. I take it you did not, Mr. Meyer."

"I finished a single semester. *Endured* is perhaps a better word. The desks, sitting still, the other students . . . A man cannot hope to understand a species by memorizing Latin names or staring at a diagram in a textbook. A plant is not merely a thing, Mr. Sokobin. It is a living creature and must be experienced in its native habitat. Observed, touched, even tasted." Meyer rocked on his heels. Suddenly a smile spread across his face, revealing straight white teeth. For a moment, he appeared quite handsome. "More than anything," he said, "what is necessary in my line of work is a sturdy pair of shoes."

Sokobin looked down. Beneath his cuffed trousers, the explorer was indeed wearing trail boots. Both men laughed, and whatever tension existed between them seemed to drift out the open window. The straw boater was sliding again, and Sokobin took it off, fanning himself. The open air felt cool against his face. "I confess that I've never stopped to consider that a plant might not be from the place where it grows."

"Few do," Meyer said. "Take Holland's famous tulips, for instance. Everyone believes them to be Dutch. Or Irish potatoes that are anything but. They are transplants, taken from one place and given new life in another. No different than you or me, Mr. Sokobin."

Sokobin could hardly imagine having anything in common with the burnished man next to him. They were standing close now, in order to hear one another over the noise. Sokobin detected the faint smell of smoke from the explorer's shirt, not from cigarettes, but like charred wood from a campfire. The explorer intrigued him. Meyer was nearly a celebrity, and not in some toshy sort of way. Sokobin wondered what sort of man would leave everything behind in order to strike out for the wilds. He was reminded of his brother, Ethan, who'd sailed for South Africa the year before and was now flying supply planes there. Sokobin knew Ethan could have found similar work stateside, but his brother wouldn't hear of it. He was set on Africa. Sokobin suspected adventure alone wasn't enough to hold his brother, he needed real risk.

Sokobin lifted his glass, then, remembering to pace himself, lowered it without drinking. "Is it dangerous? Exploration, I mean?"

"It can be. Very much so."

Meyer said the current expedition, his third to China, had been particularly tough: some two and a half years, much of it spent navigating mountainous terrain in the northern provinces. There'd been a run-in with some guards on the border between the Kansu and Shensi provinces. Neither Meyer nor his assistant used sedan chairs, and so the soldiers hadn't believed they were real American officials. Instead, the guards saw the piled wagon and accused them of trying to smuggle opium. The charge was serious, Sokobin knew, a capital offense. The guards demanded to search the wagon, Meyer told him, then demanded the explorer and his assistant strip. A nasty fight ensued; insults that erupted into blows. If not for an intervening superior officer—the man spoke better English—who actually took the time to radio in their traveling papers, Meyer and his assistant might well have been marched to the wall and summarily shot.

Meyer shook his head. "Of course, there were other troubles, the usual encounters with bandits and porters that quit and made off with equipment in the night. Once there was a close call with a near avalanche. If not for my assistant, I'm not sure I would have made it down the mountains alive. Thankfully, he is a Dutchman like me. A man of his word, of hardy disposition, and much accustomed to the cold."

Sokobin thought the character assessment sounded much like how one might describe a resilient strain of turnips. "And how exactly is it that one becomes an explorer?"

"You wish to know if explorers are born this way or made from experience? Nature or nurture? Is that the question, Mr. Sokobin?"

Sokobin sipped, wishing his glass were twice as large. It *was* what he'd meant. He was thinking of his brother again. "Yes."

Meyer told him about growing up near the Amsterdam docks where his father worked as the harbor master. Sokobin was at pains to picture the rugged man in front of him as ever having been a naïve, bright-eyed boy. But of course, they all had been once.

"These were the old wooden ships, before steamers, understand," Meyer said. "Tall things with several masts. I would imagine where they were coming from, what treasures might lie below deck. Already I dreamed of crossing the water, you see. In school, my teachers scolded me for bobbing my knees under my desks."

Sokobin remembered the notes sent home from Ethan's teachers about his restlessness, the endless fidgeting. Their mother had wrung her hands; their father delivered stern sermons and, more than once, the belt. Even as a boy, Sokobin wondered how it was possible the same blood flowed through his brother's veins as his own. They were so different. Rules, patterns, straight answers; Sokobin liked their certainty. Eventually his teachers took notice. University, they whispered, would be his ticket across the river and out of Newark.

"My father had been a sailor himself," Meyer was saying. "Each night at supper, he told us stories of the places he'd seen: Zanzibar and Cape Horn, the Dutch East Indies. You can imagine the effect of such tales on an impressionable young boy. I am afraid I also read many cheap paperback books with clever heroes in white hats."

Sokobin sipped, recalling how on stormy nights, he had lit his lantern and Ethan would cross the thin channel of floor between their beds and slip beneath the covers. Sokobin quietly read aloud, not from the picture book of Moses' life as his parents would have wanted, but from the drugstore paperbacks hidden under his bed. It seemed impossible to think the contrived tales might have had any lasting effect. And yet, just the week before, Sokobin received a letter from South Africa, the first news he'd had from Ethan in months. In it, his brother described the view from his cockpit: waves of zebras, gazelles, water buffalo moving over the plains as if the very surface of the earth itself were in motion. *The man who has never flown above this earth does not know how it feels to be free from it. I would gladly trade ten years on the ground for one in the clouds.* The letter's eloquence had stunned Sokobin. The African skies seemed to have given his brother an ease of expression he'd never known in school.

Meyer exhaled. "So, in answer to your question, Mr. Sokobin, I suppose both. The seed was there from the start, but it was watered along the way."

"The seed?" Sokobin asked. He'd lost the thread again.

"Of exploration, of curiosity," Meyer said as if Sokobin should have already guessed. "Of adventure."

Sokobin nodded. He needed another drink, but the nearest tray boy was halfway across the room. "And passion?" he asked, thinking of his brother's words.

"Passion?" Meyer's forehead was now beaded with sweat. "Certainly, that too. But understand, Mr. Sokobin, exploration is not a choice for me. It is survival. Even a city as vast as your Shanghai will soon begin to feel like a cage. Only walking keeps the dark clouds at bay."

Sokobin didn't want to ask what Meyer meant by *dark clouds*. An unsettling intimacy had crept into the conversation. He paused, fanning his hat to wipe his face, hoping the explorer would take the hint and dab his own face. He didn't.

"But you must stop me from rambling on, Mr. Sokobin. These past weeks, I have been largely alone. When I get around others, I tend to overindulge in the talking."

"What about your assistant?"

"No longer. I'm afraid not every man shares my continued *passion*, as you say, for exploration."

At last, one of the waiters passed. Sokobin was due for soda but reached for another punch. Meyer did as well and suddenly both men had full glasses. A mistake, Sokobin thought. Again, he wished Chase were standing next to him, when it struck Sokobin how unlikely it was for Arthur to let business keep him from a party, especially on a holiday. Certainly, Standard Oil would have given everyone the day off. Far more plausible was some torrid love affair that would dissolve by the week's end and leave Arthur moping in his glass. For his part, Sokobin had never really confided about Meredith, neither the seriousness of the affair nor its ignominious end, only enough to keep Arthur from attempting to set him up with another of his company's secretaries.

"When I am in the field, I can almost forget there's a war," Meyer said, looking out the window at the gunboat on the pier below. "But now that I am back in Shanghai, the war is everywhere—the papers, the cafés, the theaters." Creases fanned from the corners of his lids, and Sokobin sensed a profound weariness lurking beneath the resilient exterior.

Sokobin kept his response to a nod, remembering the CG's directive. But the silence only seemed to encourage Meyer to fill the void. He described a newsreel he'd seen in one of local theaters: a band of English soldiers charging up a forested slope. One of the men had suddenly recoiled and fallen to the ground, never to move again. Sokobin sipped, holding his tongue. The war in Europe had ceased to be small, flat photographs on newsprint but flickered larger than life. Sokobin had seen a few of the newsreels with Meredith. He would have thought nursing would have inured her to the sight of suffering. But it hadn't. He remembered her hands searching for his, the surprising force of her grip, the sobs all around them in the dark theater.

"Cut down in the prime of his life," Meyer said, as if Sokobin had never heard of the tolls of war. "And yet the camera continued to roll like nothing had happened. None of the other soldiers stopped to comfort their dying comrade. Who can say how many of them were killed within the next five minutes?"

At last Meyer withdrew a handkerchief from his trouser pocket and wiped his wet forehead. "You will no doubt think me ungrateful for saying so at a party such as this, Mr. Sokobin, but if we are to progress as a species, we must recognize our common interests. What is needed is not a United States of America, but a United States of the World."

Sokobin was disappointed. These were the kinds of slogans regularly bandied about in the papers. He found Meyer's stance naïve, somehow all the more so coming from a man who saw fit to wear trail boots to a cocktail party. The explorer talked as if men were like the plants he collected, subject only to the rational laws of evolution. But humans, Sokobin knew, were a different sort of species. A quick tour of Shanghai's dice halls and pipe dens on any given night revealed the sordid truth: let passion hold sway and it quickly made a reckless gambler of any man. It wasn't cognition, adaptation, or even language that separated humans from other life forms as most believed. It was self-destruction. Intentional or not. Sudden or slow.

"You are an idealist, Mr. Meyer," he said at last.

"I must disagree, Mr. Sokobin. I believe peace the only practical solution, indeed our only chance for survival."

Sokobin looked down to once again find his glass empty. Despite snubbing their banter all afternoon, he found himself longing to return to the chattering ranks. The explorer was wearing on his nerves. Sokobin attempted to resettle the ridiculous boater on his head for the millionth time, but no matter the angle, the hat felt askew, and he had to restrain himself from throwing it out the window.

"I have not seen my family since before the war began." Meyer was looking at the river again, his eyes on the gunship. "My father is nearly seventy now, his health failing. I must face the fact that I may never see him again in this life."

It was true. Many boats, even those sailing under a neutral

flag, were dropping anchor for the remainder of the conflict. Sokobin knew it was only about to get worse. Recent intelligence had revealed the Germans intended to expand their *untersee* attacks into a full-scale naval war. In the papers, President Wilson continued to echo the separatist position, urging *Peace at any cost*. But Sokobin suspected the official line was little more than that. It was only a matter of time before the States became ensnared, one way or another.

"Tiny, flat Holland," Meyer said, wincing as if the country lay just visible on the other side of the river. His eyes were ringed with red, rendering the irises fiercely blue. "As a boy all I ever wanted was to escape. Now I fear I may never make it back."

Sokobin pressed his lips together, not wanting to mention the three years since he'd seen his mother and brother. And Everton. Never again would he see the man whose stories of the Orient had lured him here. It was Arthur who'd heard first. Sokobin didn't know why it bothered him that Chase had been the one to tell him of Everton's passing and not the other way around. But it did bother him. Very much.

Across the room, the orchestra was taking up their gleaming instruments. The bandleader raised his hands, and the first notes blared forth—no longer the stayed waltzes from earlier but a jangly, ragtime number. Sokobin was surprised the CG had signed off on the set list, but the man himself stood clapping at the edge of the crowd, his cheeks flush with whiskey. Within seconds, the dance floor was a swell of bobbing heads and flinging arms. It was nearing sunset, and the alcohol was taking over.

Several of the nurses from the clinic climbed to the front of the stage where they formed a row and began kicking up their skirts like dance hall girls. In their shining faces Sokobin saw a joyful abandon that felt as foreign to him as China itself. He'd been wrong to break it off with Meredith; he understood that now. Even if the promotion came through in the fall, they could have had more time—six months, possibly a year before he'd be re-assigned—long enough to know if they could really make a go of it. Why had he denied himself—them—that happiness? But of course, he knew. Again, he saw the backlit shutters, Meredith's unpinned hair across his chest. Sokobin had thought he could keep whatever existed between them contained, a diversion. Instead, he'd let things go too far, let his emotions pull him under. Those afternoons he would have gladly drowned in desire.

"But you are living your dream, Mr. Meyer. Isn't that right?" Sokobin asked, impatiently fanning himself with his hat. The little flag was missing from the band; he must have lost it somewhere in the crowd.

"Yes, although even dreams come with a price, Mr. Sokobin. They are tricky, many-headed beasts and take long to die. Sometimes too long."

Sokobin lifted his glass, only to remember it was empty, and waved down the nearest server. The man wove toward them, his silver tray held aloft in his gloved hand. Sokobin was overdue for a soda, but the punch glasses glittered. *To hell with dignity and control*, he thought. It was a party after all, and he reached for his third drink in a row.

Meyer also reached. Sokobin was relieved to see the explorer's eyes were clear again, the red gone. As soon as they clinked glasses, Sokobin could move on.

"To peace," Meyer said.

"To peace," Sokobin echoed. "At any cost."

CHAPTER 3

Friday, June 6

THE OFFICE IS EMPTY. QUIET. HE'S COME IN BEFORE THE others, hoping to catch up on the correspondence he let slip in the wake of the Meyer cables yesterday. It's well before nine, too early to smoke. He bought a couple of extra packages on his way in this morning—insurance in the event he can't find a supply of Chesterfields upriver. The first two kiosks were sold out, and he'd had to walk farther down the bund before finding one stocked with the brand. An advertisement glued to the side of the stand stopped him in his tracks. *In the sea, the field, the air. Chesterfield, what a smoke!* The blue-eyed, freckled sailor looked nothing like his brother, yet something about the eyes, their far-away gleam and want, had made Sokobin think of Ethan. As if the horizon held only possibility and adventure, never death.

He opens the bottom drawer. The photograph's outline rises from the top envelope, making a faint seam across the thin paper. He hesitates, then bends and slides it out. Ethan wears tall lace-up boots, a long leather trench coat with a thick sheep's fleece collar, a white scarf tucked about the neck. Sokobin stares at the bronzed face, so close to his own, yet somehow always the more handsome in its proportions: the jaw tighter, the brow wider, the dark eyes bright as burning coals. His brother offers a half-sided smile, a slice of teeth, a slight gap between the first two. An escaped clump of curled hair from his skullcap lifts with the breeze. A lit cigarette rests between his thumb and forefinger.

His brother, the flyer. The soldier.

A scar cuts across Ethan's temple, causing a break in his right eyebrow. Sokobin has no idea how it came to be. Even through the numbing filter of the lens, he can see how his brother's skin, once pore-less and smooth, had thickened in the years they'd spent apart. His cheeks had changed too. At some point, the bones had shifted like rocks beneath the soil, leaving a sharpness Sokobin never witnessed firsthand. The picture was taken last year, when Ethan was still twenty-eight; already his brother's face bore the traces of the decades meant to come: creases at the corners of the eyes, faint lines across the forehead. The photograph, the first Sokobin received in several years, came as a shock. He still wanted to think of his brother as no more than a daring youth playing with the world, as if time would have passed them both by. But the soldier in the photograph was far from a boy. War had quickly, irrevocably aged his brother. In Sokobin's absence, Ethan had become a man, a seasoned one at that—one Sokobin had never met and now feared he never would.

A spotted sheep dog sits on its haunches at his brother's feet. The dog is a stray named Ace, Sokobin gathers from the description on the back, that the squadron took in and made their mascot. Behind them, a stilled propeller spans the frame. The plane is a Nieuport 28, French made, as the Americans have no fighters. It's nothing like the aerial tank Sokobin envisioned, but little more than a kite with wings. The 94th Aero Squadron's insignia—a stars and stripes Uncle Sam top hat—has been painted on the side. They'd dubbed themselves the Hat in the Ring Gang.

Beneath the aircraft, the flat ground is reduced to a wintery paste of mud and grass. In the distance, a set of square buildings masks the horizon; to their left, a blurred copse of leafless trees bends from an invisible wind. Time and time again, he's returned to the photograph in the hopes that the background might have come into focus, or another detail might emerge. But the image remains as elusive as before, and he returns it to its envelope and closes the drawer.

He slides a Chesterfield from the pack. Cracking his lighter, he draws the smoke deep into his lungs, then reaches for the scrimshaw. He sorts the communiqués into two piles: those requiring his personal attention and those he can safely pass on to the senior clerk, Mr. Brundage, whose prose, while quite competent, tends to be overly laced with honeyed Southern flourishes. He taps a gray slug of ash into the cracked teacup, then begins with the simplest items, thank-you notes and regrets that he cannot attend yet another edifying lecture at the local Presbyterian college. He's been avoiding the Nanking social rounds since arriving in town—teas, choir recitals, Sunday picnics, and boating trips. He makes quick work of the bunch before turning to the weightier matters of budgets, intelligence reports, and official memoranda from Peking.

He is well into the task when a knock at the door startles him, leaving a smear of ink on the page. Sokobin looks up, momentarily unable to identify the figure at the threshold. But of course, it's Windham, with his locks flopping down. The clerk wears a jaunty striped vest that looks summery and new. Tucked under his arm is a thick manila envelope.

"Morning, sir."

Embarrassed to have been caught unawares, Sokobin quickly stubs out his cigarette. His pocket watch reads 9:35. He didn't register the others coming in.

"The dossier from Shanghai?" he asks, pointing at the envelope under Windham's arm.

"Yes, sir."

"Let's have it then." The package lands on his desk like a brick. Sokobin wasn't expecting the file before mid-afternoon. "I take it there's been no word back from the patrol stations about a body?"

"No, sir. At least no Westerners."

Sokobin leans back, sending up a groan from his chair springs. He supposes he'd been hoping for a miracle, but there can be no avoiding the trip upriver now. The Meyer case has fallen squarely on his shoulders. The bottom desk drawer is still slightly ajar. Suddenly he resents the thin blue presence of the letters and shoves the drawer shut with his shoe.

"Everything settled with Mr. Lin?" Sokobin asks. He has yet to open the file containing the résumé the clerk left for him yesterday.

"Yes, sir." Windham reaches into his vest pocket and withdraws two tickets, setting them on top of the manila envelope. "For the ferry. The last boat leaves at six. Mr. Lin will meet you at the gangplank at five thirty."

Sokobin nods. "Well done, Mr. Windham."

"My pleasure, sir," the clerk says, pushing back his hair. "Would you like me to pull a Form 192 from the files?"

Windham's tone is so nonchalant that it takes Sokobin a moment to register the question. As if the clerk were asking whether the vice-consul took milk with his tea. The inquiry is anything but innocent, however, and Sokobin gleans the insinuation. *Form No. 192: Report on the Death of An American Citizen.* The clerk wants to know if Sokobin thinks Meyer is dead. After five days of going missing from a boat, there can be no other logical conclusion. And yet Sokobin's chest twists at the thought of bringing the form upriver, as if in simply carrying a sheet of paper, he might condemn the missing man to a premature end.

"Duty requires we remain hopeful, Mr. Windham. One does not simply hand over the living to the dead without proof." The lines sound vaguely familiar, of the polished sort the Consul General himself might proffer, so much so that Sokobin wonders if he's stolen them.

"Right, sir. About yesterday," he says, taking a deep breath. "I'd like to apologize."

Sokobin purses his lips. "Don't worry yourself over it, Mr. Windham."

"I spoke out of turn, sir. It wasn't my place to question. I just meant . . ."

"Thank you," Sokobin says, cutting him off, "but no need." He holds up a hand, only to find his fingers quivering like a palsied old man. He grasps the teapot to still them and pushes it across the desk.

"Please have Miss Petrie bring some tea. Cool, not hot. I have much to go over before catching the boat."

"Of course, sir. Anything else?"

Sokobin can tell the clerk is doing his best to appear unruffled. But Windham is far too young to have developed a thick veneer. Keep that clean surface, Sokobin wants to tell him. Hold on to it as long as you can.

"There is one final item," Sokobin says, hoping to avoid ending on a sour note. He attempts to summon an avuncular smile. "Perhaps see about a haircut while I'm gone? *The man in the field can't afford to let himself . . .*"

"*. . . go slack on the details,*" Windham says, finishing the line from page one of the personnel manual. For some reason, the slight scolding seems to pick up the clerk's spirits, and he grins, offering a mock salute before pivoting on his good leg and disappearing with the teapot into the front room.

Sokobin eyes the manila envelope at the center of his desk. He wonders how it's possible Shanghai has managed to amass so many pages in so little time. He rises and passes a sheaf of correspondence to Mr. Brundage in the front room as he waits for Miss Petrie to prepare the tea. Once he gets started on the file, he'll want to sift through its contents without interruption.

Miss Petrie appears, smelling faintly of peppermint. Her chestnut and silver hair has been neatly pinned, as always, into a high, heavy knot. At their small outpost, she has served Uncle

Sam the longest, though for exactly how many years Sokobin can't say. According to Mr. Brundage, Miss Petrie is a "true-blue colonial," born in-country to missionary parents, and having visited the States only twice in her life. As far as Sokobin knows, she has never married. So far, the secretary has given him no cause for complaint. He finds her to be an exceptionally tidy woman with faultless penmanship.

"It's still a bit warm, Vice-Consul. You may want to wait a few minutes." She sets down a small tray next to the scrimshaw. As she informed him his first week, she is not one for water rings. "You'll surely ruin your eyes in this dark, sir. Would you like me to open to drapes?"

"Too hot for that, I'm afraid. The light comes through anyway." He hands her several drafts. "For your typewriter, if you would."

"A busy day for you, I imagine, with this Meyer business."

"Yes, I'm afraid so."

"I'll leave you to it then."

"Thank you, Miss Petrie."

Her polished shoe buckles catch the curtains' glow as she recrosses the floorboards. Sokobin has noticed she keeps a small collection of such decorative clips, some studded with paste stones—a singular spot of vanity in a wardrobe otherwise filled with drab skirts and plain shirtwaists.

"Open or closed?" she asks, grasping the doorknob.

"Closed, please."

"I thought so." She pauses, looking intently at him. Hers is a serious, square face, one that Sokobin imagines, even when young, would have more frequently been called handsome rather than pretty.

"I do hope you find him, Mr. Vice-Consul."

"Come again, Miss Petrie?"

"Mr. Meyer. I do hope you find him." Her unrouged lips

stretch but fall short of a smile. "Of late, there are altogether too many missing people in this world."

She pulls the door shut. Sokobin stares at the knob, unsure of what to make of the secretary's words. It's perhaps the longest verbal exchange they've shared since he arrived in Nanking several months ago.

He reaches for the teapot and pours out a cup. His pocket watch reads 10:45. Plenty of time, he assures himself, to familiarize himself with the dossier before meeting Lin on the docks. His briefcase already contains the essentials: clean shirt and two collars, cuffs, tie, change of underwear, socks, razor, comb, and toothbrush. The contents assembled so that he might leave directly from the office. Anything else, he can borrow from Chase's vast stores.

Taking out his letter opener, he nudges the blade under the dossier envelope's flap and makes a swift, clean sweep. The first section offers background on Meyer, né Frans Meijer: his origins in Amsterdam, his emigration to the United States and later work for the Office of Foreign Seed and Plant Introduction, much of which Sokobin recalls from their conversation. A photograph has been attached; Sokobin is hard-pressed to reconcile the timid-looking man in the picture with the chiseled figure from the Fourth of July party. The image, most likely the duplicate from the explorer's personnel file, shows Meyer wearing city clothes: a tight suit jacket, stiff collar, and striped tie. The explorer's face is beardless, his chin soft and dimpled. If Sokobin didn't know better, he'd think the man an accountant or hotel clerk who'd never been east of Cleveland. Sokobin puts the photograph aside, reminding himself not to put too much stock in it. Whatever's happened to Meyer, wherever or in whatever state he may be, he would certainly be coming from the field and look of it.

He turns the page, moving on to the interviews. According

to the crew of the SS *Feng Yang Maru*, the last known sighting of Meyer occurred some five days before, late on the evening of June 1. The bar steward claims the explorer crossed the saloon at about a quarter after eleven p.m. and exited by the door leading to the back rails and privies. Meyer was alone and spoke to no one. Tasked with serving drinks, the steward didn't think of Meyer again until the following morning when the explorer's boy, who had slept below on the Chinese deck, came to wake his employer, and found the bed empty. It was only after the alarm had been raised that the steward realized he hadn't seen Meyer return from outside the night before.

Paper-clipped to the steward's account is a simple hand-drawn map of the steamer's top deck with Meyer's assumed route ticked out in pencil. Sokobin runs his finger from the small box marked *Meyer's cabin* through the rectangular *saloon* and along the lines marked *back rails and privies*. Whether or not the explorer ever returned to his quarters, perhaps looping back along the rails via a different way, remains unknown. Given the late hour, Sokobin thinks it likely Meyer's cabinmate, a British insurance salesman, and hitherto a stranger to the explorer, was already asleep when Meyer left their room, and passed the night unaware anything was amiss. According to the passenger manifest, both the salesman and Meyer's boy came off the ship at Shanghai and have yet to be questioned.

Sokobin slowly makes his way through the pages, pausing to pour himself another cup of cool tea before moving on to the interview with Inwood, the steamer's captain. When questioned about the possibility of foul play, Inwood claimed to be unaware of any arguments or unsavory characters aboard ship. And while Sokobin suspects that the Japanese trading company that owns the SS *Feng Yang Maru* has instructed Inwood to say this in order to avoid scandal, Sokobin sees no reason to doubt the captain's word. A thorough inspection of the boat by the American staff has revealed no signs of blood or struggle, nor have any ransom demands been received. Robbery, too, seems an unlikely motivation, in Sokobin's opinion. The explorer's possessions—personal trunk, maps, papers, herbarium, bags of seed—seem too modest to inspire attack. Even more telling is that the most valuable items, a small amount of silver coin and a box camera, were both found in good order in Meyer's cabin and are currently being held with the rest of Meyer's effects at the Shanghai Consulate. At the very least, Sokobin would expect a thief to have pinched the silver and attempted to fence the pricey camera.

He peels the page from his damp fingers and lifts his face to catch the air from the fan. He's kept the electric off—the bulbs emit too much heat—but the sun is directly behind him now, seeping through the curtains and warming his back. His pocket watch confirms it's well past one o'clock. He's lost himself in the dossier's pages, and now his stomach is beginning to make demands.

Opening the door, he asks Miss Petrie for another cool pot and sends Windham to fetch a rice bowl from the bund. As a rule, Sokobin can't identify the bowls' contents, neither the pickled vegetables nor the gristled chunks of meat. Not even the boiled eggs, which are clearly not from chickens. He gave up asking questions as to the bowls' contents after the first week, preferring not to know. Lunch, as he has quickly learned, is an exceptionally limited affair in Nanking. The Brits keep a small canteen in their office; Sokobin made the mistake of eating there once. And at the French brasserie, the hostesses are so scantily clad that Sokobin can only conclude the restaurant is a front for a brothel.

Windham returns with a bowl, after which Sokobin closes his door again. He reads the summary of findings as he eats, picking out meaty bits with his chopsticks. But in the end, there are no findings when it comes to Meyer's disappearance. Not even a working theory. The report contains abundant facts about the explorer, some of which Sokobin already knew, others not; yet none explain the man's continued absence from a steamship. He rereads the report's final lines several times:

According to those here acquainted with him, Mr. Meyer appears to have kept above the typical Eastern vices. By all accounts, he is neither an alcoholic nor gambler nor addict. He is, as far as we can ascertain, without wife, children, or romantic involvements.

The character assessment comes as no surprise. Even so, Sokobin finds it disappointing. There's nothing that might serve as a clue, no telling angle that might steer the investigation, such as money problems, a fondness for the pipe, or sexual imbroglio. It's been Sokobin's experience that the answers are to be found there, in a man's weakness. Rather Meyer sounds too perfect, too clean, almost slippery in his flawless, solitary nature. It takes Sokobin several moments to realize the same sterile phrases might be used to describe himself.

He lifts the teapot only to find it empty. He considers calling to Miss Petrie for a third round, but thinks the better of it, not wanting to spoil the room's stillness. His pocket watch reads a few minutes past three o'clock. Above him, the fan blades tick the passing seconds. The humid air feels heavy as it brushes his face, and he reaches for the paperweight from Everton, running his fingers over the ivory's smooth surface. A man steps out into the night, he thinks, never to be seen again, his fate as obscure as the dark water below.

He knocks the loose pages against his desk until they re-align and slides the report back into the manila envelope before retrieving a Chesterfield from the bottom drawer. He swivels toward the window and tugs open the curtains. The sun reflects off the river with such force that he blinks. He exhales against the glass. This case. Nothing about it makes sense. There are only three ways a man ends up in the river. He can fall, jump, or be pushed. At the moment, none seems more likely than the other.

CHAPTER 4

AT TEN MINUTES TO FIVE O'CLOCK, HE GATHERS UP HIS notes, blotting paper, a clean notepad, and extra fountain pen, and adds them to his thick briefcase. Sokobin momentarily debates the value of bringing the dossier itself, but it's heavy and there's not enough room in his case, and so he settles for his notes instead. Satisfied he's leaving nothing critical behind before heading to the docks, he retrieves the Chesterfields from the bottom drawer. The outline of Ethan's photograph is there, a barely perceptible rise on the top envelope. He's never been away from the picture, and on impulse slides it into the stiff center well of his briefcase, then lifts his suit jacket from the chair.

As he rounds his desk, his shoe slips on something. He stops and looks down to find a square white card at the rug's edge. Even without touching it, he can see that the paper is thick, like card stock. Sokobin stares, unable to understand how the paper has come to be on his floor. Perhaps it slipped from the dossier or the stack of communiqués, though neither seems likely. He would have certainly noticed it fall. And yet the white square is undeniably there, plain as day, and slightly soiled by the imprint of his sole.

He picks it up, turns it over. At once he recognizes the heavy cream stationery, the immaculate handwriting. The note is from the Consul General himself and contains a single sentence: *Should it prove relevant, several here believe Mr. Meyer to be of*

Jewish origin. Sokobin reexamines each word, certain he's misread. But he hasn't.

The chances, he thinks. The odds. He reads the sentence a third time, only to find the words the same. He sits on the edge of his desk. He feels slightly dizzy, as if the very floorboards beneath him have suddenly opened up. Surely the Consul General must be mistaken. Surely Sokobin would have sensed this about Meyer when they spoke at the Fourth of July party. But then Sokobin remembers he'd been distracted by the heavy punch and crowds. Even so, he thinks now, he would have *known*. But of course, Sokobin hadn't been looking. The truth is, he's made a point of *not* looking for such things for years. And even if he had, what exactly would he have been looking for?

The note changes nothing, he tells himself. But as soon as the thought surfaces, Sokobin knows it to be false. The sentence changes everything about the task ahead. Three days, he remembers. Three days to decently bury a fellow Jew. Old rules he thought he'd left behind long ago on Newark's sooty streets. Already it's been five days since Meyer was last seen.

The chances, he thinks again. But he doesn't have time to consider them. If he doesn't go now, he'll miss the ferry and meeting Mr. Lin. He slides the card into his jacket pocket and steps into the front room, where his staff sit working at their desks, their backs to him and unaware of his presence. The sight fills Sokobin with envy for his days in Shanghai, just months ago, when come five o'clock, the responsibility of files like Meyer's fell on someone else's shoulders. For a moment, he wishes he'd never been promoted to VC.

He clears his throat. All three turn at the sound and rise to their feet.

"Unfortunately, I've left something in my apartment." He pauses, unsure of how to explain himself. He considers mentioning the CG's note and decides against it. There isn't time.

"But, sir," says Windham. "The ferry . . ."

"I'm aware of the time," Sokobin interrupts. "I need you to head to the docks, Mr. Windham. Have Mr. Lin wait for me at the gangplank. Tell him it'll be close, but I'll make it. If need be, I can be wired via Arthur Chase care of Standard Oil of New York. As senior clerk, Mr. Brundage, you're in charge while I'm gone."

Sokobin takes a breath, certain that in his rush, he's forgotten something. He isn't sure why he's still standing there, what he's waiting for. If he didn't know better, he'd think he was deliberately trying to miss the ferry.

"No need to worry, sir," Mr. Brundage says, smoothing down his vest over his paunch. "We'll hold down the fort while you're gone. If anything important arises, we'll send word."

"Best of luck, sir," Windham says.

Miss Petrie clasps her mottled hands as if in prayer. "Do be careful, Vice-Consul." The secretary begins to say something else. *Don't forget to eat*, or perhaps *Godspeed*. But Sokobin doesn't catch the words. He is already ahead of them, exiting onto the street, splitting the wet air.

THE APARTMENT REVEALS ITSELF IN A SINGLE GLANCE: two en suite rooms and bath, its corners perpetually drenched in shadow. The heavy rugs, the crimson damask sofa, the teak furniture have all been inherited from the previous tenant, a Russian import/export type, according to the building's owner, who abandoned the rooms when the revolution broke out last year. The place was intended only as a stopgap until a suitable house could be found; something outside the city center, the CG advised, with a proper kitchen, dining room, guest rooms, and a veranda where Sokobin might entertain. *You're a man of rank now. It's important to live like one.* As a VC, Sokobin understands he's expected to maintain a flock of servants; otherwise one loses face. Still, he keeps no houseboy. A cook would be pointless, and a chauffeur absurd with the office only a few blocks away. Until now the only other person to step inside the apartment is a local woman he pays to dust and wash once a week.

Sokobin has changed nothing, not even the sheets or towels. Rather, from the first moment he stepped foot inside these rooms, he understood he belonged here. The feeling has yet to subside; he can smell traces of its former occupier's Slavic melancholy seeping through the woodwork. He knows better than to mention such ideas to others. They would label him mentally unfit, given to depressive episodes—or worse, infected with *Oriental Fatalism.* The CG has lectured on the point numerous times.

He quickly crosses the living room carpet, pushing open the double doors to the bedroom and taking a small key from the night table. At the foot of the bed is his steamer trunk. He tries the lock several times before it yields. He sifts through the trunk's contents, pulling out this and that, each item like a chronology of his life in reverse: a box of stationery printed with his old address in Shanghai; a cream-colored tuxedo jacket; a mackintosh square and rubber boots; a box containing a pair of silver cuff links from Meredith; several volumes of ancient Chinese poetry he'd once considered translating; a racket and tennis whites, both unused since college when he purchased them at great expense for a weekend at Chase's family estate; the blue and white college scarf he'd scraped for weeks to buy, now badly pilled and smelling of mothballs. He pauses at his family portrait, the last with his father in it, pressed into a stamped cardboard frame, and feels a tinge of guilt. The photograph should be out, displayed on the living room mantel or his bedside table, not locked away out of sight.

He digs deeper, scrambling now. For a moment he fears he's lost the very thing he's come for. But then he sees it at the very bottom—a small bundle flattened by the weight of everything above. He lifts it out and peels back the wrinkled black crepe paper his mother wrapped the things with when Sokobin sailed for China. His father's yarmulke and tallit. Not the purchased set his mother insisted they bury him in, but the slightly frayed versions brought from the old country and worn by Sokobin's father every *Shabbos* and service. The same yarmulke and tallit Sokobin wore as he sat *shiva* for his father in the cramped parlor of his parents' row house. He remembers the mirrors covered with black cloth, the closed windows trapping the summer heat and supposedly his father's soul, the bristle of his own unshaven face, the rendered lapel of his one good suit. His mother weeping to one side of him, Ethan unnaturally still on the other as Sokobin stared beyond the stream of mourners whispering their condolences in Yiddish, Polish, and English. Raising the bundle to his face, Sokobin breathes in and finds the life that once was. His mother's stews, his father's sweat, and Newark itself. Coal. Smoke. Chipped tenements. Factories. And the filthy stretch that bounded it all—the Passaic River.

He unclasps his briefcase and presses the bundle inside. Standing, he surveys the mess now strewn about the floor. There isn't time to put everything back. He leaves the trunk key on the bedside table, hoping the housecleaner will figure it out.

Outside he flags down the nearest rickshaw, somehow managing to convey the urgency of the departing ferry. The cart jerks forward, making him grip his briefcase for fear of losing it to the street. They turn the corner, meeting with the bund and the reclining sun. Sokobin reaches for the accordion shade overhead, but it makes little difference, and he pushes down the brim of his hat against the slanting light. He squints at his watch. 5:48. Exactly twelve minutes until the last ferry departs. He thinks of Mr.

Lin, no doubt pacing the dock with worry. Hopefully, Windham has found him and conveyed that Sokobin is on his way.

The docks are awash with motion at this hour: pedestrians, carts, food stalls, pulleys, and stacked crates. Along the waterfront, sampans jostle against the piers. The driver is deft and manages to stamp out a steady pace as he weaves them through the narrowest of lanes. Sokobin checks his watch again. 5:53.

At last, the white steamer comes into view. Passengers flit along the upper deck like colored confetti. Sokobin follows the gangplank down to the slim silhouette standing at its base, its motionless figure at odds with the surrounding chaos. *Lin*, he thinks. To Sokobin's relief, the interpreter wears Western clothes: a lightweight tan suit and a pale gray fedora. In his hand is a cognac-colored attaché; a small valise rests at his feet. Sokobin calls out to him, raising an arm overhead. The interpreter turns, his spectacles catching the light and shining like two bright suns.

The ferry's stacks sound their final warning. Sokobin orders the driver to stop and hands over several coins, not bothering with the change. Ahead two uniformed stewards begin to unwind the ship's thick ropes from the mooring bollards. Cupping his hands over the crowd, Sokobin shouts for Lin to board the ship, swings his case forward, and breaks into a run.

CHAPTER 5

SOKOBIN STANDS ON THE BACK DECK OF THE SHIP, EX-
haling smoke over the churning wake. The other passengers have
gathered at the prow to catch the breeze and sunset; presum-
ably, Mr. Lin is doing the same one deck below in Chinese first
class. For now, the stern is Sokobin's alone. He leans his elbows
against the rails, grateful for the small spot of solitude. He's always preferred the stern, its backward glance. Here he can sort
his thoughts before throwing himself into the jumbled rush of
whatever comes next.

He watches the tangle of Nanking's sampans and sleek var-
nished yachts shrink in the softening light. A bevy of anchored
metal steamers rises over the pack with their bright flags from
Great Britain, France, Holland, Japan, and the new Chinese Republic. He follows the snapping stars and stripes of an American
gunship as it huffs downriver. Coal bags have been stacked on the
deck as bullet cover for the sailors. No doubt the ship is headed to
Shanghai, and he imagines Meredith and the other nurses in a flock
of white caps and red capes there to welcome the sailors as they glide
past the bund. Few such boats remain. All the European gunships
have been requisitioned for the war; at this point, only an American skeleton crew keeps guard over the whole of China's coast.

The river bends and Nanking slips from view. Eventually the
wail of the stacks gives way to the banter of Chinese men below.
By now many of them are rolling dice and wagering at *fan tan*,

the national pastime; others are trading and making deals. The never-ending hustle of the East. For some reason, Sokobin doesn't expect to make out Lin's voice among the din. He expected there would be time enough for proper introductions and a briefing on Meyer's case in port; instead, he and Lin barely exchanged a handshake before parting for their respective decks. Beyond a passing glance at Lin's CV, Sokobin doesn't know a thing about the man. Nor has he thought to wonder until this very moment. Like the chair or the desk in his office, the interpreter has come with the job. And while Sokobin has no reason to distrust Lin, the fact is, he's headed upriver on his most significant case to date with a complete stranger.

A few sampans continue to move with the currents, but most bob on the swells, their anchors lowered and sails rolled for the night. Lanterns, like fallen stars, swing from low thatched roofs. Sokobin admires the lightness of the small boats, their simplicity of form. Unlike the heavy sea-faring junks he used to see clogging the ports in Shanghai, the sampans are long and slender, blade-like with rudderless bottoms, made for navigating the shoals found far upriver. Some boatmen will spend their entire lives on the water, fishing, trading, and sailing for hundreds of miles at a stretch, never once sleeping on solid ground.

A life forever in motion, he thinks. Like Meyer. Like Ethan. Perhaps even like himself. He exhales, watching the wind scatter the smoke, and with it, the thought. The blue-brown waters deepen color with each passing minute. It is June 6, a Friday. Sundown. *Shabbos.* The day meant for rest. Sokobin can't recall the last time he observed it.

YANGTZE. SON OF THE SEA. SOKOBIN KNOWS ONLY FOR-eigners call the whole of the river by its ancient, poetic name.

If the Chinese use a single appellation, it is *Chang Jiang*, Long River, or sometimes simply *jiang*, the river, as if it were dependent upon all others to distinguish themselves. But like so much in China, the river is a shape shifter, elusive and forever changing. And so it goes by many titles: *Yangtze* between Nanking and Shanghai, *Chuan Jiang* in Sichuan Province, *Jing Jiang* through the gorges of Hubei, *Wan Jiang* in Anhui. In Tibet it is known as *Machu*, or Red River, for the strips of burnt copper sand that lace its headwaters. But those lie nearly three thousand miles away from where Sokobin now stands, his briefcase firmly wedged between his shoes. Here among the endless floodplains and rice fields, the Yangtze spreads a half-mile wide, its depths unmeasured, its currents steeped the color of milky tea and smelling of all that has come before: clay, mud, and rotting plants. Fish guts and human excrement. Broken boats and deluged villages. Fermented garbage and factory fumes, steamer coal and the bitter scent of crude oil. Disease, famine, corruption, rebellion. Blood.

And yet Sokobin knows this smell, its ripe and rot. He has always known it. There are times in summer when a single breath is enough to transport him across the years to emerge once again as a knobby-kneed boy in Newark, Ethan still small enough to struggle to keep step as they edge past the Passaic on their way to school. By then, the local men no longer dove under the waves in search of the river's celebrated pearls, or dared to cast lines into its currents for their supper. The Passaic had become a trough for the factories lining its banks, a festering wound. Their own father worked in one of the brick fronts, processing unclean meat that would never touch his lips; unlike the other jobs he might get, the factory allowed him to work Sundays instead of *Shabbos*. And so, their father witnessed what went down the chutes: trash, tires, fabric dye, formaldehyde, saw blades, and broken engines. He warned his two sons at the supper table about the offal, dead animals, and every so often, people. As with all the other parents, at least the sober ones, he forbade *Shemeul* and *Eitan* from even dipping their toes. From a young age, Sokobin understood his life would never be his own until he crossed the river and left it behind; no different than his own parents had been made to do as children when their families fled the *shtetl* and crossed an ocean. Newark was as far as they got. Ethan must have also felt it, the need to push out, for as young men, both of them did exactly that, each in his own way, each in his own direction, but both putting as many miles between themselves and Newark as possible.

————————

HIS BROTHER HAD LEFT FOR SOUTH AFRICA UNDER the supposition that only the most clever and adventurous could survive so far afield. The illusion didn't last long. Within a year, the grand prose Ethan summoned upon his arrival was gone, re-placed by flinty words. The *Afrikaners* were a different sort, he wrote Sokobin, cut from a cruder cloth. The English tended to have more money, but Dutch or English, it made little difference. Ignorance knew no allegiance. He found the missionaries nar-row, the landowners provincial, at times hateful toward the na-tives and Indian coolies. They seemed to be compensating, bent on proving their worth, but only against people who couldn't possibly compete and had no desire to do so. Ethan concluded the bulk of colonists were either running from something—scandal or crime—or had simply shipped out after failing at home.

He despised the private clubs for whites—their guarded walls, their absurd formalities and black-tie dances—all desper-ate attempts to hold on to a superiority that had never existed. It wasn't what he'd come for: to replicate in shoddy miniature what he'd left behind. He wanted the uncontaminated, the unknown, the infinite. He wanted *Africa*. Only when he flew could he still feel her. The air. It held nothing that could be bought, farmed, mined, or stolen. No flagpoles, sentries, or borders. The air belonged to everyone. Or better yet, to no one.

And yet, he couldn't entirely avoid the clubs. It was where he was expected, where he made contacts, where he found work. It was tough enough being American, worse with a *foreign* last name no one could pronounce. He couldn't skip the dinners and dances, or else they'd cut him off, say he'd gone native.

One night he got into a fistfight with one of the members over a woman. It was stupid, he admitted to Sokobin in a letter, all the more so since there'd never been anything serious between them. He'd just been keen on her and she on him. Or so he'd thought. But then out of the blue, she had a ring. The fiancé was a cad, born with a snub nose. Ethan had come to know the type: public schoolboy, Oxbridge, and let everyone know it from the first minute. From what Ethan could see, the guy had been given everything—only to make a mess of it—and was currently running the family's sugar plantation into the ground. According to some of the rumors, he'd left England after knocking up a housemaid; in others, it was a shop girl. Ethan didn't doubt either story; they'd chatted a few times, long enough for him to make out the guy's true colors. He was also known to keep native women.

It happened at one of the dress parties. Ethan was a little drunk and asked the girl to dance. He'd held her too tightly, whispering all the while about how she might want to reconsider her options. The fiancé tried to butt in, tapping Ethan's shoulder. Ethan refused to yield, waving him off. When the man insisted, Ethan told him to wait his turn. They were drawing stares by that point. Ethan didn't care; a part of him wanted a scuffle. The man tapped his shoulder again, harder this time. Ethan stopped, suggesting they step outside. But the guy didn't wait and attempted a wild swing. Ethan easily dodged the hit, knocking the man to the ground and bloodying his nose. Even from thousands of miles away, Sokobin detected his brother's pride in landing the punch. A part of Sokobin felt it too. A touch of the old neighborhood. His brother hadn't lost it.

But then the man called Ethan a *filthy kike.*

Only after it was over did Ethan hear the girl's screams, her pleas for him to stop. At the time he heard nothing. Ethan hit the guy over and over, not caring that his opponent was already down. If he hadn't been pulled off, his brother admitted, he might have killed the guy. Even after the fact, Ethan couldn't be sure he would have regretted it.

He was shown the door and told to never come back. Several of the others wanted to ring the police, have Ethan arrested. None of them, not those he counted as friends, nor even the ones who'd previously shared their secret disdain for the fiancé, spoke up in his defense. Instead, they stood there, arms crossed, and told him he'd gone too far, mucked it up. It wasn't the real reason. They wouldn't say it, not aloud, but he knew. The tuxedoes and silk gowns were thin cover. They were kicking him out for the same reason their own parents had fled the *shtetl* as children. The small-mindedness, the hollow hearts, the same stinking old hatreds. They'd poisoned it—not just the club but the entire continent. Everything.

By the time Sokobin received the next letter, his brother was in France, volunteering with the escadrilles. He wanted to fight for something good, he wrote Sokobin, something brave and right. He wasn't the only American flyer to sign up; there was an entire squadron of Yanks. The other men didn't care about his family name, where he came from, or what he called his God. They only cared if he could face the German *Jagdstaffeln* head on and aim his gun straight; that he could cover their backs in a dogfight; that he'd sacrifice his own skin for theirs.

Somehow his brother managed to do all these things and keep himself alive long enough to see his own country join the war. Most did not.

A DOOR OPENS BEHIND, VOICES SPILLING OUT. SOKOBIN turns from the rails. The couple is young and handsome, their pale skin aglow with the dining cabin's light. They laugh a little too loudly. They are drunk. Spotting him, they cross to the other side of the railing. He remembers nights like this with Meredith, drinking a little too much brandy and wandering the narrow streets of the French concession. It soon became their favorite part of the city. Arms laced about each other's shoulders, they passed the cafés and shops, Meredith stopping them every so often to point out some little trinket in a window. He remembers how the crowd parted to let them pass, ceding the right of way to love.

By now he expected to have forgotten her, to feel nothing—at the very least for the hole in his chest to have filled itself. And yet, two years on, the memory of her body lingers inside his own, a palpable presence trespassing against the boundaries of his will. The smallest of sensations conjures her: a soft voice in the next room, a flaring skirt hem, slender fingers re-pinning a strand of fallen hair. Even now he can feel her standing with him at the rails, the edges of her hands pressing against his. Certainly, he's had other chances—many at Chase's urging—flirtations that might have cured him. Never has Sokobin pursued them beyond dinner or a drink. He's not like Arthur, forever throwing himself into one ridiculous romance after another. So quick to jump, no matter how far the fall. So quick to scramble up again, having learned absolutely nothing.

He looks down in mild panic, certain that in his absent-mindedness, he's let his briefcase slip overboard. But the case is exactly where he put it, nestled tightly between his shoes. And the bottom rail, he sees, is far too low for the bag to slide under. He reminds himself that he is a careful man. He would never have put the bag down without first having checked. His nerves are getting the best of him. It's the Chesterfields, he tells himself as he grips the rails. He's been smoking altogether too much, and now they've left him jittery and on edge.

He presses his legs more closely against the case, remembering his father's tallit and yarmulke within, the cream-colored card in his pocket from the CG. If Sokobin hadn't ceased to believe in such things, he'd think he was being tested. But he doesn't believe in such things. He's not a superstitious man.

He lights another cigarette. He's overthinking it, looking for mystical signs where there are none. Meyer's file landing on his desk is a mere coincidence of geography. Nor will anything Sokobin does now change the man's fate. What's done is done. Sokobin's only task now—his only duty as VC—is to find the man, dead or alive, and submit his Form 192. Period.

The logic is so unassailable, he nearly believes it.

He thinks of his mother thousands of miles away, still in Newark and preparing the table in the row house where she continues to live alone. The lace cloth and candlesticks from the old country, the braided challah in its basket, the chicken stew and wine. He imagines her lighting the wicks and covering her eyes as she says the blessing of the candles. There will be a prayer for him, a slightly longer one for Ethan. Or perhaps she is *not* alone. Her letters mention friends, other widows, still in the neighborhood. He prefers to picture this version.

The cigarette is a mistake, his throat too scorched to hold down the smoke, and he inhales only a few times before jettisoning the stub overboard. He follows the spark as it falls, glancing away before it hits the sloshing waves. It won't be long before they reach Wuhu. No doubt Arthur will send his new limousine to meet them at the docks. Still, Standard Oil's compound is a good half-hour drive outside the city port; Sokobin figures he can use the time to fill in Lin on Meyer. Once they arrive, however, Chase will want to stay up late, hearing about the missing man, drinking and talking too much as usual. Sokobin will be lucky if he sees a bed before midnight.

A spot of brightness flashes in the water below. The light barely registers before it's gone. Sokobin peers into the obscurity, briefly imagining the impossible: his discarded Chesterfield, miraculously still lit and floating among the waves. When the faint glow reappears, it shows the tawny patch of a boatman's face inhaling a cigarette. The small sampan is crossing dangerously close to the steamer, its thin edges nearly invisible against the black water and without so much as a lantern to announce its presence.

The boatman lifts his steering pole, and the orange gleam fades again. Sokobin waits for another glimpse, but the little boat forms only the briefest of shadows before disappearing like some shy ancient creature returned to the depths.

CHAPTER 6

S OKOBIN AND L IN WAIT SIDE BY SIDE IN THE FRONT
hall, hats in their hands, while the houseboy goes to fetch Chase.
With another man, Sokobin might attempt small talk, but Lin
exudes an almost preternatural reserve that makes him reluctant
to break the plane of silence, as if after having interpreted for so
long, Lin's voice exists only to convey the words of others.

"Soko," Chase calls out, cupping Sokobin about the shoulder.
At the sight of Lin, Arthur stops and runs a hand through his
wheat-colored hair. "Say now, your cable didn't mention you'd
be bringing anyone."

Sokobin supposes he assumed Windham would have mentioned Lin in the wire, but thinking about it now, he realizes he
never actually specified for his clerk to do so. The detail slipped
his mind. He's forgotten how tetchy Arthur can be about such
things. *Protocol*, Chase calls it.

"Arthur, this is my interpreter, Mr. Lin. Mr. Lin, Arthur
Chase."

"Pleased to meet you," Chase says, extending his hand. If
Sokobin didn't know Arthur so long, he'd think the smile
genuine. "Old college pals, Sokobin and I," Chase tells Lin as
if their history needed clarification. "Say, let's get you both
taken care of. You must be starving. I'm sure Mr. Lin would
be more comfortable in one of the rooms downstairs. It's
much cooler there."

It's an underhanded move on Arthur's part, Sokobin thinks, forcing him to make the call—up or down—on the spot. Perhaps if he'd been raised with servants like Chase, Sokobin wouldn't give the question a second thought, but men of the comprador class like Lin continue to throw him. Neither servant nor official, but both. Or neither. Sokobin can't say. As VC, it's something he should know by now. Lin and Chase look at him, clearly waiting for an answer.

"Sleep well, Mr. Lin. I'll see you at breakfast in the morning," Sokobin says, forcing a smile. It's late and he doesn't want to make a fuss. Besides, he tells himself, it's Arthur's house, Arthur's rules.

Lin blinks from behind his spectacles. The resulting bow feels unnecessarily deep. "Vice-Consul," he says, "Mr. Chase."

The houseboy leads Lin down the steps. Sokobin waits for the interpreter to glance up, but the interpreter's eyes remain fixed on his polished shoes. Somehow Lin's easy acquiescence only makes Sokobin feel worse, and he feels a familiar pang of anxiety as if he were about to be ordered downstairs as well. It's a feeling he still gets around Chase, even after so many years, even after the promotion. As if Sokobin were still the shabby scholarship boy following on Arthur's sharp heels. Sokobin wonders when, if ever, the feeling will cease.

But of course, Chase says no such thing, never has.

"Please see that Mr. Lin gets supper," Arthur calls after the houseboy. "And bring a cold plate up for the Vice-Consul." He turns back to Sokobin and gestures toward the living room. "Shall we? You can fill me in on the case while we wait."

Sokobin sinks into the long sofa as Chase busies himself at the bar. Overhead a fan quietly whirs. He knows the room, its smooth cream walls, polished floors, and chrome fittings—exactly the sort of house the CG would like Sokobin himself to occupy. But the look, as sleek and understated as an ocean liner, better suits Chase. It's why, Sokobin supposes, he continues to think of the house as Arthur's despite the fact that it, like the rest along this stretch, belong to Standard Oil of New York. Recently, the company has begun to expand its oil derricks around Wuhu, but at this point, kerosene remains Standard's bread and butter. Sokobin has seen Arthur's recruiting ads for salesmen in the papers. *Two-year commitment. Unmarried, un-conscripted men only.* At thirty-four, he and Arthur are both beyond the draft; even if Congress raises the conscription age as Sokobin expects they soon will, Chase's executive position will likely earn him an exemption, just as Sokobin would as VC. Uncle Sam needs oil as much as Chinese diplomacy. It's a point they don't discuss.

Chase hands him a whiskey, leaving the matching decanter on the low table between them, and slides into the leather chair opposite. Standard Oil's logo, a flying white horse, glints from the face of his gold wristwatch. Even at this late hour, with his sleeves rolled and bare feet stretched over the silk carpet, Chase manages to exude the effortless manners of the perennially wealthy. Privilege is his mother tongue.

"So, the missing man," he says. "I've seen his picture in the paper."

"Probably. Frank Meyer. An explorer with the Department of Agriculture."

"Let's hear it then."

Sokobin proceeds to summarize the known facts, no doubt violating all manner of confidentiality. Still, he doesn't think it right to stay in a man's house and not trust him enough to know why. There's also the fact that Chase has access to Standard Oil's resources—specifically boats and cables that may come in handy. Only the bit about the white card from the CG does Sokobin keep to himself. He'd like to think that he and Arthur are well beyond such differences after so many years, but Sokobin isn't entirely sure. They have a habit of talking around things. Even back in college, when it must have been common knowledge that Sokobin was one of twelve Hebrews permitted in their graduating class, they never spoke of it. As a general rule, he and Chase tend to stay clear of the thorny subjects from which deep friendships are normally forged: family, home, and faith. The sidestepping has been going on so long that Sokobin can't say if it's what's prevented them from growing closer or what's kept them on good terms for so long.

"Nasty business," Chase says, once Sokobin finishes the résumé. "Suffice it to say, if I'd heard anything about a white body found in the river, I'd have let you know. So, what are you thinking? Foul play?"

"Possible, although unlikely. None of the crew noted any arguments or suspicious types aboard."

Chase takes a long swill, and Sokobin knows the answer disappoints him. No doubt Arthur has been hoping to play a part in some salacious tale. He holds his glass by the rim, revealing a row of square, buffed nails. Sokobin first noticed them years ago, during one of Everton's lectures. It had taken him nearly half the semester to realize that Chase had *paid* someone to produce the tidy effect. When Arthur quietly confessed his grades were sinking at the mid-term, Sokobin had offered help. It hadn't been a kindness. Or even just about the cash. The great city with its concrete towers and polished, moneyed men might as well have been another planet. That semester and those that followed, Chase became a shadow education in trouser cuts and tie knots, the right hat and stance. Sometimes Chase took him to marbled hotel bars and fraternity parties—paneled rooms full of cavalier young men whose family names were printed on the canned goods and cleaning bottles in Sokobin's mother's pantry. Chase never introduced Sokobin by his full name, only as "my pal Soko." Eventually Sokobin learned to ape the essentials. And they have been essential, he knows. He would have never made vice-consul otherwise.

"Meyer wasn't a high roller, I take it?"

Sokobin shakes his head. "Hardly. He collected plants, species for possible cultivation in the States. Pears, lemons, shade trees, that sort of thing."

"A plant hunter." From Chase's lips, the words sound far more exotic than Meyer's official title of Agricultural Explorer. "No opium, then?"

Sokobin sips, wincing at the whiskey's searing heat on his tongue. He's never been the drinker Chase is and he lets a shard of ice melt on his tongue before answering. Arthur's penchant for the dramatic is trying him. "No."

"Could he have fallen overboard?"

"Possible, but I'm having a hard time picturing it. Meyer's expeditions took him through remote spots, over mountains, snow fields, and across deserts. He was the first white man some of those villages ever saw. This is his fourth expedition now. Hard to imagine a seasoned type like that suddenly tanking off a passenger steamer."

"No, I suppose not."

Arthur leans back, rattles his ice. Like the decanter, the crystal glass in his hand is etched with the initials *AWC*. The set may be new or some eighty years old, having been bought by Arthur's great-grandfather and shipped from the family's estate in Connecticut. Sokobin has never fully understood what keeps Arthur Wilhelm Chase IV in China, not when a manor's worth of monogrammed silver and linens await his return.

"I see your dilemma," Chase says. "A missing man who by any rational explanation shouldn't be missing."

"Correct," Sokobin says.

"And how long since Meyer disappeared again?"

"Five days."

Chase lets out a small groan. "Not so good."

"No. Not good."

The houseboy reappears and sets a red lacquered tray on the table. Sokobin is relieved when Arthur quickly dismisses the boy. Despite his years in-country, Sokobin has never grown used to being watched from the corners.

Chase tilts the decanter toward him. Sokobin declines, and Arthur releases a generous splash of whiskey into his own glass. "So, what's your next move?"

"Head down to the harbor master in the morning," Sokobin says, leaning forward to saw through the meat. Like ice, Arthur seems to have an inexhaustible line on beef and creamed horseradish. The roast is how Arthur likes it, rare, and drips under his knife. "Just to confirm, no bodies have surfaced in the last day. A long shot."

"Right. And if no?"

"Comb the water," Sokobin says, trying his best not to imagine it.

"I don't envy the task," Chase tells him. "There's a lot of river out there, Soko. Meyer's been gone some time."

Sokobin pushes a hunk of beef into his cheek. "I realize that."

"Can you even be sure he went over at Wuhu?"

"No. At this point, I can't be sure of anything."

Chase narrows his eyes. "Hold on now, you don't think he might still be alive? Not after all this time?"

"No, I don't." Sokobin can hear the irritation in his voice. "I mean, what are the chances?"

"Doubtful. Still without a body, I suppose you can never be sure, can you?"

Chase is looking at him, his head cocked, and one pale eyebrow raised. It's a gesture Sokobin suspects women find appealing. He pushes his plate toward the center of the table and takes a small sip of whiskey, letting its fire pool on his tongue before swallowing.

"It's why I'm here. To find out, one way or another. The family deserves to know."

"Well, if there's anything I can do, just wire me at the office." Chase frowns into his drink. "Damn this heat. My ice is already gone."

Arthur returns to the bar, leaving Sokobin to stare at the row of windows lining the back wall. By day the glass frames a sweeping view of the river, but at this time all that's visible is the glare from the electric spotlights lining the compound's barbed wire security fence. The Yangtze lies somewhere beyond, its waters cloaked by night.

Chase returns, sending up a sigh from the padded leather chair. Again, he holds out the decanter, and again Sokobin declines with the plea of an early rise. Meanwhile Arthur fills his glass for the fourth or fifth time. Sokobin checks his watch. He can feel himself growing tetchier by the minute. It's been over two hours since his last smoke.

"I suppose you've heard about our new iron steamer," Chase says, and the conversation shifts to business, as it inevitably does with Arthur.

Sokobin feigns interest as Arthur explains how Standard Oil has finally managed to outfit an ironclad steamer tough enough to mount the churning rapids above Ichang. Sokobin knows he's expected to applaud the American achievement, particularly as vice-consul. Until now all efforts have ended with broken ships and drowned men. Yet having once traveled up the rapids to the gorge country, it pains Sokobin to imagine the floating tank coughing its way up those tranquil green strands. He tilts his glass, only to remember he's already finished his whiskey, and sets it down.

"You can imagine what a boon this could be for us," Chase says. He has a grating tendency to use *us* and *we* whenever talking about Standard. "The kerosene market remains completely untapped that far inland. It's practically medieval."

Sokobin nods, pretending not to notice the slurred edges of Arthur's words or the flush of alcohol circling his cheeks. He can feel the Chesterfields nudging through the thin lining of his jacket pocket. His veins are ticking, and still he holds off. He hasn't seen Arthur since taking up the habit, and he's too tired to have to explain himself. He digs his fingers into his pocket to assess the number of cigarettes remaining. To his relief, the package is more full than not.

"Unfortunately, we've had to hold off with all the fighting that's broken out," Chase rattles on. "Civil unrest, it turns out, isn't so good for business. Makes one wonder what the States might be doing to stabilize the situation if we weren't so tied up in Europe."

Chase downs his whiskey in a single go and places his glass on the table. He looks at the empty cup with regret, as if he just swallowed a critical thought. After having observed Arthur at drink for some sixteen years, Sokobin knows when Chase is one round from blotto. If Arthur reaches for the decanter again, Sokobin will have no choice but to stand up and wave good night. He has half a mind to do it right now.

Arthur's eyes fix on the whiskey and Sokobin waits for Chase's hands to reach. Instead, they fall into a silent heap on his lap. "You know, sometimes I think it's best the old man didn't live to see the mess."

"Who?"

"Everton. It would have broken his heart. What China's become. The war. All of it."

Chase looks intently at Sokobin, his mouth slightly askew. It's an odd face, awkward, something Arthur never appears, even after too many drinks. The bleary expression confuses Sokobin before he finally recognizes it. Pity. Arthur is looking at him with pity.

"I don't know if I've properly said this, Soko. Scratch that, I know I haven't. But I was very sorry to hear about Ethan. I saw his name among the lists in the paper. I'm a bastard for not having written. I suppose I didn't know what to say." He blinks several times, and Sokobin fears Arthur will start to weep. "It's no excuse. I just want you to know there's not a single day that's gone by that I haven't thought of it. A damned business this war's become. A damned, bloody business."

Chase leans forward, one perfect hand aloft over the table, as if to grasp Sokobin's shoulder. The thought is unbearable, and Sokobin sits back, his spine pressed into the sofa cushions, safely out of reach.

"Do they know where?" Chase asks.

"The Channel, or so they think. They don't know."

"A dogfight?"

"No. Reconnaissance. Some sort of night mission. I don't know anything more," Sokobin tells him, now wishing he'd accepted a second fill of whiskey. If he asks for another now, Arthur will only assume he wants to talk about it. He knows now why he's been avoiding Chase these past months—not out of anger that Chase hasn't written, but because of this. To spare himself this very moment.

He looks past Chase's shoulders toward the row of windows, but the black panes only reflect their vague silhouettes. The house might as well be teetering on the great void that once ringed old sailing maps. *Sky, land, water,* his brother wrote from France. *It's not always clear where one ends and the other begins. Even with a full moon, things can get blurry.* Whatever Ethan penned after, Sokobin will never know. The censors blacked it out. It was the last letter.

"And the plane was never found?"

"No. If they had, I think they would have been able to tell us something."

Chase exhales. "Tough that, not knowing. All of it, but I imagine especially that."

Sokobin manages a nod. The spiraling plane, the fiery strands, the dark water all press hotly at the corners of his mind, demanding entry. His fingers circle the Chesterfields in his pocket. He wants to fill Chase's pristine living room to the gills with smoke.

"I take it you're not going home to see your mother," Chase says.

"I can't take the time, not so soon after the promotion. Besides, there's no point. She won't hear of it. She refuses to give up hope. And the crossing is too dangerous now. You know that."

"True. No sense risking it."

"At any rate, a lot of people have lost someone." *Lost.* The word sounds so petty, Sokobin thinks, like a misplaced cuff link or sock. And yet it fits. His brother isn't dead or alive, he's lost.

"You're not a lot of people, Soko. Not to me." Chase's eyes are so open, so blue, that it takes all Sokobin's control not to leave the room. "A fighting airman. So incredibly brave. You must be very, very proud. I hope there's some comfort to be found in that."

Sokobin's lungs cinch as something hard and shameful scuttles across his chest. Not sadness or grief, but something far less honorable. His brother's insatiable courage. Or bravado. Sokobin has never been able to pinpoint the difference. Perhaps if they'd ever talked of such things before, he might tell Arthur the truth about Ethan's bravery. How much Sokobin hates it, has always hated it. How much he hates himself for hating it. How many times these past months he's wished his brother were just another conscripted grunt in the trenches, miserable with foot rot and mad with waiting, shaken by exploding shells and mustard gas, but alive and accounted for.

He grips the Chesterfields in his pocket. "Do you mind?"

"I'm so sorry," Chase starts. He shakes his head, looking flustered. "I didn't mean to . . ."

Sokobin lets Arthur flounder longer than necessary. "I meant a cigarette," he says at last, withdrawing the package from his pocket and letting it drop onto the table. He takes out his lighter. "Do you mind if I smoke?"

"I didn't realize you did."

"I didn't."

Chase exhales, shaking his head. "I guess it's been a while."

Sokobin snaps the flint as Arthur makes his way to the bar. Years ago, Chase himself briefly flirted with the idea of smoking along with the rest of his fraternity brothers. The endeavor didn't last long. The smell, the yellowed teeth and nails, it all displeased him. In Chase's case, vanity requires traceless vices.

"Well, you might consider getting a proper cigarette case then," Chase says. He pours the remainder of the ice bucket into his glass and gulps it down, a telltale sign that he's at last ready for bed. "I must have a dozen from Standard. We're supposed to give them out as gifts to high levels. You're a high level now, you know. Fairly nice pieces, actually. Mexican Sterling. You could have it engraved."

"Thanks, but I prefer the pack. There's no need for a case. Chesterfields are waterproofed, very popular with soldiers."

"I just meant a man in your position, a vice-consul." Chase dabs at his mouth with a handkerchief. Monogrammed, no doubt, like everything else. "You know he would have been very proud to see what you've made of yourself. Everton, I mean."

It's an ungracious thought, Sokobin knows, but he wonders if not for their time at university, if he and Chase would still be friends, if indeed they ever have been in any genuine sense of the term. Or if what's kept them tethered is merely an ode to the past: Manhattan, Everton, their youth. Perhaps even less. Perhaps the connection is now nothing more than the simple fact that they are two unattached American men in China.

"I prefer the pack," Sokobin repeats and releases a thick plume of smoke toward Chase's perfect white ceiling.

IT'S A QUARTER PAST MIDNIGHT BY THE TIME HE MAKES his way down the hall to the furthest guest room. He keeps the electricity off and lifts the sash, letting the night air cool his damp skin. The river is there, a swath of shadow. From the far shore, a string of lights flicker as if transmitting signals in an unknown code.

He strips and pulls back the covers. Sinking into the mattress, he waits for exhaustion to overtake him. Branches cast a swaying filigree across the ceiling overhead. He imagines Lin installed one floor below, no doubt already sleeping the sleep of the untroubled. But the heat from the cigarettes remains lodged in Sokobin's chest, and rest refuses to come, as it so often has these past months.

He thinks about what Arthur told him, about Standard Oil's ironclad boat mounting the rapids above Ichang. It's not how Sokobin wants to remember the gorges, and he returns to drift once more through the twisting jade waters. He recalls the wet slap of the boatman's pole as they glided past rippled shores. Occasionally another sampan would appear, its ribbed sail spread like a fan on its way downriver. The trade was mostly *materia medica*, the guide told him, prized roots and berries and bark gathered from the surrounding mountains and pounded into salves or ground into tinctures. Cures for any ailment.

They sat across from one another, shaded from the sun by the boat's low thatched roof. The sides were open to the air, and for a spell, Sokobin leaned over the boat's edge to let his fingers trail through the tepid water. The guide informed them they were nearing the Cave of the Three Pilgrims, before falling silent again. By that point, the river was thin and green with silt. The sampan wound through a series of slots so narrow Sokobin could have reached out and touched the limestone walls on either side. Like secrets, each view withheld itself until they passed through the bend only to appear all at once. A dusty row of fishing huts perched on the ledge of a hill. And other small wonders: crumbling temples tucked into thickets of blue bamboo. Cliffs striped black with the trickle of a thousand years.

He recalls thinking the scene had felt so familiar, as though he'd been to the gorges before, only to eventually realize the source of the déjà vu: a set of painted scrolls Everton had once brought to class. The memory came on so sharply it nearly brought him to tears. As if all the scraping and study had been to bring him to this very place, and he remembers wishing Everton were sitting across from him, serene and smiling, the old man's fine gray hair lifting with the breeze—if only so that his beloved teacher might see the country of his youth once more. So that Everton might know that at least part of his sacred China had survived intact—eternal and hauntingly beautiful.

Eventually, the water's placid surface became riddled with currents, and the boatman was forced to steer them toward the bank. On the boulders lining either side, scores of men sat half-naked and barefoot, still and watching. Suddenly a voice called them to attention, and wordlessly they rose in a single brown motion. Bodies whittled to muscle, tendon, bone. Sokobin and the guide climbed out as the haulers trussed themselves with ropes, threw their weight forward and with impossible strength, heaved the boat up the churning water.

Men drown every year, the guide told Sokobin as they clamored up the rocks. They slipped, breaking their backs and necks. Others were dragged down by their own ropes into the whirling currents. Nothing could be done. Such men became river ghosts—the angry spirits blamed whenever a sampan capsized or a hull split over the shoals. All along the river, boatman slit the throats of chickens, tying the carcasses to the sterns as sacrifices in the hopes of being spared. In death, the haulers wielded an even greater hold over the living than they'd known while alive.

A shape flits across the plaster overhead, startling Sokobin, then disappears. A bird, he thinks; possibly a bat. Cicadas sound from the trees, their mechanical cries rising and falling like distant sirens. He listens to the river's waves brushing the shore only to realize the sound is his own breath. Of late, the pull of memory has been too strong, fissuring his thoughts and splitting him in two, plunging his mind into a dark and watery cavern while the refracted, bright world undulates above. Sometimes he can even see his own figure there, moving about the sunlit surface. But he knows it's only an imitation, a hollow form treading the currents while his real self, twisted and marred, lurks below.

Turning on his side, Sokobin looks across the guest bedroom mattress, halfway expecting to see another next to it: the narrow cot from the room he and Ethan once shared under the attic eaves, the nearly matching patchwork quilt sewn from the scraps of their mother's old *shtetl* dresses. But there's nothing there, only a blank slab of wall sheathed in moonlight.

Emptiness.

PART II

CHAPTER 7

Saturday, June 7

He sits alone in Chase's breakfast room, his every mastication observed by the houseboy hovering in the arched doorway. Sokobin does his best to ignore the man as he drinks his second cup of coffee, real Javanese as black and stiff as oil. Though it's well before eight, Arthur has somehow already managed to raise himself from the dead and depart for work, leaving behind the ferry schedule and a gently ruffled copy of the *International Herald*.

Sokobin is anxious to get to the municipal docks and interview the harbor master. He hasn't seen Mr. Lin since they parted last night and is debating whether to send for the interpreter straight off or wait for Lin to show himself. Once again, the finer points of protocol give Sokobin pause. He picks up the *Herald* instead. June 7, the dateline reads. Six days since Meyer was last seen.

As always, the front page brings news of the war. The photograph there might as well be of the moon. Sokobin supposes the Picardy countryside must have once been green and full of cattle, but he can't imagine the pocked stretch as ever containing anything but churned earth and barbed wire. Vague outlines appear in the background—felled logs or horses. Or men. Thankfully the photograph is too grainy and blurred to know.

In the columns below, he reads reports of yet more U-boat attacks. The seas turned graveyard. He reads over the dates, ship names, and death counts, but he's unable to summon the requisite sadness, or even anger. The war has spread everywhere: land, air, on the sea, under the sea. Like water itself, there seems to be no containing it—no limits or borders to its reach. Millions are dead. Entire villages are gone. Family lines have been erased. Even if the war were to end tomorrow, Sokobin can't foresee the world ever emerging from its grief.

He puts down his fork, folding and refolding the paper, but no matter which way he arranges the pages, the war stares back at him. It has been his constant breakfast companion these past years. At last he gives up, laying the *Herald* on the seat of the next chair, out of sight. He sips at his coffee, listening to his breath against the walls of his cup and wondering what the hell is keeping Lin.

———————

THE NAME HAD BEEN SLIGHTLY MISSPELLED. *SAKOBIN, Ethan.* He was used to the error; the family name was obscure, taken from the Ukrainian hamlet his parents had left as teenagers. Still Sokobin knew mistakes happened. A family plunged into grief by a *Johnson* typed instead of *Johnston*—the terrible oversight discovered only after the fact, after the anguish had cut too deep to ever fully heal. Perhaps if he'd been in the States, or even still in Shanghai, word would have come through more official channels, or at least more personal ones. Instead, he'd read his brother's name, like everyone else, in newsprint. A few smudged letters that hadn't been there the day before. It seemed impossible that so much could hang in the balance.

It was March, his second week in Nanking. He'd immediately wanted to return to Shanghai, to his old apartment, to roam the familiar rooms and lose himself in the city's dark watering holes. Even the dull routine of clerical tasks would have offered some comfort. And of course, there would have been the possibility of Meredith, of swallowing his pride and begging forgiveness. The consolation she might have offered behind closed shutters. It shamed him to think such selfish thoughts, but he wouldn't have been able to stop himself. Those first weeks he would have done anything to numb the pain.

But he wasn't in Shanghai anymore. He was in Nanking, a vice-consul, the new head of an outpost office. A man of rank. He'd endured the sympathetic looks of his staff, then to him still strangers. The CG wired, offering a few days' leave. Sokobin thanked him for the offer but declined. *We owe it to our boys to press on*, Sokobin had replied. The right words though not the true ones. The CG congratulated him on his courage; the praise only made Sokobin cringe. He wasn't brave or strong. It was Ethan who'd gone to war, who'd sacrificed. At his core, Sokobin knew, he was weak and afraid. Worse, a pretender. It hadn't been a stiff spine or sense of duty that kept him at work. He refused to stop for the simple fact that, if he did, he'd never start up again. He was teetering over a precipice; a deep pit of angry sludge waited below. Fall in and he'd never crawl back out.

Only once, with Windham, did he nearly falter. He and the junior clerk were alone in Sokobin's office, discussing some paltry errand. Without warning, the clerk reached into his jacket pocket and produced a black armband.

"You're welcome to it, sir. My mother sent an extra. She still doesn't think we can get anything over here."

Sokobin assumed the clerk too young to have lost anything. And yet he had. Two cousins, Windham explained, among the first casualties at the Western front. They were brothers; lost on the same day. They'd all grown up on neighboring farms, pitched in on each other's land come harvest time. Meanwhile, the dark band waited on Windham's pink palm. Sokobin could see the black cotton had been ironed smooth and carefully rolled.

"It helps, sir, what with us being so far away. Makes it real, I suppose."

The ensuing silence seemed to last a thousand years. Sokobin understood the gesture, however inappropriate, was meant as a kindness, a terrible sort of welcome. A part of him wanted to reach for the black band just to end it. But the thought of the cloth circling his arm made him sick. It would spell betrayal, make him his brother's murderer. Coolly he thanked the clerk for the offer but explained that the band wouldn't be fitting.

"My brother is missing, Mr. Windham, not dead."

"I'm sorry, sir," Windham said, shifting between his feet. "I meant no offense."

Sokobin's mother's letter didn't reach Nanking until April, having first gotten waylaid in the Shanghai office before someone thought to forward it upriver. His mother had recopied the note sent by the squadron leader so that her *Shemuel* might also read it. Sokobin could see the careful script, the faint pencil marks she'd drawn across with a ruler to keep the lines straight.

At twenty-nine, the major wrote, Ethan was the oldest in the group, one the most experienced flyers. Sometimes at night, he recounted stories about his time in Africa. It helped distract the other flyers, most of whom were barely beyond college. The mission had been her son's choice; Ethan had understood the risks. They were preparing to engage the Germans in air battles, and the reconnaissance was critical. *It is because of men like your son, Mrs. Sokobin, that victory will one day be ours.* Sokobin wondered how many of the words his mother had had to look up in her English dictionary. *Selfless* and *hero*, she would know. *Undaunted* or *crack shot*, she wouldn't.

The letter was short, less than a page, well-written. It pained Sokobin to think such eloquence had been acquired through practice. Only the final lines came like an ambush. *I am not a*

Hebrew, Mrs. Sokobin, nor do I pretend to know what it means to be one, and although war often forces compromise on such matters, I can say this with certainty: your Ethan will meet his maker, whenever and wherever that may prove, both as a soldier and a man of God.

He stares at the remains of his meat, the smear of egg yolk on his plate. Already his lungs are demanding a cigarette. Of course, it's far too early. Besides, he needs to ration the Chesterfields. There's no telling how long the day will last or even where it may take him. He lifts his coffee cup only to find the contents tepid. Looking at the houseboy, he taps his rim. The man comes forward, silver pot in hand, and pours out a steaming rill before retreating to the archway.

Sokobin checks his pocket watch. Five before eight. *Lin*, he thinks.

"Mr. Vice-Consul."

Sokobin turns his head at the sound of his name, unsure if the voice is real or imagined. But the interpreter is indeed there, having suddenly appeared at the edge of the room next to the houseboy. Lin holds his gray fedora in one hand, his leather attaché in the other. Sokobin notes the pressed shirt, the fresh collar, the plum and navy dotted tie. A matching plum silk square rises from the breast pocket of Lin's tan jacket. Sokobin admires the neatness.

"I am sorry to interrupt your breakfast," Lin says, offering a slight bow. Like most English interpreters, his voice sounds faintly British. For some reason, the accent only makes Sokobin feel more guilty about sending him downstairs last night.

"You are not interrupting, Mr. Lin. I hope you slept well."

"Yes, sir. Thank you."

"Would you care for some breakfast?"

"No, sir. I've already eaten."

"Very good then," Sokobin says. "We have much to do."

He expects the interpreter to join him at the table, but Lin remains at the threshold, side by side with the houseboy. His dark eyes blink behind his spectacles. Compared to the servant's long queue and traditional clasp jacket, Lin appears like a modern Continental, even more so than Sokobin himself.

"Would you care for some tea?" Sokobin asks.

But even this Lin declines. Still, he makes no sign of joining Sokobin, and at last, the vice-consul is forced to pull out the chair next to him, removing the newspaper and gesturing toward the seat. "Please."

Lin sits, placing his hat on the table. The weave is straw, very fine, Sokobin sees, and a far more sensible choice in the June heat than his own felt Hamburg. He wishes he'd thought to swap it out before making the trip.

"Mr. Vice-Consul," Lin says, looking intently at Sokobin. "There has been a development. A matter of some importance, I think."

"Regarding Mr. Meyer?"

"I believe so."

Lin tells Sokobin how the night before and earlier this morning, he took it upon himself to interview the servants—not only the houseboy, but also Chase's cook, gardener, washing *amah*, and chauffeur. "They all told the same story. A body pulled from the river. A Westerner. A man."

"They actually saw the body themselves?"

Lin shakes his head. "No. They hear this story from some men on the Standard Oil launch."

"I don't understand. Standard's boat picked up the body?"

"No, a sampan nearby. A fisherman. But the Standard Oil launch was close to the sampan, and they saw it tow the dead man to shore."

Sokobin taps the table. Assuming the story is true, Sokobin wonders how Arthur hasn't yet heard about it. "And how do the servants know all this?"

"From the other Standard Oil servants. They say they hear this story everywhere in town, in the markets. Everyone knows it."

Sokobin turns toward the houseboy, as if expecting the man to confirm the facts. But the houseboy keeps his eyes on his black felt slippers.

"Where did this take place? The body, I mean. Where was it found?"

"Upriver. Not far."

"When?"

"Three days ago."

"*Three* days?"

"Yes."

Again, Sokobin wonders how word of the body, especially a foreign one, hasn't reached Chase. It's possible Arthur's servants have assumed their employer must already be aware of all things involving Westerners. Or perhaps they are of the superstitious sort that avoids any mention of death lest they invite it upon themselves. Either way, it's clear Arthur never thought to ask. Nor, if Sokobin is honest, has he. Interviewing the servants was entirely Lin's idea.

"And they are sure the body was a white man?"

"Yes."

"What did it look like?"

"The face was black with dirt from the water and very . . ." Lin pauses, as if searching for the word. "Swollen."

Sokobin blocks the image before it forms. "I don't understand. If they couldn't see the face, how can they be sure the body was a foreigner?"

Lin turns to the houseboy. Sokobin tries to follow the exchange, but the sounds come much too fast.

"He says they say the hair was not Chinese. And the dead man has a beard. Red, not black. Mr. Meyer has a beard, yes?"

Sokobin leans back. It's entirely possible the lead he's needed has been downstairs all along, perhaps even before the Consul General first wired from Shanghai.

"Do the servants know where the body is now?"

"Ti-Kang."

Sokobin doesn't recognize the name of the village. "Upriver?"

"Yes, maybe twenty or thirty miles. The town is small but there is a patrol station. The fisherman brought the dead man there. They say everyone in Ti-Kang saw the body when the fisherman towed it ashore."

Sokobin imagines the sandaled feet circling the swollen corpse as if it were a prize catch. He sips at his coffee, swallowing his anger. Still, it's a solid lead, he thinks, far more than he expected this early in the game. Even if all the details aren't true, the story's location and timeline mesh with the basic facts of Meyer's disappearance.

The houseboy steps forward with the silver pot. Sokobin waves him off and picks up the ferry schedule. The next boat upriver leaves in just under an hour from the municipal docks. The drive alone will take nearly half that. If they leave straightaway, they should have enough time to ask the harbor master a few questions before boarding, just to rule out that no other information has come to light.

"How quickly can you be ready?" he asks Lin.

"I am ready now, Mr. Vice-Consul."

Sokobin pushes back his chair and stands. "See to it that the driver is called. I'll meet you in the front hall in five minutes. We're headed to Ti-Kang."

Lin turns toward the houseboy, and the man quickly disappears down the corridor. For some reason, the interpreter remains seated. Sokobin follows Lin's eyes to the folded *Herald* waiting on the chair.

"I should have asked if you wanted it," Sokobin says, holding out the paper. "I didn't realize you followed the war."

"Everyone follows the war, Vice-Consul," Lin says. His jaw tightens momentarily as he slips the paper into his attaché. The grimace fades so quickly Sokobin can't be sure it was there at all. "The time, sir."

"Right." Sokobin moves toward the exit, only to catch himself and pause under the arch. "Very good work, Mr. Lin," he says over his shoulder. "Very good work indeed."

CHAPTER 8

THE PATROL STATION AT TI-KANG CONSISTS OF A SIN-
gle bricked room aired by a pair of open windows and a wob-
bling fan. Sokobin and Lin sit across from its sole officer, Cheng,
a young and exceptionally lithe man whose cropped black hair is
threaded with sun-streaked strands. Sokobin deduces from his
clean desk that the outpost doesn't see much action.

"Ask the officer if he saw the body with his own eyes," Sokobin says to Lin.

"He says 'Yes,'" Lin translates. "A Westerner with a beard."

"And the clothes?"

"Trousers, no dress shirt, only an undershirt. Suspenders and
yellow city shoes. Leather."

Sokobin jots down the description in his notes. He'll need to
confirm the clothes as the same Meyer was wearing the night he
disappeared with the boy and cabinmate, once they've been tracked
down in Shanghai. Sokobin glances at his watch. 10:35 a.m. Already
he can feel the morning's cool giving way. Meanwhile, the telltale
rectangle of a cigarette package presses against the breast pocket of
Cheng's khaki uniform. Sokobin catches himself staring at it.

"But the shoes and suspenders are not on the body anymore,"
Lin relays.

Sokobin pauses his pen. "Why not?"

"The officer says he gave them to the fisherman who towed
the body."

"Whatever for?"

"He paid the fisherman eighty cents for bringing in the body. But the fisherman is an old uncle who likes to complain. He said the money wasn't enough, so the officer gave him these things to sell, to make him quiet."

The eternal negotiation of China, Sokobin thinks. The never-ending hustle. If there's anything so sacred in the country that a price can't be attached, he has yet to find it. He looks Lin squarely in the face, though what he hopes to find there—shock, outrage—Sokobin doesn't know. But Lin's dark eyes reveal nothing.

"And the fisherman," Sokobin asks. "Is he here in the village?"

The officer nods, pointing over their shoulders. Sokobin twists in his seat and follows the line of the man's finger out the front window to where a row of sampans lies beached in the sand, their sails rolled. No doubt they are waiting for the tide to change. Most of the prows are painted with totem-like faces and large bright eyes, an old-timer's trick for spotting sharp rocks and shoals, and for seeing the small boats safely through fog and night. The deeper one heads into the interior, the more the superstitions still hold.

"He says the fisherman's sampan is there. Do you wish to talk to him?"

"After we're finished here," Sokobin says, turning back to face Cheng. He taps his pen against the page as he considers how to best phrase his next question, but there's no way of putting the matter delicately. "Ask if he saw any strange marks on the body. Knife wounds, bullet holes, anything that would suggest violence or malice."

The officer puts up a hand as if refusing the very words. A dark circle spreads from the armpits of his uniform.

"He says he doesn't think so. But he does not look close. The river is hard on a body, Vice-Consul. Very hard."

Sokobin can't tell if the words are Officer Cheng's or Lin's—a statement of fact or a warning. Again he thinks of the Chesterfields in his pocket but knows it's too early to start. Besides, he doesn't want to appear on edge. So far, Cheng has been forthcoming. No doubt the officer is pleased to receive an American of rank. And yet, all that could quickly change if the patrolman senses his actions are being questioned. Sokobin has encountered the type before—quick to clam up for fear of saying anything that might be later held against them.

He senses Lin's eyes on him, waiting. Whatever was said, Sokobin's missed it. "Come again?"

"He asks if you wish to see the grave."

"Now?"

"Yes."

Sokobin rests his notebook on the edge of the desk. The body. He's been doing his best not to think of it. But of course, it's why he's here. He's the only one within hundreds of miles who can identify Meyer. He reaches for his handkerchief, wipes his forehead. "Where exactly is it?"

Lin redirects the question, and the officer jerks a thumb over his own shoulder. "He says he pays some local men to bury the body on this hill. There's a cemetery at the top."

Sokobin's eyes settle on the grassy slope contained within the peeling window frame. With few exceptions, whatever trees once grew there have been axed. A hill like any other, covered in long yellow grass and studded with dark rocks. A nameless hill that could be one of a billion in China, no more unique than a swell on the sea.

"He says it is better that we go soon," Lin translates. "Before the afternoon heat."

Sokobin can feel the sweat snaking again down his temple. He dabs his forehead but it's no use. He can't stop perspiring. Already it's too hot for the jacket. Still, he keeps it on, if only to hide the stains that must now be spreading across his back and throat.

"Vice-Consul?" Lin prompts.

"Better we speak with the fisherman first," Sokobin says. "Before he disappears with the tide. Have him bring the shoes and suspenders—assuming he hasn't sold them yet."

The officer exits through the front door, and Sokobin lifts his chin toward the fan so the whirring blades might dry his face. Through the open doorway, he can see Cheng make his way down the row of sampans. The officer stops in front of one of the boats where an old fisherman coils rope on the prow. The thatched boat is particularly weathered, its hull nearly black and painted eyes faded to dim shadows. A jumble of baskets and bric-a-brac clot the small deck.

The old fisherman continues to roll his rope. It's clear he isn't in any hurry to stop his work, not even for Cheng. The officer crosses his arms. The resulting voice is louder than Sokobin would have expected Cheng's slender frame would allow.

At last, the fisherman drops the coil and ducks beneath the thatch. He reappears moments later, holding a burlap sack. A grimace stretches across the old man's face as he bends to lower himself over the boat's edge. Bag in hand, he follows behind the officer. He is barefoot and his legs widely bowed. Rickets, Sokobin guesses. One sees it enough, especially outside the cities.

Sokobin returns to his seat and turns to a clean page in his notes as the officer takes his place at the desk. They are short one chair. Lin offers his up, but the old fisherman waves him off and stands to the side. He wears a long gray cotton shirt, sleeves rolled to the elbows, loose trousers, and a rust-colored scarf tied around his head. All are torn and exude the vinegary scents of sweat and fish. Decades of sun have weathered his skin the deep brown of tobacco.

The fisherman gives the same story. His accent is thick, even for Lin, who must stop the old man several times in order to repeat himself. But the story matches Cheng's. No, he didn't see any marks on the body. The corpse was already too swollen and floating. He figures the man must have already been in the water a couple of days before he found him.

Sokobin points to the burlap sack. "Ask him to open it."

The fisherman's fist stays tight around the bag. Several of his thick fingers appear permanently gnarled, either from arthritis or injury. He aims his words at Cheng. Sokobin hears the tone of accusation.

"He says the things are his now," Lin explains.

"Tell him that the clothes are evidence, that we must see them in order to identify the body."

The man continues to shake his head. His voice is low and slightly raspy as if his throat were coated with sand. "He says he made a deal with the officer," Lin translates. "The things are his. He intends to sell them."

Sokobin puts down his notebook and takes a breath. "Tell him the things cannot be his and are not for trading. They belong to the dead man's family. I must return them."

The fisherman points accusingly at the officer who throws up his hands and, in turn, points at Sokobin. Suddenly the men's words slap the air. The bickering lasts no more than a few seconds before Sokobin loses his patience and slams his fist down on the desk, instantly silencing them. He knows the CG would scold him for losing his temper, but the pettiness is more than Sokobin can bear. Meanwhile Lin coolly blinks from behind his gold-rimmed spectacles, seemingly unaffected. At this point, Sokobin isn't sure if he finds the interpreter's containment enviable or simply maddening.

"Tell him we will buy the dead man's things," Sokobin announces, wishing he'd had the foresight to do this from the start. In his briefcase is a small purse of cash expressly for these sorts of moments, and he comes up with a Mexican silver dollar, the preferred currency as the Republic's own keeps devaluing. It's far more than the fisherman could ever get for the waterlogged items, but Sokobin doesn't care. He wants the affair done; the old uncle gone.

The coin absurdly makes its way around the desk from Sokobin's fingers to Lin's to the officer's before finally reaching the fisherman, who lifts a small cotton purse from beneath the neck of his gray shirt, drops the silver in, and tugs it shut. At last, the old man places the sack to the desk. Sokobin watches his flat backside shuffle out the door.

Save for the fan, the silence grows ripe. Lin and Cheng both stare at the sack, clearly waiting on Sokobin to make the first move. He reaches and uncinches the strings, lifting out the suspenders first, then the shoes. Despite Cheng's earlier description, Sokobin expects to see the same trail boots Meyer wore to the Fourth of July party. But the shoes are as described: stackheeled oxfords, the leather yellowish, though badly discolored and misshapen from having been submerged. Sokobin tries not to consider what that same amount of water might do to a man's skin.

He turns the shoes upside down, tilting the soles toward the light from the window. The imprint is worn, the letters faint. Even so, Sokobin can make out the stamp, and a small wave breaks across his chest. Once again, he senses the universe toying with him. The brand is from Newark—one of the brick tanneries overlooking the Passaic. He and Ethan held their breath as they passed it on their way to school. The leather hides had to be soaked in urine; every day Sokobin thanked God their father didn't have to work there.

He lowers the shoes to the desk. "American," he says. Somehow the word doesn't deliver the relief it should.

Cheng exhales, leans back in his seat. He addresses Lin, pointing toward the hill. Sokobin doesn't need to wait for the translation. The officer is anxious to leave.

"He says it is getting hot, Vice-Consul, and will only get worse."

The officer crosses the room and lifts a cap from the hook by the door. A small mirror has been tacked to the wall, and Cheng checks his image as he settles the shiny black brim over his brow. Satisfied, he turns back to face them, his hands on his thick belt.

"He will call for a sedan chair for you, Vice-Consul. There is one in the village."

"No chair. I'll walk." Like servants hovering about in corners, Sokobin has never gone in for sedan chairs. More trouble than they're worth, in his opinion. Besides, he hasn't forgotten Meyer's disdain for them. If the grave contains the explorer's body, and all indications are it will, to be carried up the hill would feel an insult to the man himself.

"You are sure, sir? He says the hill is higher than it looks."

"Quite so, Mr. Lin." Sokobin caps his pen and slides his notebook into his briefcase. "Is there a safe place where I might keep Mr. Meyer's things while we're gone?"

The officer selects a key from the ring on his belt. Sokobin watches as he bends and unlocks the deep bottom drawer of his desk. Sokobin's chest tightens at the sight, halfway expecting to see the blue envelopes there. But of course, the drawer is empty. The officer places the burlap sack inside and turns the lock.

"Your case, sir?" Lin asks.

Sokobin knows it will be awkward lugging the briefcase up the hill, but he can't risk being separated from all the case contains: the dossier, the petty cash, his father's yarmulke and tallit. Ethan's photograph. "I'll manage, thank you," he says, clasping it shut.

Lin and the officer look at him with patience, or at least its pretense, as Sokobin pats his pockets, checking for his Chesterfields, his lighter, his wallet. But everything is there. He wipes his forehead once more before stuffing the damp cloth in his jacket pocket. Finally, there is nothing left to check, nothing to do but leave. Sokobin's eyes return to the grassy slope framed by the back window, and he realizes that what he took for dark rocks set into the grass must be, in fact, tombstones. He tells himself that there's nothing to fear. The dead, he's seen them before. Besides, there can be no avoiding the task at hand. It's why he's been sent here; what he's been sent to do. It's his duty as a man of rank.

The officer gestures toward the front door, bowing slightly.

"Whenever you are ready, Vice-Consul," Lin says.

Sokobin grips his briefcase. His heart seems to be beating from everywhere at once: his gut, his head, his hands. Silently he repeats *dignity and control* as he steps toward the door, only to have something in his chest give way at the threshold. He curls a damp hand around the frame to still his fingers.

"They used a coffin, yes?" he asks.

Behind him Lin and Cheng exchange far too many words for what should be a simple answer.

"Yes or no?" Sokobin interrupts.

"He isn't sure," Lin finally says.

CHAPTER 9

Sokobin heads for the shade of the lone surviving tree and lowers his briefcase to the patchy grass. He lifts his hat, fanning himself and reaching for his handkerchief. The climb, though short, proved steeper than expected, and now sweat encases him like a second skin. His left heel feels hot and raw. He bends to straighten his twisted sock, but it does no good. He didn't think to bring boots upriver. Or a canteen. Or a thinner suit like Lin's—his beige linen, for instance, still hanging in his wardrobe back in Nanking. The irony of the situation, his own pathetic exhaustion at tramping up a hill in search of the seasoned explorer, doesn't escape him.

Meanwhile some thirty feet ahead, Lin and the others stand a few feet from the grave in question. The grave is typically Chinese, not dug into the ground but rather piled soil, the earth too recently churned to have either settled or sprouted weeds. The diggers wear typical peasant straw hats and woven sandals. One is clearly older; the full shoulders, long faces, and hollow cheeks are too similar for them to be anything other than father and son. Each holds a rusted shovel. No doubt they are the same men who buried the body just days before.

Sokobin dips his fingers into his pocket, finds the Chesterfields there. He's waiting for the money to be settled before lighting up. It won't be long now, he tells himself. A few minutes more and the affair's price should be negotiated. As

vice-consul, he knows he's expected to stay clear of such low-
brow negotiations whenever possible. Better to stay put and
cool his inflamed heels. He's already broken rank by refusing
the sedan chair.

The cemetery runs long and narrow, like a shelf cut into the
side of the hill. At present they appear to be its only visitors.
The usual stone markers lie scattered throughout the grass, in-
terspersed with a few larger tombs shaped like honeypots. These
belong to the wealthier families, he deduces. Clay figures flank
their fronts: servants, oxen, and swine. Further up the slope, a
few headstones rise from the yellow blades. Sokobin makes out
the weathered remains of offerings: oranges, whiskey, cigarettes,
small bottles containing who knows what. As Everton used to
say, the dead are never truly dead in China. Rank and comfort
must be maintained in the afterlife. Even the humblest of families, Sokobin knows, pay tribute—weeding plots and offering
prayers, occasionally burning fake money and incense.

But on the grave in question, there is nothing, not a head-
stone to bear witness to the life lived, not even a touch of shade
from an overhanging branch. There is only churned, sunbaked
dirt waiting to sink beneath the weight of summer and vanish.
Sokobin tries to make sense of it, how an exceptional man like
Meyer could have ended up here—discarded in an unmarked
grave, on an unnamed hill, like a piece of withered fruit fallen
from the tree. Perhaps Meyer foresaw this very fate as part of
the risks of the adventuring life. Even so, the lonely sight rubs
Sokobin wrong. If he were to return to this hill in six months,
even three, there would be no evidence of Meyer's grave at all,
and with it, whatever truth existed of the man's end would have
disappeared under the wild grass.

Assuming, of course, that it's Meyer who's buried here.

Something is amiss, he thinks. The diggers should be working by now. He detects disagreement, though not in the words

themselves—these he can barely hear, let alone understand. But the tone feels off. He tells himself to give Lin another minute to sort the mess. The interpreter has already greatly impressed him, not only with his skill in translating and perfect English but also with his initiative in interviewing Chase's servants. If he hadn't, who knows how long it would have taken Sokobin to find his way here? Days, weeks. Most likely never.

The seconds grow interminable. Like so much about protocol, the situation runs contrary to Sokobin's instincts as he stands under the tree, doing nothing. He checks his watch. Half past eleven. Suddenly a knot of voices rises from the group. The officer shouts, flinging an arm into the air. Lin turns toward Sokobin, his face a mask of concern, and Sokobin understands he has no choice but to intervene.

He hesitates to leave his briefcase, but there's no one around. Ignoring the pain in his heel, he steps to the edge of the canopy and blinks against the sunlight. The tall grass rustles like paper against his trousers as he makes his way toward the group. At the sight of Sokobin's advancing frame, Cheng goes silent and crosses his arms over his narrow chest. His brimmed cap sits back on his forehead, small beads of sweat dotting his amber skin.

"Vice-Consul," Lin says, his cheeks flush with heat. "The men refuse to dig."

Sokobin directs a stern stare, but the look is lost on the pair. Despite their impressive height and full shoulders, they keep their faces timidly pointed toward the ground. Sokobin eyes their soiled, patched pants. The son's shirt, he sees, has begun to unravel at the shoulder. For a moment he remembers the sooty boys he and Ethan once ran with on Newark's streets.

"Is this about money? They should count themselves lucky to be paid twice for the same hole."

"No, sir. Not money," Lin says. "They say if they disturb a grave, they go to prison."

Sokobin exhales in frustration, more with himself than any-one. Like the boots, the canteen, the suit, the hat, like so much else, he should have foreseen this. To desecrate a man's spirit is a serious crime in China, the punishments severe. He supposes he didn't expect the rules would apply to a foreigner's grave. Yet, clearly, they do. "Tell them I am the number one man here for all things Western, and that I order them to dig."

"They know this, sir."

"Then assure them they won't get in trouble, that any respon-sibility is mine alone."

Still the older digger continues to shake his head, his voice firm. Save "No," Sokobin is unable to make out a single word. As with the old fisherman, Mr. Lin must ask the man to repeat himself.

"They say the foreigner's ghost will be angry if they dig. It will come and haunt them, make them sick, make them die. I am sorry, Vice-Consul," Lin says as if the situation were of his own making. "They are villagers, set in their ways."

Sokobin purses his lips. He attempts to summon compas-sion; the men before him are coolies, fated to a life of toil. They are poor and will never be anything but. He would be surprised if either could write his own name. But the body lies waiting and the sun overhead has begun to rob him of his patience. "We don't have time for old wives' tales, Mr. Lin."

"Not tales, Vice-Consul. Beliefs. Tradition."

Sokobin attempts to swallow the grit rising in his throat. He can't let himself lose his temper like he did in the station house. He points at the shovels. "The body must be exhumed and iden-tified, Mr. Lin. The men must dig by order of the American gov-ernment."

Sokobin waits for the interpreter's echo following his words, but Lin says nothing. Instead, he removes the silk handkerchief from his breast pocket and wipes his glasses before refolding the square into his jacket. Sokobin knows what Lin is attempting to tell him, that curt words will get him nowhere with these men. Still, he finds the interpreter's insubordination trying, if not downright infuriating. The patrolman utters a few words in Chinese; these also go untranslated.

Sokobin can feel all eyes on him as he looks at the silent mound. A man lies beneath. Meyer or some other lost soul. One way or another, he needs to know. They're wasting time. Beneath his hat, his head has begun to steam.

"If the men refuse to dig, I'll be forced to do the work myself. And they should know it will be reported." It's a lie, at least a half one. If the CG ever got wind of one of his VC's bowing to perform such a menial task, Sokobin would never hear the end of it.

Cheng's eyes widen as Lin translates, and within seconds, he is back to chastising the diggers. The older one shoves his spade into the ground. Before either Lin or Sokobin can stop him, the officer shoves the older man's chest, knocking off his straw hat. The younger one cries out, raising his shovel as if to strike. Lin attempts to calm the youth but it's no use. Sokobin can see it's about to come to blows any moment. Protocol be damned, inserts himself between Cheng and the young digger. His hands meet muscle and bone, hot furious hearts.

"This is a disgrace," he spits out.

At last Cheng throws up his hands like a captured bandit and takes several steps back. The older digger tugs at his son's arms, pulling him away and allowing Sokobin to drop his hold. The strain of keeping the two apart has left him breathless and his shirt clinging to his chest.

Still the grave is there, waiting. Sokobin inhales sharply, telling himself to think. *Think.*

"Mr. Lin, tell them that the dead man is a restless ghost, far from his people, and must be returned to them. If the body stays here, it will haunt this town and bring bad luck to everyone."

Sokobin has never liked stooping to superstition but can't see any other way. Indeed, the men's faces noticeably tighten as Lin relays the message. They step away to whisper among themselves, and Sokobin senses them relenting. After several moments, they pull scarves from their pockets, knotting the cotton at the back of their heads to cover their noses and mouths. With a wave of his hand, the father signals for Sokobin to move away from the grave, and the two men tip their shovels to the dirt.

With the task at last underway, Sokobin retreats to the shade. Again, he wishes he'd thought to bring water. The sun has left him with a slight headache. He loosens his tie and removes his jacket, hanging it from a low branch, and pulls a Chesterfield from the pocket. He snaps open his lighter and strikes the flint. His breath is still short from the scuffle, and it's a struggle to draw down the smoke.

The diggers work with their backs to him, blocking the grave as they cast off dirt to the side. Save for the growing pile, Sokobin can see little of their progress. Cheng has already moved off to the side. The patrolman pulls his cigarettes and matches from his tan shirt, cupping the flame against the faint breeze. The dark circles beneath his arms have spread. He watches Sokobin smoking under the tree as if observing a strange animal in its native habitat. Only Lin remains close to the grave, fanning himself with his pale gray hat. The soil is loose, and Sokobin can see it won't be long.

He turns toward the river, hoping to catch a breeze. Save for a few brown crusts, the cloudless sky renders the water's surface almost blue. It's about as clean looking as the Yangtze gets in the flood plain. An endless trail of ships, some large, others small, traverses the horizon. Their wakes last only a few seconds before blurring into the currents. Below he spots a group of women gathered at the water's edge. Surrounded by baskets, they dunk laundry in the shallows. He imagines his own mother among them, her hair bound and skirt knotted. Sunday mornings she and some of the others used to meet at the pump behind the tenement while the rest of the building was away at mass. Sokobin used to watch them from the window in his attic room above. Dozens of drying lines crisscrossed the air like spider webs. He wonders where Ethan was in such moments. No doubt outside, running wild. Swinging a bat, kicking a can, winning glory. Meanwhile Sokobin's schoolbooks lay waiting on the bed.

He's a few drags into his second cigarette when Lin calls his name, and Sokobin knows it's done. He takes one more pull, letting the smoke swirl against the roof of his mouth before extinguishing the remainder against the trunk. He stares at the black ash on the bark, wishing he could trade this moment for any other. He's been lying to himself thinking that his cases in Shanghai had prepared him for this moment. Nothing could.

Lin and Cheng stand side by side, facing Sokobin and blocking the grave. The officer tilts his head toward the sky and expels a thick white stream with the force of steam train, then drops the butt and crushes it beneath his boot. The diggers have moved some twenty feet from the site, their faces still covered. Watching.

"Mr. Vice-Consul," Lin says. He holds the purple silk square from his pocket to his face. The handkerchief flutters with the words.

Sokobin manages a few feet when the smell, putrid and horrifically sweet, stops him in his tracks. He presses his own handkerchief to his nose only to be met with the acrid scent of his own sweat. As he draws nearer, he sees Lin's dark eyes wince behind his spectacles.

"Sir, there is no coffin."

Sokobin barely has time to register the meaning of the statement before Lin and Cheng step to the side, parting like drapes. Sokobin stops in confusion, blinking against the glare. His first thought is of rubble, of something fallen from the sky. Three rough planks lie over the body, one below. Nothing is as it should be. He tries to decipher the pieces, how they might fit together to make a man. Two bruised feet extend beyond the wood. One leg, rigid and clad in filthy grayish trousers, juts out to the side.

He steps forward again. There is no shroud. The body itself has not been wrapped in any way. Everything is coated in soil. A mottled hand extends beyond the wood planks, the skin is the same blue-brown as the river. Sokobin reaches for it without thinking. His fingers meet with the lifeless flesh, and he quickly jerks his hand away. He'd nearly grasped it.

A tap on his shoulder. Sokobin flinches at the touch. Lin is at his side, his handkerchief billowing with talk. But Sokobin's heart is beating too loudly for him to make any sense of the words.

"Mr. Vice-Consul," Lin repeats. "The men lift the wood now. So that you can see the face."

Before Sokobin can stop them, the diggers are back, lifting the first plank and tossing it to the side. As they bend for the second plank, Sokobin tries to summon the explorer's pale eyes and ruddy face from the party, the full shoulders and heavy shanks. But it's no use. Save for the filthy beard, the wretched bluish form is unrecognizable as Meyer. What remains is hardly recognizable as a man at all.

Sokobin turns from the sight, spitting into the grass. He attempts to focus on the clean yellow blades; still the awful smell continues to seep through his handkerchief. Saliva pools beneath his tongue, and for a terrible minute, he thinks he may vomit. He orders himself to hold it together. *Dignity and control.* But neither can be pulled from the moment, only disgust. Hot bile spills across his tongue. He swallows it.

"Are you all right, sir?"

Mr. Lin's hand is on his back. "I didn't realize . . ." Sokobin stops, unsure of what he intends to say. The sun is pinning him to the spot, making it difficult to think. He manages to right himself. The body is behind him. He can't look at it.

"There are some washer women below," he tells Lin. "Have Officer Cheng buy a sheet from them and bring it here. Tell him I will pay. The body must be covered. Immediately."

Cheng stands close by, a few feet from the grave, his face somehow uncovered. He withdraws another cigarette from his uniform as Lin translates, cupping his hand over a lit match. Sokobin reaches for the Chesterfields in his own pocket, only to remember that his jacket is still hanging on the branch. It might as well be a million miles away. The officer narrows his eyes at Sokobin as Lin translates. The exchange between Cheng and Lin is short.

"He asks if the body is the American you are looking for," Lin says through his silk handkerchief. A thin trickle of sweat has begun to slip down his smooth temple, and the interpreter wipes it with the back of his hand.

Sokobin shakes his head in defeat. "I don't know. The face is too dirty."

Cheng shakes his head. Smoke curls out from his nostrils.

"He says he must know if it is the American before he goes down to the village," Lin tells Sokobin. "If it is Mr. Meyer, he will bring the funeral men with him when he comes back up the hill. If it is not Mr. Meyer, he will tell the diggers to cover the grave back up. I am sorry, sir. But he is right. We must know."

Lin holds out the plum-colored handkerchief. "Take it, sir. You will need it."

Sokobin stares at the billowing silk, at last understanding. He is to wipe the face with his own handkerchief. He presses Lin's square to his nose, taking in the faint smell of oranges and almonds. The cologne's scent lasts for only a moment before the rot eclipses it.

By then the flies have landed. Sokobin runs his own handkerchief down the neck, waving the insects away. He can't look into the face, not yet. He wipes the chest, clearing whatever skin hasn't been covered by the grubby undershirt. He reminds himself to look for gashes or holes, any sign of garroting or foul play but finds nothing. Still, he can't be entirely sure. Between the river and the heat, the skin has swollen and it's just as the officer and fisherman said: impossible to know.

He refolds his handkerchief to make a clean section, and brushes the soil from the forehead, the cheeks, the nostrils. The flies are relentless. He hesitates at the crusted lips, unsure if he should touch them. It feels too intimate, a trespass. But he has no choice. With a brief motion of the kerchief, at last, the bearded face emerges. The eyes squeezed, the mouth askew. Sokobin can see the distress of the man's final moments in them. He remembers Meyer at the party, the strain on his face as he looked out the window and spoke of his ill father.

Sokobin spreads his soiled handkerchief over the head, watching the cotton sink into the hollows. Standing, he turns toward Lin. "It's him. It's Meyer."

He hands Lin his handkerchief as they step away from the body. Lin and the officer exchange no more than a few words before Cheng heads off, jogging down the narrow trail leading back to the village.

"The diggers," Lin says.

Sokobin has forgotten all about them. But of course, they are still there waiting under the tree, their scarves tied about their necks. In Sokobin's jacket are several coins, put there just for this reason, and he motions for Lin to follow him to where his coat hangs on the branch. Like the old fisherman, the diggers wear small pouches around their necks, and they drop the coins inside, knotting them shut. The men offer small bows and take several steps backward before turning toward the trail, shovels over their shoulders. Sokobin watches their sturdy frames disappear down the slope.

At last, it is just he and Lin left on the hill. And the body, of course. Sokobin looks toward the open grave. A mistake. He tells himself not to look at it again. The sun is making him imagine things, impossible things. An echo has begun to sound in his head. His brother's name. Not Ethan, but how their parents used to call him when they were children. *Eitan*. Strength. Endurance.

"Perhaps you would prefer to wait at the station below?" Mr. Lin asks as he tucks the silk square back into his breast pocket.

"No. I must stay," Sokobin tells him. "There are certain rules," he pauses, unsure of how much he wants to go into the rules of Meyer's faith. His faith. He must keep watch over the body.

"I think it is very hot for you here, Vice-Consul. You are not used to the sun."

"I must stay, Mr. Lin. I don't expect you to understand."

"I understand, sir. Beliefs. Tradition."

Their eyes lock. Lin's spectacles slightly exaggerate the size of his dark irises. Sokobin wonders how he hasn't taken notice of this before. "If you wish to return to the station, you may do so, Mr. Lin. I don't think I'll need an interpreter with the funeral men. I'm certain they'll know what to do."

Lin removes his glasses and wipes the lenses with the ends of his tan jacket, before curling the gold metal ends around his ears. "I will wait with you, sir."

"As you wish, Mr. Lin."

Sokobin moves closer to the heavy shade near the trunk. The black ash from his cigarette is still there on the tree, and he touches a finger to the mark. A sudden wave of exhaustion overtakes him and he half sits, half collapses into the patchy grass next to his briefcase. He leans back, resting his head against the rough bark. His headache has grown, as has the soreness on his heel. He'd briefly forgotten it in the rush, but now the pain is back in full force. He loosens his shoelaces, wincing as he touches a finger to the bubble of skin forming beneath his sock.

Meanwhile Lin stands in the dappled shade at the tree's periphery. He keeps his body angled slightly away, out of awkwardness or
deference, Sokobin can't say. He finds Lin impossible to read.

"The tree is certainly large enough for the both of us," he calls
to Lin. "Come closer where the shade is better."

The interpreter steps under the branches just enough to evade
the glare. The silence expands between them as a small wind
sifts through the leaves. Sokobin withdraws a cigarette from his
jacket and manages to crack open the lighter but can't steady his
fingers enough to catch the flint. He tries again. It's no use. Meyer's face—the mottled skin and anguish—he can't stop seeing it.

Lin steps closer, holds out his palm. Sokobin hesitates, then
reluctantly hands over the lighter. Within moments, the blue
flame is up. He leans in, inhaling the smoke and hoping to feel
something—relief, sadness, anger, anything. Lin caps the lighter
and wordlessly hands it back. Despite the heat and the climb,
Lin remains preternaturally spotless, his skin smooth and his
suit crisp. At this point, the neatness is almost painful.

Sokobin shuts his eyes against the heat, but his lids sting with
sweat. "I'd offer you a cigarette, but I take it you don't indulge in
the habit."

"No, sir."

"Very wise."

Sokobin gets the feeling the word could be applied to much
of the interpreter's life. When Lin speaks, his voice hardly registers over the rustling leaves.

"I think, sir, this is the first time you see a body like this."

"I worked a few missing person cases in Shanghai." Sokobin stops before the deceit can further unfurl. "But no, nothing like this." He supposes he should be grateful, yet somehow
the answer only smacks of privilege. Thousands of ravaged men
lay strewn across Europe's fields and trenches this very moment.
Who is he to have been spared the sight?

"And you, Mr. Lin?"

"I have lived along the river all my life." Lin removes his hat, fans himself. "It is right that you bring Mr. Meyer to be buried with his people, sir. It is not good for his spirit to be left wandering so far from his village."

Lin's words take Sokobin by surprise. He's assumed, perhaps naïvely so, that along with the interpreter's modern clothes and exceptional English would come a belief in Western ways.

"I suppose you mean all that business I told the diggers about Meyer's spirit haunting the town?" Sokobin asks.

"Yes, sir."

"I don't really think that, you know. I just said it to get them to dig. I wouldn't have taken you for a superstitious man, Mr. Lin."

"I do not take myself for one either, Vice-Consul."

Sokobin exhales overhead. Light filters through the branches. He watches as the burning tip of his cigarette closes in on his lips. His brother's name is still sounding in his head. If he were to shut his eyes, the fiery plane and dark sea would be there. "The world is at war, Mr. Lin. Many men now die far from their villages."

A pained look crosses Lin's face and he stops fanning himself with his hat. "Yes, the war is a terrible thing, Vice-Consul. Each night I pray for it to end."

Pray. Sokobin's chest tightens at the word. He can't remember the last time he actually did. He thinks of his own words, spoken to Windham just two days before. *Hope demands that we do not give up the living so easily to the dead.* And yet, in his own heart, his weak and cowardly heart, Sokobin knows he has given up. Over and over again. Imagining his brother buried on some nameless hill like this or in some forgotten corner of a forest. Ethan's body dumped in a mass grave outside a prison camp. Or most likely not buried at all and simply lost, along with his plane, to the sea.

"I don't believe in ghosts," Sokobin says.

"With all respect, Vice-Consul, it is not necessary that people do."

Sokobin inhales, once again unsure if Lin means to be impertinent, if impertinence is even a word that can be attributed to the interpreter, or if Lin's mind is simply so different, the term is irrelevant. Sokobin reminds himself that what Lin does or does not think is of no consequence. He and Lin are not friends, not even colleagues. Lin is a temporary employee, no more than a hired man. And yet as soon as the thought surfaces, Sokobin knows it to be false. He does want to know what the cool and collected Mr. Lin thinks, very much so.

"See there, sir," Lin says, pointing his hat toward the edge of the hill. "The men are coming up the trail now."

Sokobin turns to find the officer's black cap cresting the ridge. He watches as Cheng's face and shoulders come into view. Under the patrolman's arm is a rolled sheet, the cotton so white it hurts Sokobin's eyes to look at it. He hears voices, and seconds later, two more heads appear. The funeral men wear round caps, long queues, neat gray jackets, and matching pants. Between them they carry a wood-framed stretcher. Sokobin was expecting a wagon and oxen. But he sees the folly of that now. There's no road, only the thin dirt trail, its slope far too steep for wheels. They'll need to convey Meyer's body down the hill by hand.

The men are close now. Sokobin takes a final drag and drives the butt into the dirt. His throat burns as he tightly relaces his shoes. It takes all his will to push himself up. The pain in his heel flares, making him groan. He'll need to lance the blister and bandage it once they get to the station.

"Vice-Consul," Lin says.

"Yes?"

"Please know that I do not intend to give offense."

"None taken."

"I am truly sorry about the loss of your friend, Mr. Meyer."

Lin places his hat over his heart and bows. From another man the gesture would no doubt appear obsequious, even absurd. And yet from Lin, it only reveals a grace that Sokobin knows he himself will never possess.

"He wasn't a friend." Immediately Sokobin regrets the cheapness of the words.

CHAPTER 10

SOKOBIN HAS THE PATROLMAN SEND SEVERAL WIRES AS soon as they arrive at the station house. The first is sent to the Consul General in Shanghai; the second, to Sokobin's office in Nanking; and the last, to Chase, requesting one of Standard Oil's steamboats right away. Cheng offers up basins for washing; the water feels cool against Sokobin's skin but leaves his face smelling of the river. As he towels off, a local merchant appears in the doorway and Sokobin buys lunch for the three of them. The fish is steamed, no doubt caught that morning, and there are greens of some sort, along with pickled vegetables. The efforts of the past hours have left them ravenous.

Afterward, the officer puts a kettle on the small stove in the corner, and they each sit sipping tea as they discuss the fastest way to transport Meyer's remains, now with the undertakers, to Shanghai. There's no doubt the Standard boat will prove faster than a sampan, but as the village is too small for a dock or mechanical lifts, getting the heavy casket aboard will prove onerous. Sokobin imagines the worst possible scenario: a rope slipping and the casket plunging into the water.

The officer suggests rehiring the old uncle. The man is always in need of money. Between themselves and the undertakers, he says, they can manage loading the coffin onto the low sampan. The larger boat will then tow the small one downriver. Sokobin nods his approval. The tea floats hot and bitter against his tongue, and he dabs his forehead with the towel. Already he is missing Miss Petrie's cool pots.

There's also the issue of timing, Sokobin explains. At this point, he and Lin won't be reaching Wuhu until well after dark— too late to catch any ferry headed for Shanghai. They'll need for the old man to stay onboard overnight and keep watch over the coffin. Sokobin knows the task shouldn't fall to a stranger, that he be the *shomer*. But the morning's efforts have depleted him, and he knows he won't have the stamina to hold vigil. He needs rest. Tomorrow promises to be another long day: rising early to catch a ferry to Shanghai, negotiating the coffin safely to the American mortuary there, then debriefing the Consul General. As far as he knows, Meyer's boy and cabinmate aboard the SS *Feng Yang Maru* have yet to be questioned. If so, the CG will want Sokobin to handle the interviews. Thinking about the to-tality of what remains to be done exhausts him. He pictures the soft mattress in Arthur's spare room, and wishes he were already lying in the dark among the crisp sheets, with the door shut.

Cheng names a price for the fisherman; the number is fair, and Sokobin authorizes the officer to go higher if nec-essary. He can't bear another shouting match. Cheng stands and settles his cap over his brow before heading out the door. At last, Sokobin removes his shoes and lets his burning heel breathe. The blister is the size of an American half-dollar, red and raw. Lin winces at the sight from the next chair, then unclasps his case and produces a packet of aspirin. Sokobin pours the powder into his teacup and quickly downs the con-tents. He cleans his pocketknife with the remnants of the kettle, and with a groan, lances the mass. The officer has left him with a bandage, and he tightly wraps his foot.

To Sokobin's great relief, Cheng returns in less than a quarter of an hour and reports the affair is squarely settled—the old fish-erman has agreed. The officer apologizes but says he must leave them again as he is late for his rounds. He says they are free to wait in the station house until the undertakers finish their work. Pausing at the doorway, he offers a small salute and then is gone.

The sun has moved, casting a slanted square of light across the scuffed floor. Sokobin stares at it as he waits for the aspirin to kick in and quiet his throbbing heel. Lin wordlessly rises from the chair and crosses the room, resettling on a bench seat spanning the width of the back window. From his attaché, Lin withdraws the copy of the *Herald* and quickly disappears behind the newspaper. The pages hang like an impenetrable wall between them. Sokobin's first impulse is that he has been rebuffed. He considers their conversation under the tree and wonders if he's somehow given offense. But the silence that ensues is indeed golden, and whatever sting Sokobin felt soon shifts to gratitude for the thin measure of privacy the newspaper affords. Perhaps the gesture is meant as a kindness to them both. Perhaps even the equanimous Lin requires the occasional release from the demands of wearing the official mask.

Meanwhile Sokobin retrieves his notebook and, sitting at Cheng's desk, turns to a clean page with the intent to reconstruct the morning's events before they slip from his memory—Lin's interviews of Chase's servants, the trip to Ti-Kang, the patrolman's statements, the fisherman's, and the examination of the suspenders and shoes. Given Meyer's employment with the federal government, Sokobin suspects he'll be asked to submit more than a pithy Form 192. The explorer has died while on official business; no doubt Meyer's supervisors in Agriculture will demand a detailed account of the investigation.

He details the climb to the hill, the unmarked grave, the diggers' reluctance, the lack of a coffin. Finally, he knows he must return to the body itself. He pauses to towel off his forehead and neck. Already he can feel a film of perspiration spreading across his neck as he pictures the mottled hand, the dirt-crusted lips, the anguished face. Of course, none of these images will make his report. To include them would be a desecration. He wants to protect Meyer, even in death, to let him be remembered as he'd been: strong, healthy, and brave.

Some soil and decomposition from water and heat present. Inspection revealed no apparent punctures, gashes, bullet holes, or ligature marks—no evidence of attack or foul play.

HE PAUSES HIS PEN. HIS TEA HAS GONE TEPID, AND HE sets the clay cup on Cheng's desk. He flips through the pages of his chicken scratch, hoping the sight of so many notes will bring some satisfaction. Instead, he feels the same frustration he experienced yesterday while reading the dossier from Shanghai. Detail after detail leading nowhere. Facts in the service of an absent theory. Now, with the body found, the only thing Sokobin knows for certain is what he suspected from the onset, but couldn't say out loud—Meyer is dead.

Although it seems grossly out of character, Sokobin must acknowledge that the most plausible explanation for Meyer's death is the most obvious one, namely that the explorer fell overboard. Inwood's report mentioned something to the effect that Meyer wasn't feeling well. The captain said he and Meyer spoke briefly; however, for the most part, Meyer kept to his cabin. Indeed, the explorer didn't appear for dinner that evening but had his boy bring soup to his room. It's entirely possible Meyer was far more ill than he appeared. Sokobin presses his pen to the page. *Fever? Nausea? Dizziness?*

He considers that Meyer was last seen heading toward the privies along the back rails. Perhaps Meyer hadn't been headed for the latrine, but to the rails themselves—seeking a spot of fresh air or, more likely, to vomit. If Meyer leaned over the rails an inch too far, or the ship suddenly rocked ... still Sokobin finds the lack of witnesses troubling, especially given that the passenger ship was relatively full. But the hour was late, he remembers; the bar steward said it was after eleven when he saw Meyer. At that hour, Sokobin supposes it wouldn't be unusual for the rails to be empty. One could safely assume the dining cabin windows wouldn't directly overlook the latrine. It's entirely possible, probable even, no one would have seen Meyer fall. If someone had, certainly they would have sounded the alarm.

He considers that Meyer's death was simply a random accident, an unlucky break. The inglorious end to an otherwise exceptional life, but the explanation only leaves Sokobin dissatisfied.

Overhead the fan blades tick out an irregular rhythm. He pulls out his pocket watch. 3:17 p.m. He has no idea how long it will take the undertakers to do their work, or when Standard Oil's boat will appear. Briefly, he considers writing to his mother; he's been avoiding sending a letter for weeks. What could he possibly say that would offer comfort? No, for now, there is nothing to do but wait. On Cheng's desk is a half-filled ashtray. Sokobin pulls it toward him, then reaches into his jacket pocket for a cigarette. He smokes slowly, methodically, trying not to see Meyer's body, seeing only Meyer's body. For his part, Lin continues to hold the newspaper aloft and turn its pages.

Sokobin looks at the beach framed by the open door, and rises from his seat. He shuffles toward the fresh air, doing his best to avoid breaking the tight skin on his heel. If there were a porch in front of the station house, he would sit. But as there are only dusty steps, he leans against the doorframe and lights another Chesterfield. He knows how he must look standing there, jacketless and barefoot, a towel around his shoulders like a ten-cent boxer down on his luck. He feels like a hypocrite for having given Windham a hard time about his hair.

Save for a few fishermen tending to their nets, the stretch is largely deserted, quiet. Even with the clopping fan behind him, he can hear the water brush against the shore. Over Ti-Kang the skies are a cloudless deep indigo. But further east, thunderheads rise up like suspended cliffs. If the weather here is anything like Shanghai, come the full heat of summer, the clouds will break under their own weight every afternoon—intense downpours that arrive with little notice, sending down sheets of rain and making pedestrians scurry for cover.

The first afternoon Meredith came to his room had been like that. It was June, he remembers, not much further into the month than now. The storm, the first of the season, had taken them both by surprise. Neither had thought to bring an umbrella. They'd already left the café, and the nurse's dormitory was obviously out of the question. Within minutes, the cobblestones were awash with streaming rivulets. Sokobin held his jacket over their heads as Meredith laced a warm arm around his back. The fit was effortless; in boots, she was nearly as tall as he. She wore a long pale-blue linen coat that day. Ivory buttons with anchors carved into them. He could feel the sharp edges of her ribs through the thin fabric, the rise and fall of her breasts as the two of them rushed down the sidewalk.

The suggestion to go to his apartment had been his, spur of the moment. Or so he'd pretended, and even let himself believe it after the fact. In truth, he'd imagined her there for months, occupying the stuffed wing chair by the fireplace, drinking from the absurdly expensive cordial set Arthur had sent for Christmas, lying on his mattress, her hair spread across the pillow. He'd begun to imagine her leaving small bits of herself on the hard surfaces as she came and went: brooches and earrings, a hat pin or scarf, items that would stay and take up residence alongside his own.

If not for the storm, he would never have suggested his place. One didn't, couldn't. Not to the missionary daughter of Iowa farmers. She'd once told him the story of how they'd passed a special plate in her church for a year to pay for her passage east. Pennies and nickels. And of the gifts that appeared before she sailed: a Bible with gilded edging, a miniature American flag, a silver locket, shirtfronts and lace collars, woolen stockings and knickers, a pair of crocheted gloves, and from her own parents, a thick coat from the Sears Roebuck catalog that must have cost them dearly. She'd never had the heart to tell them it was too heavy to wear, save at most for a few days in January.

If not for the downpour, Sokobin wonders if they would have ever found their way to his apartment. But they had, not only that afternoon but on the several that followed. Those meetings had changed things between them, things that could not be undone. Despite all the pain that followed, there are times Sokobin still wishes them back.

As if on cue, the sand outside becomes a flurry of activity as fishermen appear, some in straw hats, some with wrapped heads to push sampan after sampan down the beach and into the river. *The tide must be changing*, Sokobin thinks. He is relieved to see the old uncle's boat does not follow them out, but instead continues to remain on the sand.

Sokobin returns inside, finding the *Herald* down and folded neatly on the bench beside Lin. The interpreter is writing, his back bowed in concentration, a clipboard balanced on one thigh. On the board are several small, unlined sheets of paper that look like stationery.

Lin looks up, his spectacles catching the sunlight. For a moment, the narrow span between his eyebrows remains compressed into two dark channels of thought, and Sokobin senses he's encroached upon a private moment.

"Please keep on," Sokobin tells him. He falls into an extra chair and wipes his face with the towel. "I just need to rest my foot."

Lin looks at the letter on his lap as if debating whether or not to continue, then caps his pen and slips the clipboard into his attaché. Sokobin cannot help but feel the slight. He waits for Lin to speak, to explain himself, but nothing is forthcoming. Sokobin digs into his jacket pocket for his cigarettes, only to find the package empty. He locates the spare in his briefcase and slips a finger under the seal, breaking it. He breathes in the packed tobacco smell, heavy and sweet, almost meat-like. It never lasts.

He snaps the flint, sucking down the smoke. He gestures toward the newspaper on the bench. There, within the folded rectangle, is a headline about the latest American aerial offensive at Aisne-Marne. "Be glad that your country isn't in it," he says, sounding edgier than he intends.

"Pardon?" Mr. Lin asks.

"The war. Be glad China isn't in it."

Lin blinks. "Unfortunately, sir, it is."

Sokobin releases a thick stream toward the fan and watches the blades scatter the smoke. Technically what Lin says is true. The Chinese have declared war on Germany but sent no army. "I meant with men at the front," Sokobin clarifies. "Casualties."

Lin taps his fingers against his trousers as if considering a silent question. Reaching for his case, he unclasps the flap. Sokobin expects the clipboard to resurface; instead, the interpreter withdraws a dark square and holds it out.

"My brother, sir."

The black cardboard is thick and embossed with gilded scrolls like a book cover. Immaculate. Sokobin can tell it contains a photograph, and he rests his cigarette on the ashtray before reaching out to take the frame from Lin's hands.

Sokobin lifts the cover. Lin's brother stands straight and narrow in a fitted uniform, a long wool coat draped over his shoulders like a cape. The flat-topped cap is French and tilted forward until it nearly covers one eye. His slim trousers, much like jodhpurs, descend into gleaming, knee-high boots. A pair of gloves dangles from one hand while the other rests on a small round table stacked with books. Behind him are the typical hallmarks of a studio backdrop: a painted folding screen, fringed curtains, a potted plant.

Sokobin studies the face for any relation to Lin. The mustache and heavily bronzed skin throw him. So do the lack of eyeglasses. But a second look reveals similarities: the square head, the wide cheekbones, the flat, straight nose pointing down like an arrow. And yet, on Lin's brother's face, the sum total yields a different effect—a confident stance and direct stare. Lin's brother is a man unafraid of the camera. Or of war itself. Sokobin knows the look, for he has seen it hundreds of times staring back at him from Ethan's photograph.

"I didn't realize," Sokobin stops himself, sensing the pointlessness of the thought, its arrogance. He spent a total of sixty seconds, at most, looking over the interpreter's CV. He knows next to nothing about Lin or his background.

"He is with *Corps de travailleurs chinois*," Lin says.

Sokobin nods, understanding. Tens of thousands of Chinese, possibly far more, are in France right now. With no men of their own to spare from the lines, England and France have offered foreign labor contracts until the end of the war. For the most part, the hired men are peasants from Shandong, swayed by the promise of a steady paycheck. They wear uniforms but carry no guns as they work in ammunition factories and along supply routes. Sometimes they dig trenches or graves. If not for them, the war might have already been lost for want of manpower. Still, it's easy to forget the Corps; rarely do the newspapers make mention of them.

Yet Lin's brother is clearly not a laborer. The uniform is far too nice. "What does he do?" Sokobin asks.

"He is an interpreter between the workers and the French officers."

"Like yourself."

"Yes," Lin says. "Only much better."

"I find that hard to believe, Mr. Lin."

Lin offers a pained smile. "He was already in Paris when the war began, studying at university. I do not mind, sir. It is only right that the eldest brother be a little smarter."

Sokobin winces, knowing that his own parents took no such position. There was only Ethan coming up short, and Sokobin's own vanity. It shames him now to think of it, and he closes the cover over the photograph. On the back is the name of the studio and a Paris address. He hands back the picture, and Lin slides it into his attaché.

"It must be difficult with him so far away," Sokobin says.

"Yes, sir. Our mother worries greatly."

"But your brother is well behind the front lines, yes? Away from the worst of it?"

"Yes. She worries even so. And about after the war."

"How so?"

"The French have offered citizenship to any Chinese who completes his contract. If my brother chooses, he may stay in France. This breaks my mother's heart. We have an old saying— perhaps you have heard it, sir. *Falling leaves return to their roots.*"

"She is afraid his leaves will eventually fall in France," Sokobin says.

"Yes."

Sokobin reaches for his cigarette. "And the letter you were writing? Was it to him?"

Lin nods. "She does not want him to forget his family, his village. I am to write him every week."

Sokobin takes a drag, debating. He's not shown the picture of his brother to anyone, not even Arthur. Something tells him it's the same for the reserved Mr. Lin. He bends toward his briefcase and produces Ethan's photograph from the center well, ashamed of a small crease in one of the picture's corners. He should have already purchased a cover to protect it. As soon as he gets a chance in Shanghai, he promises himself, he'll buy a frame in one of the stores.

He holds out the image. "I also have a brother in the war in France," he says.

The only sound in the station house is the knock of the fan overhead as Lin studies the image. He cups the photograph in his palm, avoiding touching its surface, and making Sokobin wish he'd shown half as much care.

"A flyer," Lin says at last, looking up.

"Yes, with Ninety-fourth Aero Squadron."

"Most impressive, sir," Lin says.

"Yes."

"And the hat painted on the side of the plane? It's like an Uncle Sam hat, yes?"

"Yes. It's their mascot. They all have it. It's what they call themselves. The Hat in the Ring Gang." Sokobin pulls down a hot stream of smoke into his lungs. The nickname has always rubbed him wrong. Cavalier and cocksure. As if the war were just a gentlemen's boxing match, capable of dishing out no more than a black eye or a bloody nose. For a moment, he considers telling Lin the rest—the missing plane, the letter from the major—but doesn't. He wouldn't be able to bear what Lin's face would reveal, the confirmation of what any reasonable man would conclude in the face of the facts. No, Sokobin thinks, there are certain things that can't be shared, certain things he must keep contained within himself.

"I see that we have something in common, Vice-Consul," Lin says as he hands back the photograph.

"Brothers in the war, you mean?"

"Brothers in the war who are much more handsome than we are."

The interpreter's lips uptick. The expression is so unusual on Lin that Sokobin is hard-pressed to recognize it as a smile. But it is a smile, and small wisps of smoke fall from Sokobin's lips as he laughs for the first time in days. "Indeed. A fair assessment, Mr. Lin."

"I hope I do not offend."

"You do not."

Sokobin resettles the picture in his case. When he looks up, the smile has dropped from Lin's face, and a ghostly figure appears reflected on his glasses. Sokobin turns to find a young boy standing at the station's threshold. He is neatly dressed in matching jacket and trousers, both in good order, his queue smooth under a white silk cap. Sokobin can tell from the pale clothes that he belongs with the undertakers. The boy bows, addressing his words to Lin.

Sokobin takes a quick drag and extinguishes his cigarette in the dish. "Is there a problem?"

Lin shakes his head. "No, sir. They have finished with the body. Whenever you are ready."

CHAPTER 11

THE COFFIN IS AS INSTRUCTED: UNADORNED AND, AS no pine is available, made from river cypress. Sokobin braces himself as the lid is lifted, but the undertakers have done better work than he would have thought possible. Somehow the smell has been edged out by the musky scent of burning incense now filling the parlor. Though discolored, the skin has been thoroughly cleaned, and the beard trimmed. Sokobin studies the face. If there was any doubt as to the man's identity, there can be none now. It is Meyer, the great explorer who will never again take another step.

A white shirt and pants have been found and pressed; on Meyer's feet are simple cotton slippers—all as Sokobin has requested. He hesitates, then moves to slip a finger into the trouser pockets and is relieved to find they have been sewn shut as asked—just as his own father's once were. Thankfully, none of the typical pomp and finery of a Chinese funeral is in evidence, for nothing could be further from the truths Sokobin learned as a boy: in death all men, rich or poor, come humbly before their maker as the proprietors of nothing but one imperfect soul. Judgment and passage to the life beyond, if it exists, can only be measured by character, not circumstance. To think otherwise is vanity, an insult to God.

He asks that candles be lit; there is a small exchange between Lin and the men who produce a pair of tapers. Sokobin lights

them before withdrawing the tallit and yarmulke from his briefcase. Meyer's hair has been washed and hangs soft and damp
against his palms as he lifts the head. Sokobin places the tallit
around the neck, then smooths the soft folds until they lie flat
against the white shirt. With his pocketknife, he cuts off one of
the tallit's tzitzit before settling the yarmulke on Meyer's head.
Sokobin steps back. He wonders who will wash his own brother's
body or dress him in white, if kind hands will ever touch Ethan's
stilled shoulders.

He looks toward Lin. The interpreter stands in a corner, his head
bent toward his chest, his eyes closed as if in prayer. Along with his
hat, Lin has removed his spectacles, leaving moon-shaped impres-
sions on either side of his nose. Sokobin bows his own head, unsure
if it is even his place to pray for the soul of a man he met with for a
spell at a party. And yet there is no one else; once again, the task must
fall to him. He searches for the words to the *kaddish*, fearing them
lost after so many years, only to find them still there in the deep meat
of his brain. *May the great Name of God be exalted and sanctified,
throughout the world, which he has created according to his will. May
his Kingship be established in your lifetime and in your days, and in the
lifetime of the entire household of Israel . . .*

———————————

STANDARD OIL'S BOAT APPEARS OFFSHORE A FEW MIN-
utes after six. Sokobin insists he must help to convey the coffin,
and so he, the old fishermen, Lin, Officer Cheng, and the undertakers, six men in all, slowly carry the coffin over the sand. A
silent huddle of villagers watches them pass. Sokobin glances at
the faces but is at a loss to read their expressions. Fear? Curiosity? Relief? He isn't sure. At times he feels more than dialect or
nation separates him from the Chinese, but an entire language of
emotion for which he lacks even the most basic of terms.

Cheng counts to three, and they hoist the casket onto the stern. For a terrible moment, the small boat tilts under the sudden weight, threatening to discharge the coffin onto the beach. A mad grab follows. Once the weight has settled and they've regained their breath, the fisherman uncoils a rope and tightly lashes down the lid.

The tide is out, and the others strain to push the sampan down the long slope of sand. Sokobin and Lin climb aboard at the water's edge. The men push again, and suddenly the boat is weightless, floating aimlessly with the current. The fisherman wades into the shallows, and with the finesse of a man half his age, jumps onto the bow. Slowly, he poles them across the waves. At the steamship, he throws over a tow. The ship's stacks sound, releasing a black cloud as they begin to glide downriver, slicing through the steamer's thick wake.

Sokobin sits face-to-face with Lin, their briefcases wedged between their legs. A pair of upturned crates beneath the low thatched roof serve as seats. Try as he might, Sokobin can't keep his knees from occasionally bumping against the interpreter's. A tight mass of nets, baskets, and cooking pots surrounds them. Sokobin would move but the slim sampan offers no outlet, and so he and Lin must remain exactly as they are, each man a counterweight to the other.

An awkward silence pools between them, made all the worse by their closeness. Sokobin searches for some tidy phrase from the CG's repertoire that might adequately sum up the trying events of the day and release them from further conversation. But nothing redeeming can be located. Perhaps, in the end, there is nothing to say: a good man is dead, cut down in his prime.

He stares at the casket's sharp edges, their undeniable presence and unalterable end. The churning nervousness in his gut is back again. The search is over, he reminds himself, the worst behind. Against all odds, Meyer has been found. The case has come to its morbid conclusion, just as he predicted, but without the long wild goose chase he feared. Only the final logistics remain: seeing the coffin to Shanghai and submitting his reports. Soon he'll be back in his office in Nanking, he assures himself, sifting through correspondence and calling out to Miss Petrie for a cool pot or to Windham to fetch a rice bowl from the bund.

Yet the thought brings no satisfaction, only more questions about Meyer's end. The how and why of it. Sokobin tells himself they don't matter. What's done is done. Meyer is dead. Full stop.

Still the coffin is there. Silent, and waiting. Answers. Sokobin needs them. Only then will the matter be truly laid to rest.

"I could use some assistance in Shanghai, you know," he tells Lin. "An extra set of hands with transporting the body. And there's still Meyer's boy to be interviewed. I don't know how good his English is. All paid work, of course. That is, if you are available."

Sokobin stops, aware that he sounds as flustered as young Windham. He's been so focused on finding Meyer, that he hasn't thought the plan all the way through to Shanghai until this very minute. Come morning, once the casket has been loaded onto the ferry from Wuhu, Lin's contract will officially terminate, and each man will go his separate way: Lin back to Nanking and Sokobin on to Shanghai to see the coffin delivered there. The thought is enough to send a small wave of panic across Sokobin's chest. He can't explain the feeling; he only knows, with absolute certainty, this split with Lin can't happen.

A long look passes between them as Lin blinks behind his spectacles. Already Sokobin has come to understand the gesture's meaning—not thoughtlessness as he first supposed but its opposite. Lin is considering the proposition, weighing it over.

"Forget I mentioned it," Sokobin says, embarrassed for not having thought to bring up the point during the long hours at the station house. "No doubt you are as tired of the whole affair."

"I will come with you to Shanghai."

"You are sure?"

"Yes, sir. I wish to see the case until its end."

"Very good," Sokobin says, trying to hide his relief.

They move toward the center of the river and pick up speed. The loud slap of the waves makes further conversation difficult. Lin removes his glasses, wiping the spray from the lens before tucking them into his jacket pocket. He leans back, resting his head against the thatch, and closes his eyes. Within minutes, his chest takes on the slow, fixed rhythm of sleep. *The man's self-containment rivals the Great Wall,* Sokobin thinks, not without considerable envy.

Meanwhile Sokobin's own eyes refuse to close. With hours still to go, the day already feels one hundred years old. The bandage has helped the swelling on his heel, but carrying the coffin has left his foot with a dull, continuous ache. A cigarette is out of the question; he can't risk a spark catching on the thatch. The wind is too fierce.

He watches the other boats make their way over the turbid currents, mostly other sampans, but also the occasional yacht or ferry that leaves their small boat rocking with surge. Towns and villages appear and disappear, some so small that from a distance, they seem little more than flotsam washed up on the mud. Beyond the shore, the flood plains stretch for miles, offering up the sort of endless sweep that might make another man sing of freedom, but that only leaves Sokobin feeling exposed and untethered.

The sun begins its eventual drop, drenching the sky and river in shades of rich summer fruit. The golden hour, Meredith used to call it. He banishes the thought. Such memories can do him no good now. Sunset eventually cedes to dusk, dulling the palette and ending *Shabbos.*

The fisherman turns from his perch on the prow. Ducking under the roof, he pulls a pair of lanterns from the piles. Sokobin recognizes the models as among those Chase sells. The old man lights the wicks, then latches shut the small glass doors. Wordlessly, he holds out a lantern to Sokobin and points toward the stern. Sokobin crouches and carefully makes his way toward the rear, unsure of where to secure the lamp so that its light might be seen from behind. In the end, there is no choice but the casket lid itself, and pulling a length of rope from the supplies, he lashes the lantern to the crisscrossed stays. Behind the glass, the flame wavers. His throat tightens at the sight.

The boat bounces, and he's forced to grab ahold of the coffin to keep from falling overboard. One hand on the knotted ropes, he manages to withdraw a cigarette and his lighter. He figures he can safely smoke here; the backdraft will send any stray embers away from the thatch. Leaning into the coffin for support, he cups a hand over the flint.

An osprey hovers overhead, its white wings spread against the inky sky. Due east, clouds have begun to gather like sheep against the coming night; a dark veil of rain wavers below. Sokobin can't judge the storm's distance, perhaps ten miles, perhaps five, perhaps much closer. Suddenly the futility of his nation's purpose, of *his* purpose in China, hits him. The folly of thinking he might ever find a foothold in this vast country, of even hoping to understand it. It doesn't matter how long he stays here, how much he learns. He'll never be anything more than Meyer, an itinerant traveler at best, an outsider. Foreign. There was a time, when he was younger, when such an idea would have appealed to him. The romance of Everton's Orient. How easily he'd fallen under its sway. The Celestial Kingdom. The Dragon Throne. Now the notion just strikes him as sad, and rootless, and lost.

He smokes the Chesterfield down to the stub, then tosses the butt into the waves and edges his way back to his seat, ducking beneath the thatch. Night is coming on, and the breeze from the river is biting. He buttons his jacket against the cold, folding his arms over his chest. For the first time in weeks, he catches himself shivering. The water goes deep here, perhaps hundreds of feet. He has been told that giant fish, unchanged since the dawn of time, lurk in the black depths below.

The osprey is still there, seemingly content to float on their backdraft. He thinks of Ethan's small plane soaring over the golden savanna, the black cross of its shadow stamped on the backs of animals below. When he looks up again, the bird is gone.

CHAPTER 12

Once again, they arrive at Wuhu after dark. The tow is unknotted, and the steamer continues its way downriver. Taking up his long pole, the fisherman pushes them over the currents and toward the long, raised pier. The port is private, for Standard Oil's use only, and several miles from the municipal docks.

A string of electric spots sends down yellow cones of light over the boardwalk ahead. Even from a distance, Sokobin recognizes the solitary silhouette waiting there, its slim ease. Chase stands with his hands in his trouser pockets, jacketless and his vest unbuttoned, a tie softly flapping with the breeze. Sokobin wasn't expecting Arthur to come in person, merely to send his limousine, the faint outline of which Sokobin can see waiting in the lee of a nearby warehouse.

He turns to nudge Lin, only to find the interpreter already awake and sitting up, his glasses returned to his face.

"Wuhu?" Lin asks.

"Yes." Sokobin gestures toward the old fisherman on the prow. "You really think he can be trusted to watch over the coffin all night?"

"As much as anyone."

Sokobin gleans the insinuation. Trust is a commodity backed by silver. Besides, at this point, the question is moot. Short of spending the night on the tiny boat himself, Sokobin doesn't have much choice. The reality is he's lucky to have found a boat-man willing to stay the night with Meyer's body at any price.

"Tell him he'll get two more tomorrow morning," he says, handing Lin a coin, "once he gets us to the ferry for Shanghai."

Lin nods and takes the silver.

"Make sure he understands the boat leaves from the city port, not here," Sokobin says. "We'll need to leave no later than seven to make it."

"Yes, sir. I remember."

Sokobin senses he's repeating himself. He's fairly certain they went over the plan back in the station house, but that was a life-time ago, and now he can't recall what was actually said. Exhaus-tion has shrouded his brain in fog.

The waves collide with the boardwalk's thick columns, leav-ing the water choppy. As they near, Chase cups his hands and calls out, then points beneath his feet to where a metal ladder has been attached to one of the wooden piers. The fisherman shouts over his shoulder. Sokobin doesn't need the words to be trans-lated. The old man is telling him to be ready to climb; it will be hard to steady the boat.

"I'll wait for you up top while you sort out the details here," Sokobin tells Lin. "Hand me up my briefcase, all right?"

The sampan jostles, despite the fisherman's best attempts to steady the rocking boat with his pole. The thin ladder is there, de-scending into the current. Reaching, Sokobin grasps ahold of a rusty rung and with whatever breath remains, heaves himself up.

Chase kneels at the edge of the weathered planks above, one arm thrust toward Sokobin. Sheathed in the spotlight's glow, Arthur appears like an apparition sent from another world.

"Give a hand now," he calls down.

Meanwhile Sokobin clings to the gritty metal. Two rungs shy of the top, he halts, unable to move up or down. His arms hang as lifeless as sandbags.

"Come on," Chase urges. "Chop, chop."

Sokobin hesitates, infuriated by his own weakness. He clamps onto Arthur's wrist. With surprising strength, Chase pulls him onto the pier, then bends again to take Sokobin's briefcase from Mr. Lin's outstretched arms.

"I don't suppose there's any use telling you to take it easy on the smokes," Chase says once they've caught their breath.

"No more than me telling you to cut back on the whiskey."

"Fair enough."

Sokobin's shirt has gone stiff with sweat; he unbuttons the collar, shoving it along with his tie into his jacket pocket. They stand side by side, facing the river. The waves strike the piers, muffling the sound of Lin and the fisherman's voices below. The lantern is still there, tied and flickering on the bobbing casket. The air smells faintly of oil and fire.

"So, you found your man," Chase says.

"Yes."

"And you're sure it's Meyer?"

"Yes."

"So, what's the working theory?"

"About?"

"Meyer, obviously. How he died."

Sokobin shakes his head. His fingers dip into his pocket. He's running low on cigarettes and will need to buy more tomorrow. He cracks his lighter and sends up a stream of smoke. A swarm of moths flit in the lights overhead. "No way to know," he finally says.

"No marks on the body?"

"None that I could see. Hard to tell, though. Understand he was in the water a couple of days, then buried. And the weather's been so hot." Sokobin stops, remembering the blue-brown flesh of the arm, the outstretched hand. He'd almost clasped it. "There wasn't a coffin."

Chase groans. "Not an easy sight, I imagine."

"No."

Sokobin hears the familiar twist of a cap as Chase pulls a slim silver flask from his trousers. For as long as they've known one another, the flask has been there, a ubiquitous witness to their meetings. At first Sokobin took the flask for affectation—a bit of fancy flash meant to imply a weight of character not yet earned. But as with so much else in Arthur's personal stores, the flask is a monogrammed heirloom stretching back generations. By now, it must be eighty or ninety years old. Nothing of similar value survives from Sokobin's own family. Whatever had once been, if it ever existed, would have been plundered or sold for passage. Or else simply so worthless it was left behind.

Arthur holds out the flask; Sokobin declines with a wave of the hand. "Impressive finding your man like that," Chase says as he sips. "In all honesty, I didn't think you would."

"If not for Lin, I doubt I would have," Sokobin admits. He tells Chase about Lin's interviewing of his servants. "The answer was there the entire time."

"A lucky break then," Chase says.

Sokobin isn't sure what irritates him more, the slight to Lin or the idea that anything having to do with Meyer's case has been lucky. He wonders what's taking Lin so long. No doubt the old boatman is putting up a fuss or trying to negotiate more money. Further down the pier a hurricane lamp sways from the deck of a sleek yacht. Arthur has told him that the dock has become a meeting spot, a sort of floating lover's lane. The encounters go strictly against company policy; still none of the higher-ups seem bent on enforcing the rules—no doubt, as Arthur has suggested, because they are the very ones breaking them. Sokobin isn't surprised. American men do things here they'd never allow themselves to do on Main Street, USA. He'd like to exempt himself from that camp but can't.

For his part, Chase appears to see nothing, or at least pretends not to. "So, what now?" he asks.

"Notify the relatives in Amsterdam and wait for further instruction. The family may request the body be shipped back to Holland. Otherwise, Meyer will be buried in the Jewish cemetery in Shanghai. Either way, I'm taking the body there first thing tomorrow."

Chase pauses his flask. "Jewish, you say?"

"Yes."

"Astonishing that. The coincidence, I mean."

Sokobin steps out of the spotlight's beam. He can't have Chase looking at him, not right now. He doesn't want to talk about Meyer anymore. It's enough just to keep himself upright at this point. Arthur says something. He ignores it.

"Are you listening?" Chase asks.

"No."

"I said, I would have thought you'd be relieved to have found him."

"The man is dead, Arthur."

"Yes, it's tragic. But there's nothing you could have done about that. This will be a major plus on your record, Soko. The Consul General will take notice."

"I don't give a damn about that."

Sokobin hears the strain in his voice. He sounds nervy, on edge. He can feel himself splitting in two again, the world retracting around him: Arthur, the flask, the sampan, the coffin. Under the moonlight, its wooden lid appears almost metallic. The surrounding water glints like black glass, so much so that Sokobin half expects the crashing swells to shatter at any moment.

"You sound angry, Soko."

"Maybe I am."

Chase sips, then sips again. Sokobin reaches for the whiskey and takes a long pull. All the tobacco is making his nerves vibrate. Sometimes it's like gnats buzzing in his veins.

"You weren't holding out hope he might still be alive?"

"I barely knew the man."

"Soko."

Sokobin ignores him and inhales, sending the Chesterfield's burning orange line toward his lips. The small plane is there again, the white plumes of smoke, the roiling black sea, and for an awful moment he wishes it would just crash and disappear under the waves so that he might finally be rid of it forever.

"Soko," Chase repeats. "I know what you're thinking, and it's not true."

"And what am I thinking?"

"That Meyer is a sign, that the one has something to do with the other." Chase sighs. "With Ethan. But it's not true."

"I'm not a superstitious man. You know that."

Chase sips. "War makes everyone superstitious. Just know that whatever's happened to Meyer doesn't change a thing, not a damn thing. You hear me?"

And yet Sokobin knows it does, just as surely as if he'd received a cable to the effect. It's why the Meyer case landed on his desk, why he's been sent upriver. He's been deluding himself, trying to bargain with God through good deeds, as if Sokobin could somehow change the outcome from where he stands. But it hasn't worked. His brother is gone, shot down or crashed, forever lost to the sea. Sokobin sees this now; it's as obvious as the bobbing coffin in front of him. He will never know the details, where his brother's body waits. What do they matter? His brother is dead. Ethan, Eitan, is dead. Sokobin looks across the river only to find its edges erased by night. *Sky, land, water. It's not always clear where one ends and the other begins.* How much easier to simply let himself tip into the water. Pitch forward and let go. Sink forever.

He covers his eyes as they go wet, the lit cigarette wedged between his fingers. He hears Chase start to say something and then, for a blessed minute, Arthur shuts up and there is nothing but the sound of water slapping against the piers. Seconds pass. Lifetimes that will never be. He feels the warm grip of Chase's fingers on his shoulders.

"Here now, old boy," Arthur says quietly. "You're tired, that's all. You've had a long day, and things have gotten twisted up inside."

Sokobin can feel Arthur pressing something into his side and opens his eyes. Arthur is handing him a clean handkerchief, the linen spotless and monogrammed like every other damned thing Arthur owns. Sokobin drops his cigarette, crushing it with his heel. He takes the handkerchief and wipes his face.

"Keep it," Chase says. "I'm guessing yours needs a rest as much as you do. Besides, you know I have a thousand of them."

They stare over the water, passing the flask between them. Sokobin sips steadily. The taste is sweeter than Chase's usual brand and coats Sokobin's burning throat. He considers calling out to Lin but doesn't have the energy.

"You know why I came out to China?" Chase asks.

"Same as me. Everton."

Chase shakes his head.

Sokobin would say Standard Oil's money, but God knows Arthur doesn't need it. "Then no. I suppose I don't."

"To get as far away from Connecticut as possible."

Chase attempts to smile, but Sokobin isn't fooled by the tight-lipped grin. He wonders how he could know Arthur for so long and not know this basic fact.

"I've always admired you, Soko. Your drive. I spotted it right from the start, all those years ago."

Sokobin holds up a hand. Chase can get sentimental after too much whiskey.

"No," Chase says. "I wish to say it, need to say it. You see, I've never had that sort of push, never had to. I think I always hoped a part of yours might rub off."

Arthur studies the flask in his hand, pressing his thumb to the engraved initials there. Even now Sokobin can see the crease where the silver once met with a Confederate sword. Years ago, while draining its contents, Arthur recounted how his grandfather, then a Union cavalry officer, had worn the flask strapped to his chest as he rode out to battle at Brandy Station. The flask had saved his life, and several months later, Arthur's father was conceived. Without it, Arthur himself would never have come to be.

"You're your own man, Soko. Whatever you have or are is entirely of your own making. There's satisfaction to be found there, if you'd only let yourself."

Sokobin looks down, oddly humbled by the words. Arthur, his oldest friend, his anchor to the past, and last defense against loneliness. It terrifies Sokobin to think how much he needs him.

At last, he hears the faint grating sound of the ladder rungs. Sokobin quickly gives his face another go with the handkerchief, hoping the tears haven't stained his skin. Lin's pale hat, face, and torso appear in quick succession. The interpreter is already on the boardwalk before Sokobin can step forward and lend a hand. Somehow Lin has managed the climb with his attaché.

"All settled below?" Sokobin asks.

"Yes, sir."

Lin's voice sounds barbed with exhaustion, and Sokobin finally sees the toll the day has taken on the interpreter under the spotlight's beam: the rumpled tan jacket, the smudged brow, the sheen of oil across his forehead. Although Sokobin knows he looks far worse for wear, the imperfections on Lin feel sacrilege.

"Off we go then," Chase says and slips the flask into his trousers. "Forgive me for saying so, but you both look God awful."

Chase signals the driver, and the limousine's engine rumbles to life. Headlights split the dark air as they make their way toward the waiting car. The uniformed chauffeur stands next to the Pierce Arrow's open doors. Lin climbs into the front seat without a word, leaving the back seat to Sokobin and Chase. For some reason, the sight of Lin's lonely frame on the other side of the glass leaves Sokobin more uncomfortable than the memory of the interpreter's descent down the stairs the night before. Yesterday Lin was little more than a stranger. Perhaps in the larger sense, Lin still is, and yet Sokobin can't imagine having endured this day with anyone else. Something has transpired between them, something Sokobin can't put a name to; he only knows it's there now, palpable and real. Lin has ceased to be merely the case's interpreter but has become a part of its solution. He holds back Chase's arm before Arthur can slide open the window and speak with the driver.

"Lin stays upstairs tonight," Sokobin whispers. The words aren't a request.

Chase pauses, then gives a slight bow of the head. "Whatever you say, Vice-Consul."

PART III

CHAPTER 13

Sunday, June 8

Sokobin heads down the gangplank, waves down a rickshaw, and gives the driver the address to his apartment. Lin has agreed to stay onboard, the ferry ride allowing Sokobin time enough to stop off in Nanking to change clothes and check in with the office before catching the afternoon express to Shanghai. Provided the train isn't running late, he should just beat the ship carrying Lin and the casket to the docks.

He turns the key to his apartment and crosses the silent living room to find the contents of his trunk still piled haphazardly on the bedroom floor. If the housekeeper has come, he sees no signs of it. From the wardrobe, he takes down his beige linen suit and tan shoes. On the top shelf is his traveling hatbox; he lifts the lid, exchanging his felted Hamburg for the straw fedora. He makes quick work of the rest—rooting out a fresh shirt, collar, cuffs, linen, and handkerchiefs from his drawers. The suit appears loose, he observes as he inspects himself in the armoire's mirrored door. The last time he wore it would have been in September. Just nine months ago and yet a different life altogether—himself in Shanghai and Ethan in central France, then training with the Americans. Turning to the side, he tugs at the waistband. There's no doubt the suit will need taking in. He's been wearing his winter ensemble for so long the lost pounds have escaped notice. At this point, however, there's nothing he can do except tighten his belt.

His wool suit waits in a dark heap on the bed. He picks up the pieces, draping them over a chair back. He should have swapped the heavy suit out months ago. But something in him had resisted the change. That time would press forward without offering up some hint of his brother's fate seemed cruel, impossible even. And yet it had. March had ceded to April, then May, now June. Summer stands waiting on the doorstep, and still there is no trace of Ethan.

He pushes away the thought. He checks his watch and transfers the contents of the pockets from the old suit to the new. He's low on Chesterfields, but the brand will be easy enough to locate in Shanghai, perhaps even in the Nanking train station, and with the minutes running short, he heads directly to the office. The walk is but a few blocks at most; even so, the damp heat makes him perspire. He stops outside the front doors to wipe his forehead in the portico's shade and hears singing through an open window. The voice is too deep to belong to anyone but Mr. Brundage. Sokobin has overheard enough of the senior clerk's chatter to know how much the man enjoys musical revues, the bawdier, it would seem, the better. Still the exceptional voice, rich and steady, comes as a surprise. In another life, the clerk might have taken to the stage himself.

All heads turn and motion comes to a halt as Sokobin enters the front room—Windham's smile falls from his face while Mr. Brundage, his mouth still open, goes silent. Neither are wearing jackets. Meanwhile Miss Petrie lets out a small gasp as if the vice-consul were back from the dead. Not for the first time, nor even the tenth, Sokobin senses he occupies the periphery of his own office rather than its center.

"Vice-Consul," Mr. Brundage says, tugging down his vest over his gut. "We weren't expecting you back so soon. We received your wire about Mr. Meyer. Tragic."

"But where is the . . ." Windham starts.

Sokobin holds up a hand. He doesn't have time for it. "Mr. Meyer's remains are with Mr. Lin on the ferry to Shanghai, and I must be on the express in less than an hour. Some cool tea, please, Miss Petrie, but only if there is some already made."

"Right away, sir."

"Please wire the Consul General," Sokobin tells Windham. "Let him know that Meyer's remains will arrive in Shanghai this evening. Make sure he understands my interpreter is traveling with me, and that we'll both need rooms at the consulate. Two or three nights, I expect." Sokobin considers whether or not to mention the oversight about Lin with Chase, but decides that, like the full story on Meyer, it can wait.

"Will do," Windham says, pushing back his mop of ginger hair.

Clearly the haircut remains outstanding. Sokobin turns toward Mr. Brundage. "Any pressing developments?"

"No, sir," the senior clerk says. "A few communiqués from Peking, and another mail boat attack upriver. Two fatalities, neither American."

"Very well then, I'll be in my office."

Sokobin opens the door to find the room dark and stuffy, the fan off, the curtains drawn. He's been gone less than two days, and yet the absence feels like weeks. He lowers his briefcase, pulls out his chair, and sits—glad to be off his bandaged heel, if only for a moment.

"A sad end about Mr. Meyer then," Miss Petrie says, setting down her tray and pouring him a cup from the pot.

"Quite so."

"And still no sense of what happened?"

"Not yet." He takes up his tea and sips. He doesn't want to go into details, but finds it difficult to be short with Miss Petrie, whom he guesses must be near his mother's age. "We still have to conduct a couple of interviews in Shanghai. Meyer's boy and his cabinmate from the steamer. Hopefully they can offer some insight."

Miss Petrie nods, causing the heavy knot of her hair to gently sway. How she manages to keep the mass afloat with small pins Sokobin can't understand.

"I'm not sure it's my place to say such a thing, sir, but I'm glad you found him, one way or another. I'm certain the family will be relieved to know. There's nothing worse than waiting."

Sokobin looks up. There is only kindness, and perhaps memory, in the secretary's brown eyes. Still the words sting too much for Sokobin to hold them, and he stares into his cup. "Thank you, Miss Petrie, for the tea. It was missed yesterday."

"Of course, sir."

Her boots tap the floorboards as she leaves, shutting the door behind her. He checks his watch. He should be leaving for the station but can't raise himself from the chair. Just a few minutes of silence, he thinks, just long enough to gather himself before throwing himself back into the fray. Last night he'd stood at Arthur's guest room window again, watching the Yangtze's dark sweep, unable to sleep. He couldn't stop seeing Meyer's body. The mottled skin and bloated chest. And the stench. Even now his nose remembers it.

A thin layer of fresh correspondence waits under the scrimshaw at the desk's edge. On top is an invite to another lecture he knows he won't attend. He quickly thumbs through the rest. Thankfully Brundage was right; nothing requires an immediate response. He opens his briefcase and slides in the lot—he'll have time enough to sift through it all on the train. He runs his fingers over the scrimshaw's cool surface. He thinks of Everton's wry smile, his smooth gestures, and effortless elegance—traits that as a young man, Sokobin longed to make his own. But he's never been able to make them fit. Finesse. He simply doesn't have it.

He pours a second cup of tea and fishes out a Chesterfield, drawing down the smoke as he waits for the tobacco to flood his veins. But no rush comes, not even the usual jitters. Instead, his lungs feel spent, like two slabs of dried meat. His eyes fall to the bottom drawer. He thinks of the blue envelopes, and it takes all his will not to reach for the handle. There's nothing in the letters that can help him anymore, nothing new to uncover, nothing that will cut the pain.

A knock sounds on his door.

"One minute," he calls and swivels toward the window. He splits the curtains, lifts the sash and inhales once more before letting the cigarette fall to the hedgerow below. At this point, there must be a small colony of butts buried in the branches.

"Come in."

Windham enters, a thin green file folder under his arm. "Sorry to interrupt but Miss Petrie insisted I remind you of the time."

Sokobin checks his watch again; he should have left five minutes ago. "And the wire to Shanghai?"

"Sent, sir." The clerk places the folder on Sokobin's desk. "I took the liberty of pulling one of these from the files, given the circumstances, that is."

Sokobin nods. He doesn't need to lift the cover to know what's inside, and slides the folder into his briefcase. He clasps it shut, then reaches for his hat. Meanwhile the floorboards have begun to crack under the clerk's shifting legs.

"About the body, sir . . . I'm not sure how to say this."

"Well, be quick about it. I'm already late."

"Was it very bad?"

Sokobin looks at the clerk in disbelief. "What a terrible question, Mr. Windham."

"I'm sorry, sir. I don't mean to offend."

"Why would you ask such a thing?"

Windham legs have gone still. Too still. The young man is

holding his breath. "I was thinking of all the fallen soldiers, sir. How they don't get buried right away."

The lost cousins at the Western Front, Sokobin remembers. One look at the clerk's frozen expression confirms it.

"You can tell me the truth, sir. I can bear it, you know."

Sokobin stares at the smooth face, remembering himself at twenty, the worries that occupied him then. Exams, pocket money, spots on his chin. The right phrase to say to a girl. The sorts of worries he wants Windham to know—worries the war has stolen.

He takes a deep breath, forcing himself to steady his gaze. "He appeared at rest," Sokobin lies. "The end would have been quick. Painless, I'm certain."

Windham looks down at his feet and nods. His hair has fallen down over his eyes, but he makes no attempt to push it away. For a moment neither says anything, and Sokobin believes they are past the hurt. But then the clerk's jaw suddenly tightens.

"I should have been there, sir, doing my part and watching out for them. And I would have been, if not for this." He hits his heeled shoe on the floor with enough force to rattle the window. In the front room, Miss Petrie and Mr. Brundage turn in their seats.

Windham stands pinned to the spot, his fists clenched as if ready to strike. Sokobin rises and slowly rounds the desk. He hesitates to touch the clerk, unsure of even how to, then cups the young man about the shoulder. "Mr. Windham. Mr. Windham, look at me."

Windham glares, his eyes narrowed. For the first time, Sokobin sees anger, rage even, in the clerk's speckled face. Sokobin knows the look all too well. For months he's seen it staring back at him from his own bathroom mirror.

"You serve your country here, Mr. Windham. Very well, I might add. Don't ever forget that."

The clerk covers his eyes, rocking on his heels. Miss Petrie rises from her chair, but Sokobin shakes his head, and she sits back down. Windham's tears last a few seconds at most, just long enough for Mr. Brundage to bow his head and make the sign of the cross.

"I'm sorry, sir," Windham says, wiping his face with the back of his sleeve. "I don't know what came over me."

"Don't concern yourself with it," Sokobin says, at last dropping his grip from the clerk's shoulder. In the front room, Mr. Brundage and Miss Petrie turn back to their desks. "Flag me down a rickshaw to the station?" Sokobin asks, taking up his briefcase.

Windham nods. "Yes, sir. Right away."

There's no time for goodbyes, only a quick wave as Sokobin passes through the front room. Windham is already there on the street, his face slightly swollen as he holds open the cab door. Sokobin places his briefcase on the seat and climbs in.

"About the other, sir," Windham says as he shuts the door.

"The other?"

"The haircut, sir. I have an appointment. I didn't want you to think I'd forgotten."

Sokobin can't help but smile and holds out his hand. "Be well, Mr. Windham."

"You too, Vice-Consul. And thank you, sir."

The rickshaw bumps forward; the driver's long black queue swings hypnotically as they bounce over the cobblestones. Meanwhile the heat of Windham's shoulder remains on Sokobin's hand. *You serve your country here.*

Like so much else from his mouth, Sokobin is certain the words are borrowed. Still, he hopes they are true, for unlike his clerk, his own legs are even and able.

CHAPTER 14

HE LEANS BACK INTO THE PLUSH SEAT, STRETCHING HIS legs toward the empty bench opposite. Padded leather and polished brass. Electric lamps. A foldout table large enough to write on. The first-class compartment feels like an exercise in privilege. Sokobin supposes it is—one of the cushy benefits of the vice-consulship he's still not accustomed to and feels a small, rebellious streak against. His Newark roots.

But for now, first class means space. Better yet, privacy. The compartment is his alone, at least until the next stop. It is a quiet Sunday, the seats of white first class more empty than full. Scattered among the rest of the car sit serious-looking men with attachés, headed to Shanghai in anticipation of Monday morning's business, and one unwieldy group of British tourists. Clad from head to toe in khaki canvas, they boarded with Sokobin at Nanking where they'd taken over the platform, their faces flush as they loudly nattered on about the weekend's adventures like children who'd eaten too much candy floss at the circus. Sokobin was relieved when they took seats on the opposite end of the car. Even so, their laughter occasionally erupts, startling him and filling the corridor between.

He glances at his briefcase on the seat beside him. By now he should be making his way through the correspondence. Instead, he reaches for a cigarette and lets himself sink under the hypnotic clacking of the wheels, grateful for the brief reprieve from the chronic *appropriateness* required of his new office. For the first time in days, he's not due somewhere ten minutes ago, and he has to remind his feet to hold still, his lungs to breathe.

Farmland flashes outside the windows; summer fields thick with rice, wheat, and rapeseed. There are hills to the southwest, he's been told, but for now there is only the flood plain; its rich soil sliced into highly cultivated plots. Row after row of crops pass by, along with dense villages compressed onto the dry patches between the omnipresent water. One is never far from water in Kiangsu. *A pretty puddle*, Mr. Brundage calls the province. The Yangtze is miles to the north; nevertheless, water seems to seep into every inch of ground. Indeed, every few minutes the train must slow to cross another bridge, forged from concrete and like the locomotive itself, English steel, while below some paddy or pond glints like quicksilver with the afternoon sun.

He taps on the glass as the rolling cart passes, overpaying for a meat pie and a newspaper. Both are faintly gray. Once, he had made the mistake of ordering a tea only to have it spill all over his shirtfront when the train took a sudden turn around a cemetery. Such jolts happen fairly frequently on the line, given the Chinese's refusal to relocate graves, even for track, and so the railway must compete with Kiangsu's dead for solid ground. Unfortunately, the quick twists also make it nearly impossible to doze off in the nearly two hundred miles separating Nanking from Shanghai.

He suffers the pie, then unfolds the paper. The dateline reads June 8. Eight days since Meyer went overboard the *SS Feng Yang Maru*.

The front photograph shows a never-ending line of ambulances transporting the wounded to a field hospital. The German army is now within thirty-five miles of Paris, the article reports, with the French government on the verge of evacuating south to Bordeaux. Meanwhile the fighting at Belleau Wood has intensi-fied, with unknown casualties to the American marines there. Turning the page, he reads about the fighting at Chateau Thierry, the latest push in the Aisne-Marne offensive. Thirteen American aero squadrons have been deployed—the first large-scale show of aerial force from the States to date. He feels a small pang reading of the dogfights, knowing how much Ethan would have wanted to be there. It was how Sokobin imagined his brother would go down, if he went down at all. A battle, somewhere with a name, a place Sokobin could utter and people would knowingly nod. He tells himself it shouldn't make a difference, despises himself for even thinking it. But it does matter for the ones left behind, the ones who will have to explain.

Further into the paper he finds another photograph: a class of French schoolchildren outside Reims, according to the cap-tion. Sokobin eyes the thin bodies, the worn coats, sagging knee socks, and scuffed boots. Monstrous gas masks cover their small faces. He closes the paper, leaving it on the table while he smokes his cigarette to the end.

When he picks it back up, he focuses on a bright spot in the box scores: the Yankees 1 to 0 over the Browns in Saint Louis. It's an unexpected victory in an otherwise miserable season for New York. Sokobin is far from being a dyed-in-the-wool fan, even of baseball itself. As a boy, he'd been average, at best, at stickball, never coming close to his brother's crackerjack swing. Still Soko-bin feels a small loyalty to the New York team—a remnant from his college days. And a reminder, he supposes, or perhaps reassur-ance that despite the war and the thousands of miles between, home still exists somewhere.

He neatly folds the paper, sliding it next to the crumbled re-mains of the pie. The tourists are laughing again. The rolling cart porter forgot to close the compartment door, and Sokobin leans over, tugging at the handle. He pulls out another cigarette, only to find it's the last man standing in the package and decides to hold off. By his estimate, they are a little less than halfway to Shanghai's North Station.

He pops the clasp of his briefcase. His fingers pass over the correspondence, pausing on the corner of his brother's photograph. The urge to look at the picture is there, just as strong as his incessant desire for a smoke. Devotion. Compulsion. He can no longer make out the difference.

Instead, he extracts the green folder from Windham, opening the cover to reveal a single sheet inside.

United States Consular Form 192:
Report on the Death of an American Abroad

Place and date of report:
Name in full of the deceased:
Age of deceased:
Date of death:
Place of death:
Cause of death:
Disposition of remains:
Disposition of effects:
Names and addresses relatives contacted (2):
Remarks (optional):

Sokobin stares at the form, wondering how he's managed to miss its evasiveness until now. As a clerk in Shanghai, 192s inevitably came across his desk. He read every one before filing it away in the cabinets. But only with mild, distant curiosity, never with a burning need to know. Form 192 isn't so much a report as it is a checklist. There's no description of the deceased or their occupation. No reason for them being abroad. Nothing to suggest the life that came before whatever ignominious end awaited them. The single page is so tidy its reader might easily forget the nature of what's being described. Perhaps, he thinks, this is exactly what Form 192 is meant to do. Neatly box in the dead, and move on.

Only the last entry, *Remarks*, located just above the consular seal, allows for any deviation. Three pre-printed lines follow. Unlike the other fields, most of which Sokobin could fill in with Meyer's details right now, *Remarks* is optional. And yet these are the very lines he most wants to fill. The very lines that refuse to be written.

The train slows. Sokobin looks out the window; they are coming into the station at Soochow. Along the platform the passengers have already divided themselves in anticipation of boarding: the spare anemic line headed to white first class; the rumpled, pulsing crowd destined for Chinese coach; the contained cluster of black robes and silk for Chinese first. Sokobin remembers the explorer mentioning that this last was how he preferred to travel in order to save a bit on train expenses.

They jolt to a stop, and the doors open with a slap. The English tourists spill onto the platform in a small khaki wave. No doubt they've come to view the ancient city's famous gardens. Heels sound along the corridor, and Sokobin senses his solitude about to slip away. In quick succession, he slides the green folder back into his briefcase and snaps it shut, then removes the newspaper from the table and deposits the pie remains in the rubbish bin. The small cabin has grown thick with smoke, and he pulls down the window to clear the air. Sitting up straight, he resets his face just in time to greet the tap on the compartment door.

CHAPTER 15

"One minute," the Consul General says, his silver head pointed at the paperwork in front of him.

The CG sits in a leather armchair, his slender silhouette framed by the tall windows and blue silk curtains behind. A set of thin sheers covers the panes, obscuring the boats along Soochow Creek and washing the massive mahogany desk with pale light. To the right stands a brass flagpole and an easel with a portrait of President Wilson; to the left, a large fern overflows from an antique porcelain Chinese pot.

Sokobin hovers over the opposite chair, trying to keep himself from shifting about like Windham as he awaits the instruction to sit. He knows the room well from his years of ferrying reports and files, though today, he reminds himself, he's come not as a clerk but as a VC. Just four months ago he stood in this very spot listening as the CG dispensed his parting advice before Sokobin left for Nanking to take up his new post. Since then, the office seems to have grown; Sokobin would wager it must be six times the size of his own. Even the June heat proves no match for the deep brick walls. Here, the air remains cool through late afternoon, the room's corners shrouded in shadow and its surfaces smelling of lemon wood polish.

At last, the Consul presses his fountain pen to the page, releasing his signature, and places the dossier in an otherwise empty *Out* box. Only in his dreams will Sokobin ever know such a clear desk.

"Samuel, good to see you again," the Consul says, removing his glasses and reaching across to shake hands. "Rather, I should say, Vice-Consul." His thin lips offer a tempered smile.

"You as well, sir."

"I'm sure we both wish the circumstances were different."

"Indeed."

"It's quite late. Brandy?"

"No, thank you."

They take their seats, and for a moment, the room's only sound is the ticking of the electric fan overhead. The CG wears a slim-fitting three-piece, fashioned in seersucker, his Yale sporting tie, and spotless white bucks, all of which make Sokobin relieved to have left his tired winter suit back in Nanking. As always, the Consul's silver hair has been cleanly parted and oiled into a singular gleaming wave of the like Sokobin's wiry locks can never achieve. The CG's pinched nose and trim mustache exude moderation; only the gray eyes, shining like two wet stones, hint at something fiercer beneath.

"So, Meyer," he says. "A tragic end."

"Yes, sir."

"I didn't know him personally, but an extraordinary man by all accounts. And a great service to the country. Imagine braving all those backwaters and mountaintops in search of plants. To be honest, I'm not sure I could have done it, even when I was young." The Consul exhales. "And Mr. Meyer wasn't exactly young anymore, was he?"

"No, sir. Forty-two."

"Remarkable. I'm told he didn't use sedan chairs."

"Correct, sir."

"Remarkable," the CG repeats, tapping his blotter with his pen. "Your wire mentioned some trouble at the cemetery."

"Yes, sir. The diggers were reluctant to uncover the body. The village, Ti-Kang, is very small. Traditional," Sokobin says, remembering Lin's word.

"Fear of evil spirits or some such, I'm sure. But clearly you persuaded them."

"Yes, sir." Sokobin catches his fingers before they reach into his pockets and drops them to his lap. The CG has made no secret of his disdain of the "smoking habit" and forbids even celebratory cigars in his office. "Mr. Meyer was in the water, most likely for a couple days before being buried. There was also the heat, sir. No coffin was used." Sokobin does his best to push away the images and meet the Consul's solemn stare.

"I realize that executing that particular task must have been quite difficult—an unfortunate part of our duties as men of rank, I'm afraid. I wish I could tell you it won't ever happen again, but we both know that would be a lie." He purses his lips. "And you're sure the body is Meyer's?"

"Hard to be absolutely certain, sir, given the state of it, but I believe so. The funeral men did a surprisingly good job." Sokobin thinks of the coffin, the dead man dressed in white, his father's yarmulke and tallit, knowing better than to disclose these details. He's still trying to convince himself that it was right to give such precious things to a near stranger. "Bear in mind that I met Mr. Meyer only once," he adds, "at the Fourth of July reception the year before last."

A smile passes over the Consul's lips. "Our first in the new building."

"Yes."

"Quite a day that was."

Sokobin detects a hint of sentimentality in the CG's voice. Nothing could be further from Sokobin's memory of the experience, and it shames him to think of his anger at the dead man that day. For that's what it was, Sokobin realizes now. Meyer had refused to don his party mask, refused to be the bold, brave explorer Sokobin had wanted him to be. He recalls Meyer standing at the window, his eyes creased with loneliness and regret. Sokobin now wonders how many times, these past months, his staff in Nan-king have witnessed the same worn expression on his own face.

"At any rate, all the facts would point to the body being Meyer," Sokobin says. "The face and build certainly resemble the man I recall. And the time and location of the fisherman who towed it ashore are both consistent with Mr. Meyer's reported disappearance from the steamer. I've also checked with all the patrol stations along that stretch of river, and no other Westerners have been reported missing. At this point, it's hard to imagine the body could be anyone other than Mr. Meyer."

The CG nods. "I agree. At this point it's more of a formality. Still, any particularities that might confirm identity? A birth-mark or tattoo?"

"No, but I was able to retrieve a pair of suspenders and shoes from the fisherman. It's my hope Meyer's cabinmate and boy can corroborate them. I suppose the boy could identify the body, though after so much time, it seems cruel and unnecessary."

The CG nods. "Wise choice. Let's just get confirmation on the items, and I'll send word to the family and Meyer's supervisor. Given his line of work, it's possible Meyer left final instructions. And the body is at the American mortuary here, yes?"

"Yes, sir. I didn't feel it right to leave Mr. Meyer buried in Ti-Kang, given your note."

"My note?"

"About Mr. Meyer's faith, sir."

"Right," the Consul says. "The Hebrew angle."

Sokobin presses his lips together. He's always suspected the CG didn't welcome his promotion so much as tolerate it.

"Yes, sir. The family may wish the remains to be shipped back to Holland. If not, Mr. Meyer can be buried in the Jewish cemetery here. Either way, Shanghai seemed the only logical choice."

The CG leans back in his chair and tents his hands on his lap. "Rather astonishing that Meyer's file fell to you, isn't it? One might even be tempted to say, the hand of God."

The resulting stare lasts too long for Sokobin's comfort, and he looks past the CG's shoulder, to the river contained in the sheers. The truth of the matter is Sokobin can't shake the feeling that Meyer is a sign. But like the tallit and yarmulke, and as with so much else, he knows to keep such ideas to himself. The Consul is testing him, he knows, waiting for him to trip up.

"Tempting to say, sir. But one has nothing to do with the other," Sokobin says, repeating Chase's words from the night before. "A mere coincidence of geography."

The Consul nods. He leans forward again, sending up a cracking sound from his chair. "Good to hear you say it, Vice-Consul. I'd hate to think of you falling prey to Oriental fatalism. I've seen it take too many men in the field already." He presses his hands to his desk. "At any rate, a job well done, especially with your being so new to the area. I'll be making a note of it in your file."

"Thank you, sir, but I'm not sure how much of the credit belongs to me," Sokobin tells him and briefly explains Lin's interviewing of the servants.

"That proves only one thing," the Consul says, raising a finger. "Your good judgment in picking the right man for the job. Don't sell yourself short, Sokobin. You do us all a disservice when you do. Still, I don't understand why you felt it necessary to bring your man to Shanghai when we have so many approved interpreters here. The list must be a mile long. All the old Mandarins desperate for work now."

"It seemed the wisest course, sir, given that Mr. Lin is so versed with the facts of the case. Plus, his English is excellent." Sokobin delivers the lines clearly and without hesitation, precisely because he has practiced them on the train in anticipation of this very question. "Mr. Lin has also shown a calm disposition in the face of trying circumstances."

The Consul releases a breathy laugh. "Well, that is a rarity. But putting him up here?"

"I'd rather he stay close, sir. More efficient with coordinating our remaining tasks." Sokobin stops, knowing that to say more will only make him appear defensive.

The CG purses his lips. "I'm going to make an exception, given the late hour. But let's not make a habit of it. There's a certain natural order to these things that must be observed. Otherwise, it all quickly gets *muddled*, as the English say. Anything else?"

"The cabinmate and the servant boy, sir. I believe someone in this office was tracking them down?"

"Yes, you can ask Mr. Welch about that. He's handling the file here. I've asked him to come in order to give you whatever you need. You know Welch, don't you?"

Sokobin smiles at the name. "Of course, sir." His first two years in Shanghai, back when they still occupied the old building, Welch had the desk next to his. Sokobin and Theo were close in age and got on from the start. More than anyone else, it was Welch who showed Sokobin the ropes, Welch who made him laugh. "I'd also like to take a look at Mr. Meyer's effects, sir. They may shed some light on the situation."

"Yes, we have them here somewhere. Welch can help you with that as well. But is all this really necessary?"

Sokobin stares in confusion. "It's not clear what caused Mr. Meyer's death, sir."

"The man drowned, correct? Certainly, there's no question of that."

"No, sir. I mean the question being why. Mr. Meyer died while on official duty. I'm certain his colleagues will demand to know the circumstances of his passing. And the family. You did say to leave no stone unturned, sir." These last words, though not rehearsed, come as sharply as any before.

The Consul taps his blotter. His eyes narrow until the brows, still black, nearly touch. "Yes, I did," he says at last. "But I don't understand. You suspect something other than accident?"

"At this point, I have no clear theory, sir. It's difficult to believe such an experienced explorer would simply fall from a passenger ship."

"At first glance, I'd have to agree. However, if I'm remembering correctly, there was some mention of sickness. It's possible Meyer was with fever."

"Perhaps, sir. I'm hoping the cabinmate and boy can clarify the extent of any illness. I can find Mr. Welch in his office?"

"Yes. We've moved him, though. He's at your old desk now. I'm sure you remember where that is."

"Of course, sir."

The Consul runs a finger along his mustache. "I want to make myself clear, Sokobin. Once we have a positive identification on Meyer, I expect a Form 192 on my desk. It's terribly sad what's happened, but I need you back in Nanking with your mind squarely on the Chinese situation. I'll spare you the latest report," he says, picking up the top dossier from the tray and letting it fall back down. "What I'm trying to say is I don't want you getting over-involved."

"Over-involved, sir?"

"On account of the other."

"The other, sir?"

"Mr. Meyer's faith. I think you understand what I'm saying, Vice-Consul."

Sokobin blinks. "Yes, sir," he says, knowing he has no intention of pulling away.

The CG lifts his watch from his vest and exhales. "I must go. I'm frightfully late."

"Diplomatic dinner, sir?"

The Consul emits a quick laugh. "If only it were so easy. My wife. Trust me, there are no more difficult negotiations. The twins are about to enter high school, and let's just say there's some disagreement as to where."

He reaches for the silver picture frame on the desk. The image isn't visible from Sokobin's chair, but he knows it well from having stood so often at the Consul's shoulder—the two bright-eyed boys in matching sailor shirts and caps, taken years ago when they were just five or six years old.

"I hesitate to think of where'd they be if only they were a few years older," the Consul says quietly and carefully lowers the frame. "My poor sister hasn't been so lucky. Terrifying what comes down to chance."

He looks at Sokobin with a weary, furrowed expression, his mask briefly forgotten, and for a moment, it's possible to imagine the Consul as he must be away from the office: an ordinary man, no different from Sokobin himself, waking from the depths of a dark dream and reaching for the lamp chain. Sokobin almost forgives him. Almost.

"I don't suppose there's been any further word on your . . ."

"No, sir," Sokobin interjects. There's no need to hear the words. He's seen the look enough to know what comes next.

The Consul nods. He plants his hands on his desk and rises from his chair. Sokobin stands, taking up his briefcase. "One must never give up hope," the CG says, his face once again composed. "Duty requires it."

"Yes, sir," Sokobin says.

CHAPTER 16

Sokobin leaves the CG's office and immediately heads to the service stairwell where he lights a Chesterfield. He doesn't expect Lin back from dinner until after eight—time enough to see Welch and locate Meyer's things.

He heads up the stairs, exiting at the third floor. His footsteps echo as he passes down the long corridor. Nearly everyone is gone; only a skeleton crew remains on weekends—a few security guards and a pair of operators to monitor the cables. Sokobin turns the corner and crosses the secretarial pool, its dozen typewriters now silent and covered with dust cloths. Lowering his cigarette, he breathes in traces of perfume: lavender, lemon verbena, and rose.

By the time he reaches his old office, the Chesterfield is already half gone. Welch sits with his back to the doorway, his white linen jacket slung over the chair. Beneath his vest is a striped shirt. He smokes a long brown cigarette as he turns the pages of a magazine. Counting the minutes, Sokobin is sure.

"Who the hell is that sitting in my chair?"

Welch jumps at the voice. Turning, he catches sight of Sokobin and breaks into a wide smile. Theo's is a handsome face, with a clean-shaven jaw, wide cheeks, and large hazel eyes rimmed with thick lashes the secretaries used to tease were wasted on a man. Theo stands, as slim as ever. He kowtows theatrically, and

Sokobin notices a patch of scalp where Welch's auburn hair has started to thin. It's been a few years since he's observed Theo at such close range.

"Vice-Consul Sokobin, to what do I owe the honor?"

"Sam still works fine, thank you very much," Sokobin says, waving him off. He knows Theo is only playing, but the dramatic gesture makes him uncomfortable. "For God's sake, sit."

Welch lowers himself into the chair while Sokobin sets down his briefcase, relieved to be free of its weight. He perches himself on the edge of the desk that for seven years was his own. He runs a hand along the familiar grain; somehow the desk kept following him despite several moves and reassignments. A collection of coffee cup rings, the likes of which would certainly incur the wrath of Miss Petrie and to which Sokobin knows he greatly contributed, stain its surface. Even so, he notes subtle changes under Theo's reign. Welch has shifted the in/out box to the opposite side and gotten himself a new brass lamp. He's also added a pair of lacquered picture frames. Sokobin remembers them from before: the first shows Welch's three pretty sisters in winter coats and ice skates, and the other their handsome parents outside the leafy Cincinnati home where Theo grew up. Sokobin used to study them like scenes from a travel brochure whenever Welch was away from his desk. Their perfect American normalcy fascinated him.

"So, how's the old gal treating you?" Sokobin asks, tapping his ash into the glass ashtray. Another change.

"All right. But that won't open," Welch says, pointing toward the right drawer with his long cigarette. Theo's tastes have always run to the expensive, all-Turkish blends.

"It never did," Sokobin says. "There could be gold bricks in there for all we know."

"And here I was thinking it held your old stash of girlie magazines."

Sokobin shakes his head, unable to suppress a smile. "Do you ever stop?"

"Not until they catch me."

They laugh, and Sokobin recalls how easy it once was between them—the effortless banter that felt like a private language unto themselves. It didn't last. By the time they moved to the new buildings, Sokobin had been promoted to a different floor, and his and Theo's interactions were reduced to the occasional passing greeting on the stairs. He digs into his pocket for another cigarette.

"So, you partake now," Welch says. "The hefty demands of rank? Does the CG know?"

Sokobin shakes his head and cracks his lighter. He sends a stream of smoke out the side of his mouth.

"What's your poison?" Welch asks.

"Chesterfields."

Welch cocks an eyebrow. "Soldier smokes, eh?"

Sokobin guesses Welch hasn't heard about Ethan, and he isn't about to tell him. He knows better than to try to broach sensitive matters with Welch. Welch isn't Chase.

"I just like them, that's all," he says.

Welch releases a tight curl of smoke out the window. He looks disappointed, and Sokobin wishes he'd thought of a snappier comeback.

"And how is little Nanking?"

"Little."

Welch grins and taps his ash. "How many in your office?"

"Three plus myself."

"Sounds like a wild party. Any lookers?"

"Enough," Sokobin tells him, suddenly defensive. He doesn't like Theo making quips about his staff. Besides, it's getting late, he reminds himself; he still has to examine the explorer's things. "About Meyer. The Consul said you have contact information for the cabinmate and boy."

Welch sets down his cigarette. "Right, the business at hand. I almost forgot." Theo shoots him a look—the same he used to make whenever their supervisor dropped off files too late in the day. Sokobin's let himself forget this side of Welch, the petty barbs that used to spill from his mouth, especially when it came to the higher-ups. There was a time Sokobin found them wickedly funny and was glad to be in the joke. Cheeky, indulgent, and free. Alive. It was how Welch once made him feel, like a man without constraints. But he's not Welch's audience anymore. As a higher-up, he can't be.

Theo pulls the stack of files from his tray, extracting one and lifting the cover. "Here," he says, handing over a sheet of paper. Sokobin glances at the two names.

"Isley Drysdale. British. Insurance salesman," Welch explains. "He and Meyer briefly shared a cabin on the boat. I'd call Drysdale's hotel this evening if I were you. He's staying at the Imperial. It's written down. At any rate, you'll need to move quick. He's scheduled to leave for Hong Kong on business the day after tomorrow."

"Will do. And the boy?"

"Yao-feng Ting. Given the address listed on the passenger manifest, I'd say you'll want to interview him here. No telephone that I know of. You'll need to send a messenger."

Sokobin taps his ash into the tray. If Theo were Windham, he'd praise him on a job well done. But Welch isn't his clerk. Even if Sokobin is technically Welch's superior now, Theo is still Theo. Once they'd sat side by side. "Thanks for this," he says, folding the paper in half and slipping it into his jacket. "And Meyer's things? Are they in the basement?"

Welch nods. "Everything except the silver and his camera. Those are being held in the safe. Otherwise, it's all there. Storage room three." He withdraws a key from his desk and slides it across the wood. Sokobin drops the key into his pocket. "It's not much, really. A small trunk, some burlap bags. Seeds."

"Have you gone through it?"

"Nope." Welch takes up his cigarette, still alive in the tray. The all-Turkish blends burn slowly. "That's for the lead man. You, I suppose. So, are they putting you up in one of the rooms next door?"

Sokobin nods. "Me and my interpreter."

"The royal treatment." Welch takes a long pull from his cigarette, narrowing his eyes. In this light they appear more gold than green. "Anything else, Vice-Consul?"

Sokobin senses the impatience. "No."

"I'll be heading out then."

"Got a date?"

"Hope springs eternal," Welch says, tamping out his cigarette and shutting the window. He pulls a small mirror from the desk's shallow center drawer and sets about examining his teeth and hair, and for a moment, Sokobin is back to those blurry months when come sundown, neighboring desks gave way to neighboring stools. Somehow Welch always seemed to be in the know of the latest watering spot, especially the ones that never closed. More than once, Sokobin had left Theo at the bar before staggering home at 2 a.m. He used to wonder if the man ever slept.

Theo snaps the mirror shut, exchanging it for a bottle of cologne. "Tell the truth, Sam," he says, unscrewing the cap. "You miss it."

"What?" Sokobin asks, pretending not to understand.

"Shanghai."

"Not that much."

Theo shakes his head. "Bullshit."

Sokobin holds his tongue as Theo dabs his neck, knowing that whatever he says, Welch will easily best him. Theo's not moving up the line has not been for lack of cleverness, only for lack of push. The absence of ambition used to stymie Sokobin until he realized it was calculated. Welch did just enough—never more, never less—to ensure he stayed exactly where he wanted to be. Shanghai. It was Theo's playground. At this point, Sokobin would wager Welch loves the city more than his own country.

Theo slides the drawer closed and lifts his jacket from the chair. Crossing the room, he takes the last remaining hat from the rack. "Follow me down?" he asks, angling the brim.

Sokobin stubs out the rest of his cigarette. "No attaché?"

"No need." Theo raises his arms up like a magician. "I'm a free man until 9 a.m. tomorrow morning."

They head down the stairs. In the lobby, the armed night guard stands next to the locked door. The man is new. Sokobin doesn't know his name.

"What happened to McGuinn?" Sokobin whispers.

"Joined up. If they don't end this thing soon, the place is going to be guarded by dames." Welch pauses at one of the console tables and pulls a sleek cigarette case from his jacket. The container is long, meant to hold after-dinner lengths—precisely the sort of case Chase would like Sokobin to buy. "Hold up a second."

"I thought you had a date," Sokobin says and immediately wishes he hadn't. He sounds uptight, rushed for time.

"Give it a minute," Welch says. "You can't be too punctual, you know." He tilts the case toward Sokobin. "Any interest in a real smoke?"

"No, thanks," Sokobin says, lowering his briefcase to the tiles with a thud. He takes a Chesterfield from his pocket and draws from Welch's lighter. "I'm partial now."

"Aren't we all?" Welch says, sending up a white stream. "Say, why not come along tonight? Just for drinks. You'd like the place." He smiles from the corner of his mouth, revealing a slice of teeth. "Dark and a little seedy. Just your style."

Sokobin inhales, delaying. "I'd only be a third wheel."

Welch laughs. "Without a doubt. But who knows, maybe we'll find you a fourth?"

"You know I can't. The Meyer file."

"What? Stay here and sift through a dead man's things when the dissolution capital of the world awaits your return? "

It was something they used to say over the third drink, justification for the fourth, the fifth. One morning after a particularly long night, Sokobin threw up in the men's room. He thought he was alone, but he wasn't. *Rough night there, sailor?* another clerk had called from the next stall. Sokobin knew the story would make its way around the floor and down the stairs before noon. He'd need to make a choice, he understood—stop or get passed over. He suspected some in the office would have welcomed any excuse not to see him go up the chain. He'd put an end to the nights of oblivion after that, pleading work and staying late at the office. At a certain point, Theo stopped asking. Sokobin has always wondered if Welch held it against him. Now he knows.

"Another time perhaps," Sokobin tells him. "Before I head back to Nanking." A lie. He's pretty sure Theo knows it too.

"Going once, going twice . . ."

"Gone," Sokobin says.

"To each his own." Welch taps his ashes, ignoring the tray and letting the ashes fall to the floor. He dips his hat. "Good to see you again, Sam."

Welch calls out to the guard who reaches for the key ring on his belt and unlocks the door. Outside, the sidewalk is thick with bodies, and the bund rushes with traffic. The sky has turned dark and the streetlamps glow. Across the road, boats strung with lanterns glide along the black creek. Welch leans toward the guard, giving him a small punch on the arm and making the man laugh. Sokobin can't make out the words over the din from the street. Theo steps down and deftly inserts himself into the passing crowd, disappearing before Sokobin can count to three.

"Going out, sir?" the guard calls to Sokobin.

Sokobin stands next to the table, inhaling a mix of smoke and exhaust. He shakes his head, and the door closes again, its bolt echoing across the floor tiles.

CHAPTER 17

HE RINGS THE IMPERIAL, ONLY TO BE TOLD DRYSDALE is out for the evening. Sokobin leaves a message, resolved to try the hotel again first thing in the morning. He's not expecting to learn very much from Drysdale given that he and Meyer shared a cabin for a day at most before the explorer went missing. Still, Drysdale was one of the last people to see the explorer alive.

Sokobin stares at the silent telephone. His stomach has begun to make noises, and he considers putting off Meyer's effects until tomorrow. The last time he ate was the miserable pie on the express from Nanking, and at this point, his body wants nothing more than to down a whiskey and crawl under the guest room sheets. But not reaching Drysdale has left him feeling dissatisfied, and the conversations with the CG and Welch uneasy—as if somehow it were Sokobin himself, and not Meyer, who was under investigation. Better to sort through the explorer's things tonight, he decides. If he attempts sleep now, he'll only twist the sheets into knots.

He heads down the service stairs, his stomach clamoring with every step. One hand to the railing and the other on his briefcase, he sinks into the dim. Apparently, no one has thought to keep the basement lights on at night. By the last steps, the disorientation is nearly complete, and he suddenly stops, unsure of his own footing. If not for the railing, he'd pitch headfirst into the obscurity.

He stands immobile, his heart sounding in his ears. He reminds himself that he knows this place, having come down these stairs dozens of times in search of this item or that. He moves forward again, and his shoes find the flat plane of the basement landing. Reaching out, he locates the exit door, and hears it click shut behind him. He blinks only to realize it makes no difference if his lids remain open or shut. The basement is entirely belowground, come night its corridors reduced to pitch black. He gropes about for the switch, but his fingers can't find the button. Frustrated, he stops, swearing at himself for having already forgotten its location.

Damp air presses against his face. Save for the sound of his own sour breath, the resulting silence is absolute—without a single voice or car horn or banging water pipe. An eternity passes in dark suspension as he waits for the images to flash against the dark. Not the falling plane, but the body on the hill, the swollen skin, the hand reaching for his. He steadies himself against the wall's cool bricks, breathing in deeply until his heart quiets. The fear evaporates, replaced by shame. A grown man afraid of the dark. At moments like these he understands what kind of soldier he'd make. A dead one. He wouldn't last a week in the trenches. Or worse—a coward, a liability to the others.

He makes another attempt to find the switch plate but to no avail. He's about to quit when he remembers the lighter in his pocket and snaps the flint. The flame quickly reveals why he couldn't find the button. There isn't one, only a short pull descending from the fixture overhead.

———————

HE INSERTS THE KEY, SWINGING THE DOOR WIDE AND letting the hall light filter in. A bare bulb flickers on. The first sight of the columns of boxes and crates is deflating, but he

quickly realizes these are filled with old files and office what-
not and have nothing to do with Meyer. He finds the explorer's things neatly stacked, just as Welch said, against the side
wall. Pinned to the top of the pile is a sheet of yellow paper with
MEYER, FRANK spelled out in Theo's clear, stick-like letters.

Sokobin lays his jacket over his case and rolls up his sleeves.
The topmost item is a burlap sack—one of the seed bags, he
figures. He works open the drawstring; indeed, hundreds, perhaps thousands, of tiny black seeds rest inside. Of what variety,
Sokobin has no idea. He inspects the three other sacks, running
his hands through the contents; these too contain nothing but
seeds, he piles them to the side.

Working his way down, he finds Meyer's walking stick. The
sight of the staff's stilled and lonely frame strikes him as pro-
foundly sad, and Sokobin takes it up, curling his fingers around
the grip. His fingers don't come close to filling the worn grooves.
A snake has been carved into the length of the wooden shaft.
Sokobin runs a finger over its rippled shape.

Two items remain, a canvas rucksack and a small wooden
trunk. Sokobin hesitates; he's not in the habit of rummaging
through other people's private belongings, let alone those of dead
men. But there's no way around it. The pack's top flap has been
tightly knotted, and it takes a minute before he can tease out
the strings. From inside, he removes the wool bedroll, placing it
with the walking stick and seed bags. One by one, he empties the
left pocket, spreading the items over the trunk lid. As he does,
a canteen in miniature appears: bouillon cubes, nuts, a pouch
of dried rice, pocketknife, metal cup, spoon, and waterproofed
matches. From the right pocket he pulls a compass, basic medical
kit, needle and thread, safety pins, comb, compact mirror, small
towel, thin slice of soap, two pencil stubs, and a brass skeleton
key—this last item he pockets. There are also several folded maps
and a small notebook, all of which appear to have been scribbled

on. These, too, Sokobin sets aside to examine in his room where the light promises to be better.

From the main compartment he withdraws two changes of linen and a wool shirt—well used, judging by their smell. Additionally, he finds a bandanna, leather gloves, boot laces, a mosquito net for the face, and a mackintosh square. At the very bottom of the compartment his fingers close around a small, sharp bundle. As he lifts it, Sokobin knows it contains a gun. Carefully, he turns back the chamois to reveal a thin, black barrel and back-jutting grip. Sokobin has never been one to carry a pistol, finding them more nuisance than they're worth in the city; even so, he recognizes the model as a Luger 9mm—current standard issue for the German army.

Sokobin can feel his mind chewing at the bit, anxious to run with half-baked, cloak-and-dagger scenarios. Experience, however, tells him that few, if any, of these possibilities will bear scrutiny come the light of morning. The fact is, nothing in Meyer's record suggests him to be anything other than the man he presented himself as: a plant hunter and a pacifist; the type to find God in the quivering petals of an orchid. Besides, Sokobin knows, Lugers are common enough, and China's backroads littered with thieves and slit throats. Given the remote territories Meyer traveled through, it would have been tantamount to suicide not to carry a rifle or pistol; preferably both. He rewraps the Luger and makes a mental note to ask Meyer's boy about it when they meet.

Sokobin returns the pack's contents and then on impulse slips its padded straps over his shirt. He takes a few steps, attempting to imagine bearing such weight day after day, mile after mile, but having lived only in cities, the pack feels as alien to Sokobin as a monkey on his back. Setting it down, he turns his attention to the steamer trunk, and fishes out the brass key from his pocket. To his relief, the lock yields. At the top of the open trunk sit

Meyer's field boots, wiped clean of dirt and resting on a cotton towel. Sokobin lifts them out; beneath he finds no shortage of papers: U.S. government documents identifying Meyer's purpose in China and requesting safe passage for the explorer and his crew, inventory sheets and accounting forms, a small stack of Office of Foreign Seed and Plant Introduction stationery, a blotter, several fountain pens, and a nearly expired bottle of ink. There are also several bundles of letters, some of which appear to be personal, others from his office, all of which Sokobin adds to the pile destined for upstairs. Digging more deeply, he finds a box of ammunition, a matching green cap and scarf—the knit stretched and pilling—and two volumes: *History of European Botanical Discoveries in China* and Whitman's *Leaves of Grass*. The covers of both books are dented and their bindings cracked.

A cardboard film box holds no negatives but contains several photographs. Two of the photos depict Meyer posing in a garden next to men who might be friends or colleagues. Another shows a younger Meyer, dressed in city clothes and standing at the center of a handsome group with their arms laced about each other's waists. Sokobin looks from one smiling face to the next. The family in Amsterdam, he thinks. The resemblance is too clear for them to be anything but. Meyer's people appear happy, well-kept, respectably trimmed out. By now, they would have certainly received the message bearing the terrible news. He imagines the same group, minus Meyer, now huddled together, their backs bent in grief and faces swollen from tears.

However, it is the final image that most holds Sokobin's attention. A bearded Meyer and another man wear thick boots, heavy coats, and beaver fur caps. Meyer grips his walking stick, the second man a rifle. Each ceremoniously bends a knee to a cobblestone street patched with dirty ice; meanwhile a block of sooty brick buildings rises behind. The two men stare defiantly at the camera like a pair of seasoned soldiers fresh from battle.

This was the real Meyer, Sokobin thinks, the hardy explorer he'd been looking for at the party, not the nostalgic idealist or the timid-looking man shown in his personnel photo, but the adventurer in his element: formidable and undeterred. And something else, Sokobin thinks, as he studies the explorer's face and stance. A certainty of purpose so intense it borders on faith. He flips the picture and reads the inscription.

Peking February 6, 1915.
Together we stand or fall.

He can already tell from the other papers that the scrawl is Meyer's. Sokobin turns back to the image. Blond hair rims the edges of the second man's fur cap. He appears younger than Meyer, perhaps by five or seven years. Despite the colorless image, Sokobin can make out the deep flush of his cheeks from the cold. The assistant, he thinks, the one who left. He remembers Meyer mentioning something about the man when they spoke at the party. But Sokobin is too exhausted to remember anything more, and adds the photograph to the stack he intends to carry upstairs.

At the bottom of the trunk, he finds a bundle wrapped in dark crepe paper. For a moment, Sokobin thinks it must contain a yarmulke and tallit. Instead, he pulls back the paper to reveal a tuxedo jacket. The sight is so unexpected and strange, he nearly laughs. He can hardly imagine the same man who wore field boots to a cocktail party ever agreeing to wear such formal attire. He holds up the jacket; the sleeves are deeply creased as if they haven't been unfolded in years. Faint speckles of mildew dot the fabric.

Save for the small pile destined for his room, he replaces the trunk's contents and closes the lid. Between his briefcase and the stack under his arm, closing the storage room requires some maneuvering. At last, he manages and makes his way back along the corridor. He stops under the pull chain, then thinking better of it, leaves the light on.

HE REACHES THE GUEST HALLWAY AND LOWERS HIS briefcase, then Meyer's things, to the carpet. He sifts through the keys in his pocket. Next door, a slice of yellow light spills across the threshold to Lin's quarters. A shadow passes, momentarily blocking the glow. Given the long day, Sokobin expected Lin to be in bed and already asleep. He checks his watch. Half past nine. Sokobin isn't sure which shows greater respect: knocking and checking in or simply letting the man be.

He knocks.

Lin cracks the door and blinks. "Vice-Consul."

Lin steps back. The interpreter stands in his socks, his collar off, his jacket and tie on the valet stand, his shoes placed neatly beneath. He isn't wearing his spectacles. Sokobin has grown so used to the sight of the glasses that Lin's features appear incomplete without them. Sokobin spots them resting on the desk across the room, next to a sheath of papers. He recognizes the stationery as the same from the day before, and senses he's made a mistake in knocking. He's trespassed again.

"Sorry to disturb you," Sokobin says, remaining in the hall. "I just wanted to make sure you're settled. You were able to find a decent dinner?"

"Yes. Too many choices, sir. We do not have this problem in Nanking."

Sokobin emits a small laugh. The interpreter's humor is so spare and dry that when it comes, it continues to take him by surprise.

"And you, sir?"

"I'm afraid not. I've been busy, meeting with the Consul and going through Mr. Meyer's things," Sokobin says, pointing at the stack on the floor. "I've left a message with Meyer's cabinmate from the steamer about meeting tomorrow. And we still need to bring in Meyer's boy for questioning. I'll have you send that message in the morning."

Lin nods but says nothing, and Sokobin feels slightly foolish; certainly, he could have simply waited until morning to speak with the interpreter. He glances at the untouched bed, then back to the papers on the desk. "Well, it's late and I don't want to keep you. I'll see you at breakfast then. Good night."

"Good night, Vice-Consul."

Sokobin's room is the twin of Lin's: tidy and tasteful with damask gold drapes and coverlet, framed prints of sampans and temples, a sprig of white silk orchids in a painted Chinese vase. He sets down his briefcase on the floor, finds the bedside lamp and stacks Meyer's things on the desk. Opening the small interior door, he gives a small sigh of relief. The room has a private bath. Hot water. He hasn't had it since moving to Nanking.

He opens the tap, waiting for the steam before setting the plug. He lifts the window sash and pulls out a cigarette while he waits for the tub to fill. It's started to drizzle, cooling the night air. His room overlooks Soochow Creek, the second slice of water that divides the city. He thinks of Welch out there, doing who knows what by now. Sokobin can't say, only that whatever it is, Theo won't be applying the brakes. The dissolute life. It could have easily been Sokobin's own. But he'd chosen differently. Maybe Chase was right. Maybe there was something in him pushing him forward, a drive. Maybe it wasn't even so much a choice, Sokobin thinks, no different than the explorer—just the way he was made.

He tamps out his cigarette and strips, submerging himself. Sweat drifts from his skin, leaving iridescent smears on the water's surface. He stares at the cake of soap left on the sink, willing himself to lift his body and reach for it. Gradually the tub water goes tepid. He closes his eyes. The day has exhausted him. If he could, he'd fall asleep right here.

He becomes aware of a voice coming from Lin's room. Sokobin stills himself, trying to make it out. The wall muffles the words, but even so, Sokobin can tell they aren't English—the rhythm is too different. He waits for someone else to speak, but Lin's is the only voice: steady and rhythmic. It takes a moment before Sokobin understands. Mr. Lin is praying.

CHAPTER 18

Monday, June 9

"UNFORTUNATE," DRYSDALE SAYS WHEN SOKOBIN IN-
forms him that Meyer's body has been found.

They sit in the Imperial's paneled salon, Drysdale in a rattan
armchair, Sokobin and Lin side by side on a red velvet settee that
seems garishly pretentious for the modest hotel. A trio of faux
Ming vases rests on a low cocktail table between them. Drysdale's
message came this morning, just as Sokobin and Lin were finishing breakfast in the canteen. A notebook sits on Lin's lap, open
to a clean page. Sokobin has asked him to take notes during the
interview, so that Sokobin may fully concentrate on the questions.

"Do you recall what Mr. Meyer was wearing that night?"

"I didn't think to take notice," Drysdale says.

Sokobin withdraws the cloth sack from his briefcase. He uncinches the top, placing the suspenders and shoes on the table.
Drysdale winces as the river's murky rot fills the air between them.
He has a soft-boiled British face—pink, lipless, and balding—the
sort that strikes Sokobin as being at complete odds with China itself.

"Yes. I'm almost certain now that I see them," Drysdale says,
reaching for his cigarette case. He wears a three-piece, beige plaid
in summer-weight wool, and a complicated tie knot. "He mentioned something about having to buy the braces in Hankow
before boarding the boat. Apparently, he and his boy had been
trapped in Ichang for several months. I gathered the fighting

had been pretty nasty, and they'd had to go to rations." Drysdale pauses, blowing smoke toward the open window. "He did look somewhat gaunt."

Sokobin returns the suspenders and shoes to his briefcase. "Did Mr. Meyer seem ill to you? Any sign of fever?"

"If he had, I certainly would have demanded to be moved to another cabin. He said he wasn't feeling tip-top and kept to his bed. I assumed it was just the typical stomach upset one gets on a steamer. He ate a bit though. Soup, I believe."

"What about any arguments on board? Did you witness or hear anything?"

Drysdale shakes his head. "No, nothing like that."

"So no one suspicious or unusual, perhaps another passenger who might have meant Mr. Meyer harm?"

Drysdale leans forward and taps his ash. "Hardly. Aside from Meyer's disappearance, the trip was dull as paste." He frowns, signaling the Chinese waiter in the corner. "We're still waiting on the biscuits," he tells the man as he steps forward to refill their teacups. The waiter departs, and Drysdale flashes Sokobin a conspiratorial look of exasperation.

Sokobin averts his eyes and reaches into his pocket for a cigarette. He's met plenty of Drysdale's type before—the Shanghai Club type. Sokobin has seen the brass placard on the front doors: *No Chinese or dogs allowed.* Other than to offer the briefest of handshakes, Drysdale hasn't cast a single glance in Lin's direction.

Sokobin cracks his lighter and draws down the smoke. "When did you last see Mr. Meyer?"

"Half past ten or eleven. I can't say, really. The light was out, and I was already in bed. He said he was stepping out for some air. I assumed he meant the privies. One doesn't press for details."

"And did Mr. Meyer return to the cabin after that?"

"I don't know. I must have fallen asleep. I didn't realize he wasn't there until his boy knocked the next morning and I saw the empty bed. If I'd known, of course . . ." Drysdale lowers his teacup to the table, leaving the thought unfinished.

"You said that Mr. Meyer spoke of his time in Ichang. Did you two speak about anything else?"

"We chatted a bit, as one does, just to pass the time. I gathered he was originally from Holland but worked for your government now. Mostly he talked of the war in Europe. He seemed to take the affair as a personal affront. *Civilization's lowest point*, I believe he called it."

Sokobin inhales, remembering his conversation with Meyer at the party, how quick he'd been to dismiss the explorer's idealism, its embarrassing honesty. But that was before Ethan had volunteered with the French or the United States had joined the war.

The waiter returns with a small stack of pale biscuits. Drysdale lifts one, inspects it and returns it to the plate. "He was also quite upset about Ichang. The town was surrounded for months. He said he'd nearly lost his mind being cooped up. I take it he witnessed some terrible things in the fighting."

"Such as?"

"He didn't specify, but war is war, Vice-Consul. Have you ever been?" Drysdale asks, as if combat were some curious, little-known European capital.

Sokobin taps his ashes, willing himself to meet Drysdale's stare. "No."

"Well, count yourself lucky. I did a tour in Afghanistan myself when I was much younger. Too young." Drysdale sucks in his cheeks, holding the smoke and narrowing his eyes. "Let's just say there are things that stay with a man long after he leaves."

Sokobin feels Lin shift next to him, his pen pausing as he reaches for his tea. Perhaps the interpreter is thinking of his brother. Even if Lin manages to convince him to return home to China, the man who comes back may not be the same one who left.

"And how would you describe Mr. Meyer's mental state?"

"I only knew him a matter of hours, hardly enough to proffer an opinion."

"But if you were to?"

Drysdale exhales, tilting his head toward the ceiling. He runs a hand over his trouser crease. "A bit down, I'd say. If I'm honest, morose. Let's just say that with certain types, it's simply a matter of time before they go overboard, one way or another."

"I'm not sure I follow, Mr. Drysdale."

"The extreme sort, Mr. Sokobin. I'm sure you've met them. They keep pushing until they can't."

Sokobin inhales. He and Lin exchange a brief look. The interpreter blinks.

"Did Mr. Meyer tell you why he was headed for Shanghai?"

"We didn't discuss it. In general, I'm not one to pry." Drysdale crushes out his cigarette. "If that's all, I must finish packing now."

Sokobin looks at the plate of uneaten biscuits. He knows there's no point in asking the question, that it will get him nothing, and yet he can't stop himself. "One final thing. Did Mr. Meyer say anything to the effect of being Jewish?"

Drysdale tilts his head. "I don't understand."

"We're in the process of making final arrangements."

"Well, in that case, he didn't say anything. But I think I would have known, Mr. Sokobin."

"How so?"

"One can generally tell with Hebrews." Drysdale stands, buttoning his jacket. "Good afternoon."

———————

SOKOBIN AND LIN STAND OUTSIDE UNDER THE IMPERIal's striped awning. Lin asks for a couple of hours in order to find a laundry and post office. Sokobin can hardly refuse the request, and they agree to meet at 3 p.m. in Sokobin's room to take a closer look at the stack of Meyer's things he brought up from the basement. Perhaps by then they'll have heard back from Ting about an interview. Sokobin reaches for a cigarette, contemplating his next move. The interview with Drysdale has left him rattled; other than confirming the suspenders and the shoes, he's not sure what's been gained from the meeting aside from a sinking feeling.

The rain let up hours ago, and beyond the awning's shade, the sun is back in full force, drawing steam from the damp cobblestones. He looks across the rolling tide of pedestrians, motor cars, wagons, and rickshaws. Down the street, a cloud of dark smoke rises over the roofs of the buildings fronting the Quai de France. The Imperial stands two blocks north of French Town and a few east of the bund.

He reminds himself he's back in familiar territory as he taps his cigarette. A Shanghailander returned to the same kinetic avenues and alleys that used to thrill him. At one point, the city had been a great source of pride—proof of just how far he'd come from Newark's squalor. And yet now, Shanghai strikes him as something else, its flux excessive and manic. The endless run of hanging banners and shop windows that once felt like captured energy, now seem loud and desperate. After less than four months away, what Sokobin most feels from Shanghai is its exhausting racket. Even the city's air feels depleted, its every breath already inhaled and stripped of oxygen.

Across the street, an unescorted Western woman waits at the curb—an anomaly among the roving crowd of black pants and jackets. She wears a white hat and plain suit. Sokobin thinks he recognizes her. She lets a tram pass before stepping down onto the stones and making her way to his side. Yes, he's certain now, recalling the long, loping gait. She isn't in her nurse's uniform, but he remembers her—she'd been among the crew who'd snubbed him at the Fourth of July party. The tall, skinny-as-straw girl with the dull hair. Sharp mouthed, quick. She and Meredith were roommates. Sokobin attempts to dredge up her name. Anne. Mary. Beth. *Beth.*

She walks at a clipped pace despite the heat. At any moment, she'll turn the corner and disappear. He lowers the brim of his hat down against the glare and steps away from the awning. If he thinks about it too much, he'll talk himself out of following her. The meeting has to happen on the street, as if by chance. Once she reaches the mission, it will be too late. He'll never ring the bell, never ask to be let in.

She veers north, in the same direction as the mission hospital, not noticing him among the sea of men. He rounds the corner, catching sight of her white hat among the bobbing crowd. He weaves through the bodies, closing the gap until he is right behind her, matching his stride to hers. With a swing of his briefcase, he pushes forward, bumping her leg as he pretends to pass.

"Sorry about that," he says, turning just enough to show his face.

She looks up, their heads nearly level. Her dark eyes lock on his. "Sam? Sam from the consulate?"

"Yes."

"We've met before. I'm Meredith's friend. We work at the mission clinic together."

"Of course, I remember."

They stop, forming a small island on the pavement. She offers a hand, and he grasps her damp fingers. The grip is pronounced, certain.

"Miss Winters, correct?"

"Wenders, but please call me Beth."

Bodies stream around them, and they edge out of the crowd, stopping in the shade of a nearby building. Her skin is more yellow than fair, absent any hint of the powder or rouge that Meredith favored in public. The discordant features seem plucked from several women at once—the too-thick eyebrows, the soft chin, the upturned, puggish nose.

"I thought you'd been transferred," she says. "Or promoted to vice-consul or some such."

"Both. I'm in Nanking now."

"So why are you here?"

A frown passes over her face, and Sokobin suspects the question holds more distrust than curiosity. No doubt by now she's remembered that he's *persona non grata* and that she shouldn't be talking to him at all. He stops himself from reaching for a cigarette, knowing how it will look. Nervous, fidgety—exactly how he feels.

He feigns a smile. "Official business. I'm not at liberty to discuss specifics."

"I see."

Her eyes dart ahead, as if already formulating an excuse to move on. He needs to keep her, if only for a minute.

"And how are things at the hospital?"

"As busy as ever. She's still there, you know. That's what you're after, isn't it?"

There's no sense denying it, he supposes. "And Meredith?"

"Why not see for yourself?"

Sokobin shakes his head. "I wouldn't want to presume."

"She fell for you hard, you know. You led her to think there was a real future between you two. She was crushed."

He does know. He remembers Meredith's face, the terrible way the skin fell from her bones in the moment before her hand shot out to slap his face. His fingers dip into his pocket for a cigarette. He cracks his lighter, searching for the right phrase. "Certainly, that's all water under the bridge by now."

"You're a terrible liar," she tells him, her stare unwavering. "Even worse than before. I'm not sure if that's a good thing or bad." Her eyes search his. "You don't know, do you?"

"Know what?"

She shakes her head, refusing his question. It was a mistake following her like this, he thinks. He's remembered her quickness but not the power of her punch. She'd never liked him, even at the start. He never mentioned anything about it to Meredith, not wanting to stir up trouble between friends or seem difficult. After all, it was nothing he could put his finger on, more of an instinct.

"Know what?" he repeats, raising his voice.

She holds up her hand like a shield. Faces turn their way, eyes on him. He knows how it must appear—some jerk harassing a lone female. He takes a step back like a thief caught in the act.

"Look, I know there's no point in talking about it now with you," she tells him. "Still, I'd say she was owed a little more. A proper explanation. An apology."

"No doubt," he says, angry with himself for so easily conceding the point, for allowing himself to air his dirty laundry on a crowded street. But mostly for continuing to stand there. For caring so much. He's still thinking of her question. *You don't know, do you?*

She checks her wristwatch. "She'll be on her shift. I'm headed back there now. I'll tell her we ran into one another."

He dabs the sweat from his face. "I'm not sure hearing from me would be welcome at this point."

"I don't know entirely either. But I think so, given the circumstances. We've been roommates for years. Understand, I'm not saying any of this for your sake, to make you feel better. I couldn't care less about that. I'm saying it for Meredith, to give her some peace of mind."

He suddenly understands, clear as day, why Beth would suggest a meeting. She's banking on him failing again, a conversation ending in shambles, knowing she'll be the shoulder left to cry on.

She pats her throat with a handkerchief. "Look, it's hot and my shift starts soon, so you better say yes before I change my mind. We both know you won't come calling without a card. It's why you've followed me, right? Pretending to knock me with your briefcase?"

What she says is true. He won't come to the hospital, won't even send a message. No, the invitation has to come from Meredith herself. Now or never.

"She can reach me at the consulate. If she wishes to."

Beth turns without saying goodbye. Sokobin watches until her white hat is swallowed by the crowd. He exhales a thick stream of smoke into the humid air. Her words continue to sound in his head. *You don't know, do you?*

The things he doesn't know could fill an ocean.

SOKOBIN STANDS IN HIS ROOM, SMOKING AT THE OPEN window—not the one overlooking the bund but the other that views the settlement. From here he can just make out the edge of the mission clinic's tiled roof. By now, Meredith would be off her shift. He taps his cigarette against the sill, scattering the ash into the air. She owes him nothing, he reminds himself. It's entirely possible she dismissed the idea of meeting him out of hand. For all he knows, Beth never intended to deliver the message and simply played him for a fool—building him up, only to make the fall come that much harder.

A soft knock sounds on the door. Lin, he thinks, glancing at his watch. Quarter to three. He takes a last pull from the Chesterfield and crushes it into the tray on the desk, next to the stack of Meyer's papers. In truth, he's glad for the task; otherwise, he'd sit here inhaling endless cigarettes, waiting for a message that is unlikely to come.

The two of them settle in, Lin in the desk chair and Sokobin on the edge of the bed. They keep the windows open for air, attempting to ignore the sounds of traffic from the street as they divvy up the papers. Lin has changed from his tan suit into a sobering gray and navy pinstripe, the fabric slightly heavier and more suitable for fall. Like himself, Lin appears to be a man of few suits. Despite the English education and brother in Paris, Sokobin gleans Lin isn't from some coddled family but has humble roots. A fellow scholarship boy.

"A few of the letters are in Dutch," Lin says. "Perhaps from the family?"

"I don't suppose you happen to know it?"

Lin shakes his head, and Sokobin tells him to put them aside. Meanwhile Sokobin makes his way through Meyer's journal; unfortunately, the pages don't prove the intimate diary of an adventurer, only a dry daily log. The parsimonious entries, one or two lines at most, amount to little more than a list of dates, locations, and tasks. Sokobin guesses Meyer was required to keep a paper trail—justification for his salary at the taxpayer's expense. Most of the items involve searching for pear seeds. Sokobin knows from having read the dossier that finding them was Meyer's first priority for the expedition—certain Chinese pear varieties that had proven resistant to a blight currently decimating the American industry. As Sokobin reads through the pages, he can feel Meyer's incessant frustration and the tedium of waiting in the remote town of Kingman for the fruit to ripen, the subsequent negotiations with the pickers, and the additional weeks of waiting for seeding. Hardly the riveting stuff of newspaper exposés.

Lin holds out a letter, his head tilted. "A fit of nervous prostration?" he asks.

"It means a nervous breakdown. Meyer suffered one?"

Lin nods. "It seems so. Sometime last spring."

When the Americans joined the war, Sokobin thinks. He

reaches across the mattress and takes the letter from Lin. The sender is David Fairchild, Meyer's supervisor at the Office of Foreign Seed.

Should you feel the need to return to the States, I'll arrange for your passage and find you a position in one of the substations, but I doubt a man of your restless nature will be satisfied with the sedentary work of a plant breeder.

How different things might have turned out for Meyer had he only accepted Fairchild's offer. And yet as soon as he imagines it, Sokobin knows it could never have been. He can no more picture the explorer sitting day after day at a desk than he could a lion living as a house cat. No, Drysdale was right about Meyer being the extreme sort, the type who couldn't stop.

———————————

OVER THE COURSE OF THE NEXT TWO HOURS, THEY piece together a rough timeline of the year leading up to Meyer's disappearance, little of which appeared in the official dossier: the breakdown in Ichang, followed by a monthlong convalescence; the resignation of Meyer's longtime interpreter that summer; at last, locating adequate quantities of pears outside Kingman, only to learn the variety fruited much later than expected; the monotony of waiting week after week and the subsequent gathering of one ton of seed. Then, as winter approached, Meyer's fateful decision to return to Ichang so that he might trek the surrounding mountains. The letters show the explorer chomping at the bit and desperate to satiate his own curiosity, all the while stubbornly downplaying the growing threat of the fighting around Ichang until it was too late and the town was cut off by warring factions.

"Sir, you should read this," Lin says, handing over an oddly shaped bit of paper.

Sokobin takes it up and sees what it is—or was—an envelope once addressed to *Frank Meyer c/o the American Legation in Peking*, now slit open at the sides and turned inside out. The paper's surface is covered in the loose scrawl Sokobin has come to recognize as the explorer's handwriting. He looks at Lin in confusion.

"I think he was running out of paper, sir."

Sokobin nods; it takes a moment to decipher the penciled words.

Notes re: proposed resignation
Not feeling as well as I used to—lack of energy, difficulty
sleeping
Mentally, I grow tired and can't accomplish what I used to.
Age? Fatigue?
This never-ending war paralyzes me, and I can do nothing.
CORRESPONDENCE. ACCOUNTS.
Weighed down by oppressive quantities of baggage.
The incessant filth, poverty, disease. The refusal of this country
to change, to care for its people.
Trouble sending material, limited shipping due to submarine
attacks.
No garden of my own to see my work grow.
No assistant or prospect of one. Loneliness.

Sokobin puts down the envelope. Meyer was trying to convince himself to quit—knowing he needed to stop exploration, but knowing he never could. His restlessness would never allow it. The chronic push and pull. Sokobin has lived it all too well. He lights a cigarette, watching the smoke drift out the window. He can feel Meyer's desperation so keenly that he must keep reminding himself the man is dead.

Lin shifts in his chair opposite. He looks toward Sokobin and blinks. "Mr. Meyer was still employed by the American government at the time of his death, yes?"

"Yes."

"There's a copy of a resignation letter here."

"Let's see it." Sokobin quickly reads through the paragraphs. Across the top is the word DRAFT written in bold letters. "He must have changed his mind and never sent it."

Lin nods. "This is Mr. Meyer, yes?" he asks, pointing to the photograph Sokobin left propped against the wall—the one taken on Peking's snowy streets. "And the other man?"

"His assistant, I think. Not for this last expedition but the one before. Meyer wrote something on the other side."

Lin turns the photograph over, then carefully puts it back. For a moment neither says anything as Sokobin smokes his cigarette to the end.

As Lin gathers up the letters into a neat stack, someone calls Sokobin's name through the door. He lifts himself from the bed and turns the knob. A young clerk stands in the hall. "Two messages for you, sir," he says, handing over the slips. A black band circles the arm of his jacket, and for a moment, Sokobin thinks of Windham.

"Would you like me to wait, in case of reply?"

Sokobin tells him yes. The first message is from Meyer's boy. "Ting can meet us here tomorrow morning," he says, turning toward Lin. "Send an affirmative reply," he instructs the clerk before unfolding the second message.

Le Continental. Tonight, 8 p.m.
—M.

Sokobin closes his eyes, his shoes rooted to the carpet.

"Sir?"

"No reply," he says and slips the note into his pocket.

PART IV

CHAPTER 19

HE LINGERS NEAR THE BRASSERIE'S GLASS DOORS, casting his eyes over the room, making sure she hasn't somehow beaten him here. The hotel still hasn't converted to electricity, and the large gasolier overhead emits a wavering glow. He's ten minutes early and considers taking one of the empty stools along the bar, but knows she'll prefer one of the padded banquettes. So, he waits for the nearest aproned *serveur* to finish clearing a vacated table. He vaguely remembers the man from before, the stocky shoulders and thick mustache, the entrenched scowl that strikes Sokobin as definitively Gallic.

His task completed, the waiter looks at Sokobin and holds up two fingers. Sokobin nods and follows him toward a small banquette at the back. How the man can be so sure he's meeting someone else, Sokobin doesn't know. Perhaps the waiter recalls them from before, though it seems a stretch after such a long time. Meredith and he weren't regulars, preferring instead the narrow alleyway of restaurants along the Rue Corneille. More likely, Sokobin suspects, his nervous anticipation is written all over his face.

He sinks onto the bench facing the street, fairly certain he and Meredith once sat at this very table. The waiter returns, depositing a carafe of water, two smudged glasses, and a *carte*. Sokobin is unsure if he should order a drink or wait; in terrible French, he tells the waiter to come back.

Only a quarter of the brasserie's tables are occupied. A thin smattering of voices—French, Dutch, Russian—bounces across the tiled floor. Many foreigners in the city are effectively marooned, waiting out the war until they can return home. Or to what's left of it. After four years of conflict in Europe, and now the revolution in Russia, every bar in the concessions slightly reeks of exile and desperation. Shanghai has become a holding cell. Occasionally men run out of money or hope and off themselves. The papers don't write about it, of course. Compared to the tolls from the battlefield, a death here and there in some sordid rooming house hardly seems worthy of mention.

He checks his watch. Five after eight. He thinks about lighting a cigarette but doesn't want a cloud of smoke to be her first impression of him. He grasps the package of Chesterfields in his pocket, wishing he'd always smoked them so he wouldn't have to explain himself. The waiter returns, his voice impatient. Sokobin orders a Scotch whiskey at three times the price of what it was just two years ago.

His drink arrives too quickly. Sokobin takes a sip and knows it's been watered down. He paces himself, making a point to rest his palms on the cool marble tabletop between sips. There are no Chinese tray boys in sight; only two servers in black vests and long aprons. Both appear directly imported from Paris. It was one of the reasons he and Meredith came here from time to time, not for the food or the service, but for the anonymity. Anywhere in the English and American settlement and they were bound to run into people they knew; sometimes they did even in the small spots along the Rue Corneille. But the brasserie has never attracted many Anglophones. Meredith liked the look of the place and knew French well enough to manage for the both of them. Here, they could sit together unobserved.

They'd tried to be careful like that. The hospital was strict about men and dates. More than once, Meredith had been forced to arrange a story with one of the other nurses in order to avoid curfew. Sokobin didn't mind her having to fib; rather, the mild deception suited him just fine. He preferred to keep his affairs private, especially when he began to come in line for promotion. He'd heard the stories of men ruined early on in their careers. Just a whiff of scandal, deserved or not, and the rumors stuck. A man like that could expect to get passed over time and time again, wasting away his years in one burro and dung hovel after another until typhoid or dengue fever did him in.

He puts down his glass, needing to pace himself. He watches the front, the blur of Chinese men passing by the window. Dusk is giving way to night. His watch now reads quarter after. Perhaps she intends to stand him up. Perhaps this is the very reason she sent her message—to even the score. A part of him yearns for the punishment.

He decides he'll give her another five minutes, then down the rest of his drink and go. But by the next sip, he already knows it's a lie. He'll wait, drag out the whiskey to the last drop, then order another until there's no possible hope.

When he looks up, she's there, just inside the glass doors. She stands coatless, in a rose-colored sheath that rises halfway up her calves and a matching feathered toque, neither of which he remembers. She looks thinner, he thinks. At first, she doesn't see him, and it takes all his control to keep himself from standing too quickly and overturning his drink. He tells himself to hold steady, to draw the moment out. No matter what else happens this evening, he can leave with this: her face searching for his, still wanting to find him.

Her eyes stop at his table. He raises a hand and she moves toward him, the crisp pleats of her dress skirt shifting like armor. A lace placket, dyed a slightly deeper pink than the rest, trails down the front of the bodice. She stops several feet away, her ungloved hands clasped in front of her. There is no wedding ring.

"Samuel."

"Meredith."

He stands, and they kiss cheeks. Her perfume has changed—more spiced than floral. He would take her coat, but there is none, no chair to pull out. There are only their bodies, face-to-face, as they used to meet.

"Please," he says, gesturing.

He takes the hard wooden chair, leaving her the padded bench. For a moment neither says anything. Only the little marble table separates them. If he were to cross it, it would detonate like a minedfield. He wonders how it was possible they once managed to be so close and at ease. And yet there was a time when they would have sat even closer, sharing the bench thigh to thigh. He hasn't forgotten the charge of it, pricking and alive.

She sips from her water glass. He sees appraisal in her eyes—his face and figure, his clothes. How he fares in the assessment he can't say. He takes in the darkest points of her skin: the red lips, her pale eyes lined with kohl, the carved jade pendant hanging in the dip of her neckline. Yes, she is thinner, he thinks, her face more defined. The last two years have changed her. What remains is beautiful but sharper. The girlish roundness that once so charmed him has been whittled away, replaced by a saturation and depth that didn't exist before. Her work at the hospital, he guesses. The war. This country's slow unraveling. But also, him; most certainly him.

"Do you still take sherry?" he asks.

"Yes."

He signals for the waiter but when the man comes, she raises a finger and says she's changed her mind and asks, in French, for cognac. The server offers a nod of approval, and they exchange a few phrases. Sokobin orders another Scotch, a choice that earns him only a frown.

"Your French is much improved," he tells her once the man leaves.

"Yes. We have two nurses from Marseille on staff now. I'm also fairly certain the waiter recognizes me. We've come here a few times."

"We did as well, I think." *We.* The word sounds foreign from his mouth. The multitudes contained within just two letters.

"Yes, I remember. Though less crowded now, I'd say."

She surveys the room, and he loses himself in the exposed nape at the back of her hat. Her hair hasn't been pinned up as he first thought, but cut short. The dark ends curl around her earlobes, flaring out. He wants to touch them. Not so very long ago, he could have.

"You're staring," she says, turning back to face him.

"Your hair."

"Oh, that. It kept getting in the way every time I bent over a patient. Besides, it never stayed put in pins. You remember how it was always coming loose."

You remember. Proof she hasn't erased him from her memory.

"Short as a boy's now," she says. "You must find it shocking."

"No. It suits you. You look well."

"Thanks. Beth says I'm simply ahead of the fashion. She thinks once women get the vote, more of us will start cutting it off." She reaches for her water and leans back. The pink feather in her hat sways like seagrass. "I'm blathering, aren't I?"

"A little," he says, and they both laugh. "I don't mind," he tells her. He doesn't. The ordinary talk of the day. Not memoranda or politics or urgent cables, but the chatter of silly things. He misses it.

At last, the server returns to deposit their drinks. She circles her hands around the bell-shaped goblet, swirling the golden liquid inside. He raises his whiskey. "It's good to see you again."

He waits for her to say something. She doesn't, and they clink glasses. She takes a sip, leaving a faint red crescent on the rim. He can still see the true shape of her mouth under the rouge. "Beth told me about the ridiculous stunt with the briefcase." She smiles in a way that makes it difficult for him not to as well.

"Then I don't regret it," he admits. "It got you here."

"To be honest. I almost didn't show, but she told me it would be a good idea."

"Is that why you came tonight?" he asks, trying to keep his voice smooth. "Because Beth told you to?"

"In part."

She takes the smallest sip of her cognac. He's forgotten what a maddeningly slow drinker she can be. Meanwhile he's already halfway through his second round, and the Scotch is starting to flow through his blood. At another time he might welcome the slow undertow, but not tonight. He needs to stay afloat, sharp.

"To be honest," she says, "I'm not entirely sure why I came."

He curls his fingers around the table's edge. "To tell me what a rotten snake I was?"

"Tempting, I admit. I practiced a few scripts, none very kind. But now seeing you, somehow I don't feel them anymore."

"How so?"

"I've moved on, Sam."

He's unsure what to make of her words—if he's been forgiven or is simply no longer important enough to warrant her wrath. He doesn't ask, preferring not to know.

"So, vice-consul now."

"Yes."

"And how is Nanking?"

"Quiet, at least compared to Shanghai. I have my own office. The staff is very small, just three. But I can concentrate on work. Less temptation."

"Temptation. Yes, Shanghai is full of them."

He knows what she's implying: she herself was once one. He's still thinking about what she said, about moving on. He knows he should be relieved, and yet he's not. He thought that when he saw her, it would feel complete—that he would see her through a different lens and know it was finally over. But what he sees is exactly what he saw before. A beautiful, talented woman. A woman who could sit across a café table, and with just her stare, make him think he mattered.

"So, aside from overpriced, watered down drinks, what brings you back to Shanghai?" she asks.

He taps his glass, sets it down. "An American went missing from a steamer upriver about a week ago. An explorer named Frank Meyer."

"I think I've heard the name."

"Very likely. He made the papers from time to time. He collected plants for the Department of Agriculture. Nanking was the nearest office, so I got the file."

"He went overboard?"

"Yes." Sokobin pauses, unsure of how much to offer up. With another woman, he'd avoid going further, but at this point, he supposes there's very little Meredith hasn't seen from her patients at the clinic. "Unfortunately, he's dead. We found the body yesterday."

"Where?"

"In a small village upriver of Wuhu. A fisherman towed it to shore, and the local patrol officer had it buried in the town cemetery up the hill." Sokobin reaches for his whiskey glass, sees that it's nearly empty and puts it down. "There wasn't a coffin."

"I'm so sorry," she says, reaching across the table. Her hand touches his. "What happened?"

"We're still trying to determine that. My interpreter and I interviewed Meyer's cabinmate this morning and are supposed to meet with his hired boy tomorrow. To be honest, the case doesn't make a lot of sense." Meanwhile his fist sits on the marble, immobile under her fingers like a frightened animal playing dead. "I probably shouldn't even be talking about it."

"Of course."

She withdraws her hand, and he downs the last of his whiskey. He doesn't want to think about the Meyer file, not now. He wants to draw a circle around himself and Meredith and keep everything else outside.

"So, what do you feel?" he asks.

"What do you mean?"

"This. Us. You said you don't feel what you thought you would."

"The jury's still out. But you needn't worry. I won't be slapping your face again, however deserved."

She purses her red lips coyly. He remembers the smirk. Usually, he had to wait a couple of drinks before it surfaced. He'd relished it, thinking it only for him. But the smile doesn't belong to him anymore, and he senses it's become a thin cover for something pricklier beneath.

The waiter arrives to refill the water carafe and Sokobin holds out his empty cup. At this point, the tab will cost him a day's wages. He doesn't care. He asks Meredith if she wants another, knowing she'll decline, which she does.

"How is work at the clinic?"

"Busy. Hard to believe it will all be over soon."

"How so?"

She tilts her head. "I'm going back, you know."

"Back?"

"Yes, to the States. I've accepted a position in one of the army hospitals outside Washington, DC." She attempts a smile. "I'm sorry. I assumed Beth had told you."

He reaches for his glass, only to remember the waiter has

taken it. "For good?" he asks, as if he hasn't already guessed. *You don't know, do you?*

"Yes. I'm tired of reading about the war in the papers. I need to act, to do something. Even if it all ends tomorrow, thousands of men will be coming home. They'll be damaged and need care. I've learned enough now that I can be of help."

But Sokobin is only half listening. Something inside him is dropping like a stone kicked off a cliff. Even if he hadn't reached out these past years, he'd taken some comfort in knowing that Meredith was here in Shanghai, that he could still find her. But that's all over now. Soon she'll be gone and whatever they shared, whatever did or didn't happen, will vanish with her.

At last the waiter appears with his drink. Sokobin swirls it, then takes a long swallow. "But you can't sail now," he says as soon as the man has turned his back. "Not with the Germans sinking everything in sight." He can hear how he sounds—pathetic, pleading.

"It wasn't easy to find a berth. I'll have to take my chances. Our soldiers do it every day."

"And there's nothing I can say to change your mind?"

She looks into her glass. "Not anymore."

He sips, then sips again. He's still waiting for whatever is falling inside to crash. "When do you go?"

"Ten days."

It's why she agreed to come tonight, he thinks. Not to give him a dressing down or even to demand some long-awaited explanation, only to say goodbye. Tying up a loose end, checking him off her list.

"You know I never meant to stay so long in Shanghai. It's been five years, Sam. I don't want to become like this," she says, gesturing toward the nearly empty room. "Or your Meyer."

"Meaning?"

"One of the ones who never find their way back."

Like himself, he thinks. She won't say it, but he knows it's what she means. After seven years in-country, he's become a man between nations, out of bounds. American yes, but something else. He can hardly imagine returning home—wherever that is. Newark. Washington, DC. Manhattan. Main Street, USA. Regular life, whatever that constitutes, no longer appeals. He sips, letting the whiskey's heat idle on his tongue. For a time, she'd tethered him to Shanghai, made him feel like he belonged here. To need someone like that frightened him.

The silence stretches between them. He reaches for the Chesterfields, puts them on the table. "Do you mind?"

"When did you start that up?"

"I don't know exactly," he lies.

"Go ahead, but know they might as well be poison."

He cracks his lighter, drawing down the burning air. The smoke mixes with the Scotch, seeping into his bones and pulling him under.

"I don't care what anyone says about how good they are for the lungs," she says. "I've seen enough insides to know. It's like breathing coal smoke."

Sokobin releases a stream toward the ceiling. "Reminds me of my childhood." He wants her to laugh, to slap his arm, to do anything, but she doesn't.

"You used to say you hated the smell."

"I changed my mind."

She shakes her head and takes a long swallow. She's sipping more steadily now and nearly done with her drink. "The truth is it will be hard to leave. I try not to think about it too much." She closes her eyes, and for a moment he thinks she may cry. "You grow closer to people here. It's like everyone has to count for a little more."

He'd like to think she's including him on that list. Once, he surely would have been. He inhales, holding the smoke, weighing his words. A braver man might tell her the truth. He'd made a mistake. But he's not brave. He stares at the remains of his sweating glass, unable to look at her face. "Those afternoons in my rooms," he says. "We were reckless."

"Yes." Her fingers tap the table. Even with the nails clipped to the quick, they are beautiful hands; long and elegant. "I assumed you thought less of me for it."

"Never. It's how things ended that I regret."

"They didn't end, Samuel. You ended them."

She finishes her drink and lays the glass gently on the table. Her hands reach across the tablecloth again to cover his. Faint lines fan from the edges of her eyes; he knows the furrows on his own face run much deeper.

"I'd like to be with you like that again, once before I go," she says. "Nothing to hold us, no obligations. Isn't that what you've always wanted?"

He leans back, certain he's misheard, but her hand stays clasped over his, anchoring him to the table. "I don't want you thinking I came here expecting that," he says.

"Not expecting, only wishing."

"I came in friendship." Another lie.

The coy smile is back. "Come now, Samuel, we've never been friends."

———

LATER, HE WILL REMEMBER THIS: THE CLICK OF THE door, the silence of the thin coverlet, the hot, still air. It is a hotel room like any other: an iron bed frame, mirrored wardrobe, and a writing desk with an enamel pitcher and basin. She sits on the edge of the bed in the half-light, her back to him, unpinning her hat. They do not bother with the lanterns.

He stands at the window, his hand on the curtains. "Open or closed?"

"Open."

He tugs at the drapes and lifts the sash. The street is in the French style, lined with plane trees, the canopy thick with summer growth. A steady stream of men passes below the leaves. The cobblestones are awash in sound: clattering rickshaws and roaring motorcar engines, the din of the wandering crowd. It is how he thinks of the city—always in flux, always en route, never arrived. A tram approaches, its beam like a searchlight.

Beneath the curtains is a set of sheers. He pulls the voile across the window and watches as she unbuttons her dress and hangs it on the bedpost. She rolls down her stockings and unbuckles her shoes. She leans back on the bed, the fringes of her cropped hair fanned on the pillowcase. The light from the street makes her silk slip glow.

He drops his clothes. His heart flaps against his ribs like a trapped bird as he moves toward her, sitting at the end of the bed. Shadows pool beneath her eyes, her neck, and along the ridges of her collarbone. He lowers the straps of her slip. He moves slowly, tracing the edges of her face, her neck, and her shoulder, knowing it is the last time he will ever touch her this way. He wants to ration her skin. He runs his tongue over the swells of her breasts, ribs like rippled shoals, trying to convert each moment to memory. He wants to remember everything. Her body is like a beloved country he stands on the shore of, never to see again. He needs to be able to return to this moment in his mind once she is gone.

She lies back, and he parts her legs, running his tongue down her chest and stomach, further below. He can hear her breathing. Her hand reaches out and finds his. Work has made her fingers strong, her grip fierce.

AFTERWARD, SHE ASKS IF HE WANTS HER TO GO.

"No," he says. "Stay a while."

He crosses the room, feels for the Chesterfields in his jacket pocket. On the opposite side of the street, two Chinese men are waving their arms and shouting at one another; a crowd has begun to form.

"What is it?" she asks.

"I don't know. Some kind of argument."

She joins him at the window. They stand side by side, their nakedness muted by the sheers as they watch with laced fingers. A *gendarme* appears and stands between the two men. A few more insults and the men go their separate way. With no blood or arrest, the crowd soon disperses. The entire episode is over in less than two minutes. He could have stood with her like that for years.

She sits on the bed, her back to the iron frame. He pours her a glass of water from the pitcher on the desk and brings it to the mattress. There's an ashtray on the night table, and he sits on the edge of the bed, snapping the flint. He can still feel the sticky friction of her skin on his. This desire to have her near him. He can't kick it.

She puts down the water and holds out a shadowy hand toward his cigarette. "Give me a try."

"I wouldn't want to be responsible for your corruption."

"A little late for that."

The cigarette tip glows as she inhales. Her lips look swollen and the kohl around her eyes smeared. The hair at her temples is streaked with sweat. All the people in the street below, he thinks, none will ever see this, know this moment.

"Not as smooth as Turkish," she says, handing it back. He expects her to cough. She doesn't. "What's the brand?"

"Chesterfield."

"Ah, soldier cigarettes." She reaches again. "Let's have another then."

"I thought you didn't smoke."

"I don't. Just like you."

They pass the cigarette back and forth. The tip grows damp from her mouth, and he has to remind himself that she's destined to leave, no longer his to keep.

"So, why Chesterfields?"

"My brother smokes them."

"I remember. The bush pilot."

"Yes. He's in France now."

She groans softly. "The war, you mean."

"Yes. Ninety-fourth Aero Squadron. Before that he volunteered with the French, the escadrilles."

She inhales, watching him. "Impressive. And terrifying."

"Yes."

"It must take a certain kind of mindset. Have you ever been in an airplane?"

"No."

"I haven't either. Honestly, I can't imagine it. Let alone the rest."

He taps the ash into the tray on the table. He knows he could tell her about the major's letter, and she would put her arms around him, but then the moment would change and become about that, about Ethan, and himself reduced to the anguished brother. Sokobin doesn't want her sympathy or pity. Only her. Whatever scarce minutes remain, he wants them all to himself.

"Wasn't he supposed to come out and visit you here?" she asks.

"We tossed around the idea. Nothing ever came of it."

He exhales, aiming the smoke away. He'd been so caught up with work, he hadn't pressed, thinking they'd have more time later. A part of him wanted to wait until he'd secured the promotion. It was how he wanted Ethan to see him—as a VC. A man of rank. He sent word of the news in a letter at the start of February. He doesn't know if it reached France in time or not. Looking back, the vanity disgusts him.

"After the war then," she says.

He nods, grateful to be in the shadows. They each take a final drag before he extinguishes the stub in the ash tray.

"Another?"

"No." She reaches for the water glass, drinks the rest. She sits up, and a thin stream of light from the window catches her face. "There's something I need to tell you. I'm engaged to be married."

He stays there, his feet rooted to the rug, uncomprehending. For a moment he thinks she means to hurt him. But that would make her petty and she's never been that. He searches her face just to make sure she's not making some brutal joke. He can see she isn't. *You don't know, do you?* At last, he understands the full meaning of the statement.

"You're not wearing a ring."

"No. It's not practical for work."

"But you're not working tonight. And it's not on your hand."

"No. Would it have made a difference?"

He reaches for the cigarettes on the table and cracks the lighter. "No," he admits, turning away. He can't look at her. "Where is he now? Is he an officer?"

"No, he's like you, just beyond the draft. But we agree about needing to help in our own way."

"A doctor?"

"Yes. He came to do a stint at the clinic."

"When?" He hates the sound of his voice, aggressive and disbelieving, as if she were a suspect under questioning.

"About six months ago. He's based in DC. It's why I'm headed there. He's a good man, Samuel, a good doctor. Reliable and giving. Kind."

Sokobin inhales, letting the words sink in, knowing they represent everything she thinks him not to be. He reminds himself her engagement changes nothing; she's leaving anyway. But it does matter. If he'd only asked, she might have followed him upriver to Nanking. But he didn't and now he'll never know. He can hear her crying and turns back, handing her the cigarette. She takes a few puffs, then waves it away. She covers her eyes, and he crushes it in the tray.

"I need to go," she says.

He reaches for her shoulder. "No, stay a little longer."

"I can't. It's almost curfew." She wipes her face and swings her legs to the other side of the mattress, keeping her back to him. "I'm sure you remember that."

"What does it matter now? You're leaving. Just stay a minute."

"Stop. You're only making it worse."

Pressing her hands to the mattress, she pushes up and gathers her clothes from the bedpost. She quickly buttons her dress, not bothering with her stockings but stuffing them into her handbag. He stays on the edge of the bed as she crosses the room. He hears the scrape of the desk chair along the floor, the metal of her shoe buckles.

"Goodbye, Samuel." She stands by the window, her body silhouetted by the streetlamps. She is fully dressed, her hat resettled. "Say it," she tells him.

"I don't want to."

"Say it."

"Goodbye, Meredith."

The door opens, and the hallway light spills in. Her form momentarily fills the threshold and then she is gone.

CHAPTER 20

Tuesday, June 10

SOKOBIN ARRIVES TO BREAKFAST THIRTY MINUTES late, his head clouded and in dire need of coffee. He threads his way through the tables, trying to make his way to Lin, seated alone in the far corner, where he is sipping tea and reading the paper.

A pack of secretaries calls out as Sokobin passes, forcing him to stop and field questions about life upriver. There was a time when he would have welcomed the attention, but not this morning. The night with Meredith has left him feeling raw and exposed. It had been after midnight before he returned to his room, only to lie with his eyes open, missing the feel of her skin and making knots of the sheets. He had awakened with a jolt, his chest damp with sweat, and the sun already brightly shining through the window. The mirror only confirmed how much worse he looked for wear. Shadowy and wrung out. Slightly deranged—nothing at all like *the right sort.*

Meanwhile a few of the women niggle for information, claiming to have met Meyer. He understands it's the real reason they've stopped him—for gossip—and does his best to evade their questions. Besides, there's little definitive he can tell them aside from the fact the explorer has drowned.

At last he breaks free of the questions and reaches Lin's table, pulling out a chair and putting his back to the room. "Apologies, I suppose you've already eaten," he says, avoiding eye contact. The memory of last night remains so strong he thinks it must be written all over his face.

The Chinese server arrives with coffee. Sokobin orders eggs, hash, and buttered toast—the same combination that used to resuscitate him from the dead after a long night with Welch. His muscles feel gritty and sore, as if he's coming down with the cold. Too many cigarettes, he knows. And the third whiskey. He drains his cup of coffee and signals for more. He needs to get his head straight before meeting with Ting.

In contrast, Lin's tan suit appears pressed, his collars and cuffs starched. Clearly he's been to a laundry. "Your brother's aero squadron, sir," he says, sliding the newspaper toward Sokobin. "You said the Ninety-fourth, yes?"

"Yes." Sokobin looks down at the headline: *America's First Flying Ace*. The photograph shows the beaming young pilot, Douglas Campbell, posing next to his plane. The Nieuport 28 fighter looks the same as Ethan's, down to the painted Uncle Sam's hat on the side. Campbell wears his army uniform and tall boots; he is trim and good-looking in a swarthy way, like a swashbuckling actor from the pictures. Sokobin tries to hand the paper back.

Lin waves his hand. "No, sir. Keep it, please."

The server arrives carrying a plate piled with food. Grateful for the excuse, Sokobin pushes the paper to the side, turning it over so the photo faces the table. He quickly downs several forkfuls of steaming eggs, blanketing his insides with the warm, salty food. He eyes the crisped potatoes, then reaches for the ketchup bottle, knowing he can't get it upriver. The server returns to refill Lin's teacup, and Sokobin starts in on another cup of coffee. The only good thing about feeling hungover is that he isn't yet craving a cigarette.

Lin tilts the creamer, releasing a thin stream into his tea.

"You take milk," Sokobin says between bites.

"Yes, sir. When I can get it."

"Very English of you."

"I developed the taste for it there. At university."

Sokobin chews, certain he should know this already. No doubt the fact is salient on Lin's résumé. It would certainly explain the accent. "Remind me, Oxford?"

"Cambridge, sir. I was there two years."

"I've never been personally, but I have a hard time imagining you bundled in a heavy coat and scarf, Mr. Lin. Eating mutton pies, drinking pints, and tramping through the snow."

Lin lowers his spoon and blinks. "Yes, England is a cold place, Vice-Consul." His smile is short and strained. "In many ways."

Sokobin waits for Lin to say more, but nothing is forthcoming, and once again, he's struck by the disparity between the man and his chosen profession. The interpreter makes his living relaying information from others and yet so rarely offers it about himself. Reserve surrounds him like a moat.

"And your degree?" Sokobin asks.

"From Nanking, sir. I completed my studies there. At home."

The little Presbyterian college, Sokobin thinks, remembering all the lecture invitations he's declined. He can feel the coffee kickstarting his brain. "About Ting," he says. "It's important we get everything we can out of him. He's our last chance to learn about Meyer's final hours. He may have seen or heard something Drysdale didn't."

"Understood, sir."

"If you sense I'm not asking the right questions, or going about things the wrong way, say something. You won't offend me. Do you know if he knows Meyer is dead?"

"I can't say, sir."

"You didn't mention anything about finding the body in the message?"

"No, sir."

"Good. We'll see his natural reaction then."

Although Sokobin has no reason to suspect Ting of wrongdoing, he's had to consider that if anyone were to have fought with Meyer, at least enough to want to push the explorer over the rails, the likely choice would be Ting—some sort of argument over money, perhaps, or the terms of their contract. A slight or insult that cut too deep. Men have been killed for less, and despite the fact that the bar steward reported the explorer was alone when he crossed the saloon, as Meyer's boy, Ting would have been allowed up on the deck. He could have crossed paths with Meyer outside, arriving at the back rails a different way without anyone in the saloon taking notice.

"Vice-Consul," a voice calls from behind.

Sokobin turns in his seat, his mouth full of hash, to find the clerk who delivered the messages to his room yesterday standing nearby. The man has changed his jacket since; the black armband, however, remains.

"Sorry to interrupt, sir, but the Consul asks that you come to his office."

Sokobin wipes his face with his napkin. "Now?"

"Yes, sir."

Sokobin exhales; half his plate has gone untouched. He takes another slug of coffee and pushes back his chair. "Don't wait on me," he tells Lin. "There's a small conference room on the ground floor. Meet me there at nine forty-five."

He follows the clerk up the stairs to the Consul's office. The clerk raps twice, waits and then raps twice more—the same code Sokobin was taught. The man must be the Consul's new gopher.

The CG peers over his reading glasses as they enter. His secretary, Miss Greene, stands at his side, pointing to an open file on his desk. Both are sheathed by the pale morning light filtering in from the side window. The Consul scribbles his signature, and she closes the dossier, taking it up and reminding him of several tasks—letters to Peking that must be drafted before lunch and his afternoon meeting with the textile exporters. Though no one would ever dare say it aloud, it's understood the Consul wouldn't last three days without her.

"Vice-Consul," she says coolly as she passes him on her way out. The clerk also exits, closing the door behind him, and suddenly Sokobin finds himself alone with the Consul. Yesterday's seersucker suit is gone, replaced by crisp white linen and a chartreuse striped bowtie.

"The Meyer file," the CG says. "Where do we stand on it?"

"We still have one more interview to conduct," Sokobin says. "Mr. Meyer's boy. We've arranged to meet him here this morning."

"Glad to hear it. A cable came in overnight from Mr. Meyer's supervisor at the Office of Foreign Seed. He's asked for a full report, with a timeline of your movements."

"David Fairchild," Sokobin says, remembering the name from the explorer's papers. "I figured as much, sir. I've kept notes. If one of the secretaries can type it up, I can submit it before I return to Nanking."

"Miss Greene will see to it." The CG exhales, pointing toward the chair. "Sit a moment. It seems there's been a small mix-up about Meyer."

Sokobin lowers himself into the seat. "Mix-up, sir?"

"Yes. It appears Meyer *wasn't* Jewish after all. Protestant, though not particularly observant, but definitely not Jewish. Mr. Fairchild was quite firm on the point."

Sokobin's chest cinches, thinking of his father's tallit and yarmulke. "And why did we assume he was?" he asks, attempting to steady his voice.

"Jewish? A general impression among some of the staff here."

"I'm not sure I follow, sir."

"Well, the name of course, and probably something to do with his being foreign. From all accounts he was a rather brooding sort. Innocent mistake."

Sokobin looks past the CG's shoulders toward the wavering blur of water contained within the window sheers. For years he's understood his professional survival hinges on the smallest of moments—the pause needed to take a breath and swallow the rage.

"I brought Mr. Meyer's body here to Shanghai, sir, believing him to be Jewish. Your note."

The CG's eyes narrow. "I'm aware of what I wrote, Vice-Consul." He shifts in his chair, smoothing down his trousers. "Best not to make a thing of it."

Not to make a thing of it. Sokobin thinks of the plain coffin, the white pants, the sewn pockets. His father's tallit and yarmulke. The prayer said for Meyer's soul. A Jewish soul. At the time, Sokobin was certain the words had been heard by God himself. He still wants to believe they were, that his best efforts to see the body properly cared for have mattered, that they've counted for something. That his good deeds—*mitzvot*—haven't gone unnoticed.

"And the body, sir? What happens to it now?"

"It stays here. Mr. Fairchild has already cabled the family in Holland, and they have no intention to press for its return. Apparently, Meyer left specific instructions with his superiors that no fuss was to be made in the event of his death in the field. 'Bury me wherever I fall' or something to the effect. Look, you were right to bring Mr. Meyer's remains to Shanghai. No doubt about that. He was a distinguished employee of this government. Despite whatever he said, his remains should be properly marked, not left half buried on some forgotten hill."

"And the funeral?"

"Nine o'clock tomorrow morning. Miss Greene is making the arrangements with Bubbling Wells now."

The Protestant cemetery, Sokobin thinks.

"It's all a bit rushed, but given how long it's been, better not to wait. We're expecting a small gathering—myself and a few of the staff, perhaps some university types he knew here in the city. You needn't bother yourself, if you're not feeling up to it."

"I'd like to attend, sir. I'm fairly certain Mr. Lin would as well."

"Entirely your choice, Vice-Consul. I wasn't aware that you and Mr. Meyer were particularly close."

"We weren't," Sokobin says, although he isn't sure that's true anymore. He's gone through the man's things, read his letters. And the body itself. He couldn't forget it if he tried. It's not a connection Sokobin would have ever wanted, but it's there all the same. Undeniable. "And what about Mr. Meyer's boy? Should I invite him as well?"

"I'll leave that to you. But do use judgment. We're hoping for a quiet affair. Funerals are trying enough even without all the typical dramatics." The CG taps at his blotter as if counting the seconds. "I'll need the 192 as well as your report before you go. Just so there's no confusion, we are talking about an accident, yes?"

Sokobin holds the Consul's gaze. The prudent thing would be to simply say yes and be through with the matter once and for all. But Sokobin can't; he isn't done with Meyer. Not understanding isn't an option.

"About that, sir. I've had a chance to look through Mr. Meyer's things. His letters and journal entries."

"And?"

"And it seems he may have been suffering from depression for quite some time. One of Fairchild's letters referenced a nervous breakdown last year. I also found a draft of a resignation," Sokobin nearly said *we*, thinking of Lin, but knows the CG wouldn't like the interpreter going through Meyer's papers. "It would seem Mr. Meyer no longer wished to continue with exploration."

The Consul holds up a hand. "I'd keep these items to yourself,

Vice-Consul. For Mr. Meyer's sake and those of his colleagues. No sense exposing any ill feelings or personal issues. At his death Mr. Meyer was a federal employee in good standing. But I fail to see the relevance of any of this for the 192."

"It speaks to his state of mind, sir. Mr. Meyer was deeply opposed to the war and makes mention of it in his letters. His cabinmate aboard the steamer said that Meyer and he discussed the war, and that Meyer seemed quite down about it."

"Plenty of people oppose the war. No sane man would want it."

"I understand, sir. It's just I'm not sure Mr. Meyer..."

The Consul's lips funnel to a point as he leans forward, one finger pointed at Sokobin. "I know exactly what you're implying, and I'd strongly urge you to reconsider before making such an accusation. What's your proof?"

Sokobin blinks, his face hot. "Just a very strong feeling."

"A Form 192 isn't about *feelings*, Vice-Consul, only facts. Can you say for certain?"

"No, sir."

"Then don't. Consider the ramifications. We're talking about a man's reputation, not to mention that of his family and this government." The CG leans back, folding his hands over his lap. "Look, you've done your task admirably, and it will be so noted in your file. But now it's time for you and your interpreter to return to Nanking. There's an express tomorrow afternoon. Do I make myself clear?"

Sokobin understands. He's being sent back upriver. The Consul's patience for the Meyer affair has run out. "Yes, sir," he says, taking up his briefcase.

"And Sokobin," the CG says, running his finger under his jaw. "Consider getting yourself a professional shave and trim before tomorrow. Remember, the man in the field can't afford to let himself go slack on the details."

Sokobin is no sooner out the door than he withdraws a Chesterfield and his lighter.

"I wouldn't smoke that here, if I were you," Miss Greene says. "He won't tolerate the smell anywhere near his office." Her station is composed of two desks shaped like an L with a type-writer facing the corridor. Meanwhile a steady stream of clerks and secretaries moves past them. "Everything all right, Mr. Sokobin? You appear a bit peaked."

"Fine, thank you," he says. He's repeated the words so many times over the last months that they mean nothing anymore. The truth is he's not all right. He's still thinking of his father's things, given away for nothing and about to be buried in a Protestant cemetery. "Just a bit drained from all the back and forth."

"If you wouldn't mind then, a small housekeeping matter," she says as she feeds a sheet of paper into her typewriter. "It's about your old mail slot. I'm afraid they never took your name off. The old clerk enlisted, and unfortunately his replacement isn't particularly thoughtful. I've asked him to remove your name, seeing as you're no longer in this office. But in the meantime, it's gotten chock-full."

He looks at her, his mind too crammed to take in what she's asking. He takes out his watch. He was due to meet Lin in the conference room three minutes ago.

"Sorry, come again?" he says.

"I'm saying you might want to look before it all gets tossed." She snaps down the metal guard on her machine, and the register slides into place with a heavy *thunk*. "If not now, perhaps after your interview with Mr. Ting?"

Sokobin looks at her quizzically, unsure how she could possibly know this.

"Oh, I'm aware of everything that happens here, Vice-Consul."

Her words barely register as Sokobin steps down the corridor.

Lin and Ting are waiting. A last chance. As much as Sokobin has tried to treat Meyer as just another Form 192, he can't. It doesn't matter what the CG has said, warned even, Sokobin won't be able to rest until he has the answers to this mystery.

CHAPTER 21

THE WIDE-BRIMMED FELT HAT RESTING BESIDE HIM ON the table is Western; otherwise, Ting wears the usual black cloth pants and slippers. An oiled queue hangs down the back of a plain gray clasp jacket that does little to hide the thin frame beneath. It's clear the last months have taken their toll. Ting's face is deeply brown and dry from the sun. Sokobin would have guessed him to be at least thirty, but his identity card puts him at just twenty-three.

Sokobin pours cool water from the pitcher and slides it across the table. He waits for Ting to drink, then put down his glass. "I am sorry to inform you that we have found Mr. Meyer's body."

Ting's dark eyes hold Sokobin's, as if waiting for him to say more. When nothing comes, Ting reaches into his jacket and withdraws a package of cheap Chinese cigarettes and a small box of matches. His cheeks go hollow as he inhales. Seeing him in person, Sokobin thinks it highly unlikely Ting could have overpowered Meyer even if he'd wanted to. Ting is a good four or five inches shorter and far thinner about the arms and shoulders.

"Mr. Meyer does not like cigarettes," he says flatly. "He tells me I burn my insides."

"You understand Mr. Meyer is dead, drowned in the river."

"Ai-yah," Ting says. He stares at the table.

Sokobin hears the soft scratch of Lin's pen. Both he and Lin have open notebooks in front of them. If the circumstances were different, Sokobin would ask one of the secretaries to transcribe the interview, but in this case, his gut tells him not to. It's been his experience that the Chinese can be particularly hesitant to speak of difficult details; Sokobin suspects throwing an American female into the mix would only make it more so. Ting's English, though heavily accented, seems competent enough. However, when Ting talks again, it's in Chinese. Lin pauses his pencil. The switch doesn't entirely surprise Sokobin. Even those with strong English can lapse when upset.

"He asks where we found the body," Lin translates.

"Better, I think, if you explain," Sokobin tells him. "The short version."

Ting smokes, his face blank, as Lin speaks. Sokobin's first impression is that the young man looks detached and unemotional. No doubt he is in shock, unable to process that his employer is actually gone. It's how Sokobin has been thinking about their relationship until this moment, but now he isn't sure the term feels adequate to describe the connection that would have existed between the two. Given the intense nature of Meyer's work, Ting would have been much closer to the explorer than the typical servant—more like the assistant Meyer once had. A companion.

"Did you know Mr. Meyer was dead?" Sokobin asks once Lin has finished.

Ting shakes his head. "No. But it is the only thing possible," he says in English. "We look everywhere on the boat. He is gone."

"How long did you work for Mr. Meyer?"

"About six months. Maybe more."

"And what did you do for him? What kind of tasks?"

"Everything. I carry things and go to the market and help him when he is sick. And sometimes like you," he says, gesturing toward Lin with his cigarette.

"An interpreter."

"Yes, interpreter. Guide. Everything. What Mr. Meyer needs, I do. I am his number one boy. Only boy."

"Did Mr. Meyer have another interpreter before you?"

"Yes. He has another man long time. Mr. Meyer says he is no good. He gambles and drinks and refuses to walk. This man does not like it here in the south or care about plants. So, he quits and goes back to his family in Peking." Ting taps his ashes. A smile briefly crosses his face. "Mr. Meyer has a funny name for this man. He calls him Little Darling."

Sokobin waits for Lin to catch up before reaching for the burlap bag and placing the suspenders and shoes on the table. "Do you recognize these?"

Ting leans forward, one hand out, then stops. He murmurs in Chinese.

"He says these are Mr. Meyer's things."

"How can he be sure?"

Ting and Lin quickly exchange phrases. "He was with Mr. Meyer when he bought them in Hankow. It was the morning they boarded the steamer. They spent the night before in a hotel. He says they stopped in the city to rest and buy food and clothes before boarding the steamer for Shanghai. Meyer needed the suspenders. They both lost weight when they were in Ichang. The boats had stopped running supplies because of attacks, and the town was surrounded with soldiers and fighting, so they couldn't get much food."

"Why the shoes?"

"Meyer's boots were worn out from the walk and needed new soles. He said he wanted light shoes for the steamer. City shoes."

Ting stubs out his cigarette in the tray. He remains turned in his chair, his eyes averted from the waterlogged items. Sokobin returns them to the burlap sack and places it on the floor out of sight. He turns to a fresh page.

"How long were they trapped in Ichang?"

Ting's shoulders slump at the question. He closes his eyes.

"Five or six months," Lin translates.

"How was Meyer during that time? In terms of his mood, his health?"

"He says not good."

"How so?" Sokobin asks although he already knows the answer. He remembers Meyer telling him about being unable to sit still in school. *The dark clouds.*

"He says if Mr. Meyer doesn't walk, he gets depressed. Also, they saw bad things in Ichang during the fighting there."

Sokobin pauses his pen. "Bad things?"

Ting taps out another cigarette from the package on the table. He lifts his head as he exhales, revealing a tight bundle of tendons along his neck.

"He says he does not want to talk of it. He still has nightmares."

Lin gives him a look, and Sokobin understands not to press. "How were they able to escape?"

"He says there was a break in the fighting, and Meyer decided they had to leave, take their chances. They left most of the equipment and specimens behind in Ichang. It was only the two of them, no porters to carry the rest. They walked inland, away from the bandits along the river. They had left bags of pear seeds and Meyer's trunk in another town, Kingmen, back before they came to Ichang. So they went there, retrieved their things."

"Mr. Meyer had a pistol, yes?"

Ting nods.

"He says Mr. Meyer kept his gun out. He worried constantly about running into soldiers. Mr. Meyer told Mr. Ting they would kill them both."

"How did they get to Hankow?"

"They walked for four days to Kingmen, then two days more

to the river," Lin translates. "By then they were far enough from the fighting that there were boats running south. They took a small one to Hankow and got off to rest and wait for the steamer to Shanghai."

Sokobin realizes he's stopped writing, and jots down a few notes. "Did Mr. Meyer have any enemies on the boat to Shanghai?"

Ting shakes his head.

"Did he argue with any of the other passengers?"

"No," Ting says in English. "He is sick and stays in his room. I pour him some tea."

"How was Mr. Meyer sick?"

Ting points to his stomach with his cigarette. "The walk from Ichang is hard. Not a lot of food." He pauses, then slips into Chinese.

"He says most villages they came to had been looted and burned."

"We know that Mr. Meyer suffered periodically from malaria," Sokobin pauses to let Lin translate the disease. "Malaria can cause hallucinations. Was Mr. Meyer sick like this, with a fever?"

Ting shakes his head again. "Maybe a little fever but not bad. It is his belly."

"And you stayed below on the boat, in Chinese second class? Did you see Mr. Meyer the day he disappeared?"

Ting nods.

"When?"

"All day. Three, maybe four times. He eats some soup at night in his room. He does not go out."

Sokobin pauses. So far Ting's account squares completely with Drysdale's.

"Mr. Meyer was last seen walking toward the back railings. Do you think it's possible that he leaned over the railing to be sick and fell into the water?"

Ting takes a long pull from his cigarette. A sound escapes him, sharp, not quite a laugh. "Mr. Meyer does not fall from a boat like this. He is very strong and walks very far, more far than any man I know. He walks over snow and high mountains in the north." He shakes his head, takes a drag, and crushes the butt in the tray. "No, Mr. Meyer does not fall from the boat."

Lin looks up from his notebook. From behind his glasses, his dark eyes lock on Sokobin's. Perhaps the interpreter is thinking the same thing Sokobin has suspected from the start. Ting is right; it wouldn't be like the veteran explorer to fall from a ferry boat. Indeed it's absurd. Sokobin remembers his first view of Meyer calmly perched on the open windowsill at the consulate party—his back exposed to the cobblestones several stories below.

Sokobin reaches into his jacket for the Chesterfields, offering one to Ting before lighting up himself. "Mr. Meyer's cabinmate said Mr. Meyer seemed depressed on account of the war in Europe."

"Ai-yah. He says the world does not get better, only more bad. He does not see his family for two, maybe three years because of the German submarines. He says his father is old and sick and he never sees his father again."

Sokobin taps his ashes. Meyer had told him as much at the party. Only now the father had outlived the son. "Do you know why Mr. Meyer was headed to Shanghai?"

"He wants to ship seeds to Washington, DC. He says the Americans here in this building help with this. After we go to Chefoo."

"Chefoo? Up the coast?"

"Yes. Mr. Meyer has a friend there."

"Who?"

"His assistant from before."

The photograph. Sokobin sees the picture in his mind's eye.

The two men on the snowy Peking street. *Together we stand or fall.* It hadn't proved true. In the end, Meyer fell alone. "This man in Chefoo, do you know anything about him?"

"He is Dutch, like Mr. Meyer. Together they walk many places. Mr. Meyer says this man saves his life."

Again Sokobin recalls the story: the border guards who'd nearly shot Meyer and his assistant, thinking them opium smugglers.

"Mr. Meyer and this man work for two or three years together," Ting says. "Mr. Meyer calls this man *broer.*"

"Broer?"

Ting repeats himself, but Sokobin still doesn't understand, and Ting and Lin trade quick phrases. Lin taps his pencil against his notebook. "He says it's Dutch for brother."

Sokobin inhales, holding in the smoke. The fiery plane is suddenly there at the edge of his mind, demanding entry. He pushes it away. "But Mr. Meyer's assistant didn't continue with Meyer. He quit, yes?"

Ting nods. "When his contract is over, he finds different work in Chefoo with the ships. Mr. Meyer is alone then. He says he is sad. He misses this man long time."

"Do you know this man's name?"

Ting tries several times before Lin intervenes. "Johannes."

"Last name?"

Lin shakes his head.

Sokobin draws down the smoke. No doubt he can find it written in one of the Dutch letters back in his room. "Why would Mr. Meyer go to see this man if he quit?"

For a moment Ting says nothing. He looks at his cigarette. "Mr. Meyer says he thinks a lot about this man in Ichang. He tells me he understands why this man leaves, why he quits this work. Finally Mr. Meyer says we must escape. He wants to tell Johannes he is not angry now, that they are still like brothers."

Mr. Lin pauses his pen. Sokobin stares at Ting. For a moment the room feels suspended.

"But Mr. Meyer didn't make it to Chefoo," Sokobin manages.

Ting shakes his head. He seems to be avoiding Sokobin's eye.

"Why didn't he make it to Chefoo?" Sokobin repeats.

Ting looks toward the window, blinking against the light. Sokobin sees his jaw clench. He can sense Ting is holding something back.

"Tell me," Sokobin orders, his hands now on the table. "A man is dead. You were supposed to take care of him."

"Sir," Lin says.

Sokobin pushes back his chair and walks to the window. Frustration curls within him like a tight wave, ready to break. He presses a hand to the glass. Outside the bund is awash in sun. He draws down the smoke, watching the bodies move over the cobblestones. Dozens of people, all strangers. What he wouldn't give for just one of them to be his brother. Behind him, Ting is trying to talk, choking on the words.

"He says Mr. Meyer told him he knew he would die in China before he left the United States," Lin translates, "that nothing can be done for a man like this."

The extreme sort. They keep pushing until they can't.

Sokobin turns from the window. Ting sits slumped in the chair, looking at his lap. His cigarette has gone out on the tray. Tears run down his face. Lin hands him a handkerchief, and Ting wipes his cheeks.

"He says the night before Mr. Meyer went missing, he told Mr. Ting he had a dream."

Sokobin grips the back of his chair. "Please explain that we're not concerned with dreams, only the facts." He knows he sounds like the CG and hates it.

"He says the dream is a fact, and that Mr. Meyer does not talk about dreams very much except this one. In the dream, Meyer told him, his old father came to see him and his brother and sisters in Holland. His dead mother was there and many friends from America. All come to say goodbye to him and wish him well. He says Mr. Meyer told him the dream was a sign."

"A sign of what?"

"Of things to come," Lin says. The words can only be his, for Ting has said nothing.

Sokobin takes a long pull from his cigarette before stubbing it out in the tray. "Thank you for your time, Mr. Ting. We are very sorry for your ordeal and loss." He reaches across the table to shake the young man's hand and tells him about the funeral. "If you would, Mr. Lin, please show Mr. Ting out."

Sokobin sips from his glass, but the water has gone warm. He opens the window, hoping the air will dry the sweat on his neck as he waits for Lin to return, but the day is too humid. Outside the traffic clatters down the bund. He lights another cigarette and watches the smoke drift out toward the street. He remembers what Meyer told him about dreams: how they came at a cost, how they were many-headed beasts and took too long to die. Sokobin didn't understand at the time. Now he does.

Lin closes the door behind him and retakes his seat. He removes his spectacles, rubbing the sides of his nose where the pinchers have left marks. He dabs his forehead, then refolds his handkerchief with excruciating precision.

"Did Ting say anything else?" Sokobin asks.

"Only if I thought you believed him."

"What did you say?"

"I thought so. Do you?"

"Yes."

"All of it?"

Sokobin knows what he should say as vice-consul, the expected thing—only the material facts matter. But he can't, not when he himself has lived so intimately with visions. Invoking them, craving them for any hint of truth they might transmit from another dimension. Who is he to say another man's dream isn't a sign?

For several moments, neither speaks until Sokobin can't bear the weight of the silence anymore. "Meyer jumped. Am I right?" He thought he would feel better once the words were finally said. But he doesn't feel better, only sad and defeated. It's not the ending he wants for the adventurer. Anything but this.

"It's not for me to say, sir."

"Yet you have heard everything, read through Meyer's things."

"I'm just the interpreter, sir. It's not my place to . . ."

Sokobin cuts him off. "But you're not disagreeing?"

"No."

Sokobin paces the narrow channel of floor between the table and the window. "What I don't understand is why not keep going, after he'd finally managed to escape Ichang and walked all that way? And why buy the suspenders and the shoes in Hankow? Why not go onto Chefoo and see this man he calls his brother, Johannes?"

"Only Mr. Meyer can know."

Sokobin reaches for his cigarette resting on the tray, but it's gone out. Ashes clot the dish. "True as that may be, Mr. Lin, it doesn't help me write a report."

"I think what matters most for a man like Mr. Meyer is not how he died but how he lived. You've done all that you can, sir. Not everything has an answer."

"I'm well aware of that," Sokobin tells him, hearing the tension in his voice. He cracks his lighter, sucking down the flame until the cigarette glows again. There's a lot he could tell Mr. Lin about not having answers.

"You look very tired, sir. I do not intend to give offense."

Smoke drips from Sokobin's mouth as he releases a breathy

laugh. "Yes, the Consul has already mentioned it. I didn't sleep well last night."

"I think more than just last night."

Lin is correct, of course. It's been months, but Sokobin doesn't want to go into it. "I'm afraid you haven't seen me at my best, Mr. Lin. Will you be attending the funeral tomorrow?"

"Yes, if you would like me to."

Sokobin nods. "Very well. I'll see you at breakfast then. We can go over to the cemetery together, then take the train back to Nanking. There's an express leaving in the afternoon." He taps his ashes. The thought of tomorrow, of getting from point A to point B, exhausts him. He feels like a car coasting on gasoline fumes, ready to give out at any point.

"Is there anything more I can do, sir?"

The only tasks remaining fall to Sokobin alone: his report to Meyer's supervisor and the Form 192. "No. You are free to go."

Lin stands, settling his gray hat. His spectacles catch the light from the window, reflecting the bund's frantic energy like a moving picture from a strange future. He lifts his attaché and unclasps the buckle. "You forgot this at breakfast," he says, with-drawing the folded newspaper and sliding it across the table.

Sokobin looks down to find the photograph of the smiling American ace. If only Ethan had lasted a few more weeks, he thinks, it might have been his brother's face on the page. He feigns thanks and puts the paper in his case, knowing he won't look at it again.

Lin blinks. "May I ask, sir, why it is so very important for you to know about Mr. Meyer? How he died?"

Sokobin closes his eyes, trying to summon patience, only to find none. "You may not, Mr. Lin. Good day."

Lin shuts the door behind him. Sokobin draws the curtains and sits in the dim room, listening to the traffic outside as he finishes his cigarette. He stares at the Chesterfield's glowing tip.

He can feel the fiery plane and the black sea waiting for him. A plane that may or may not be real flying over a black sea that may or may not exist. A brother who is neither here nor there, neither alive nor dead. And Sokobin's own grief that cannot be grief, but a nameless pain and endless waiting whose only certainty is that it refuses to fade.

CHAPTER 22

SOKOBIN SETS DOWN HIS BRIEFCASE IN THE NARROW mailroom and tugs at the thick wedge of papers in his old box. Most of the pages prove irrelevant—internal memoranda dated from many weeks ago. One by one he drops them into the wastebasket as the new mail clerk hums a tune and rolls his cart down the rows. Sokobin recognizes the melody from Mr. Brundage's repertoire.

Bending at the knees, Sokobin sees a second bunch of items shoved to the back of the slot and reaches in to retrieve the clump. It takes several tries to tease it out, as the contents have become quite compacted. When at last he succeeds, he finds among the crumpled contents several envelopes from the personnel department, all regarding his transfer, all come too late. He flips through the remainder of the stack and stops. The last envelope is pale blue. He stares at the pointed back flap, his face hot. For a moment he is afraid to turn the envelope over in case he is mistaken. But he is not. His name is there, spelled out in sepia ink across the front, the handwriting unmistakably Ethan's. *Soldier's mail*, the stamp reads. *Passed by censor.*

He tilts the envelope toward the window, trying to make out the post date. But the mark is faint, and only the month— March—is visible. Otherwise, the censor's initials cover the day. Sokobin quickly does the math. The envelope would have likely arrived here in Shanghai sometime in April, after he'd left for

Nanking. Anger floods his veins. All this time he's been desperate for another letter, begging God and the universe for one, and it's been here, stuffed into the back of his old mailbox and waiting to get tossed in the bin. And would have, if the Meyer case hadn't brought him to Shanghai by chance. The thought is enough to make Sokobin want to throw a brick through the window.

He holds up the envelope for the humming clerk to see. "How long has this been sitting in my box?" he demands.

The clerk shrugs, barely giving the envelope a passing glance as he pushes his cart forward. "I can't say. There's lots of mail that comes through."

"You will look at me when spoken to and address me as sir."

The clerk's head snaps up. He turns and stares at the envelope, then at the name on the slot. Sokobin can practically see the little wheels turning in his skinny head, the exact panicked moment of recognition as the young man grips the handle of his cart.

"I'm sorry, sir. I didn't realize."

"Didn't realize?" Sokobin demands. "A letter from the front and no one thought to forward this on to me in Nanking? Is that so very difficult to figure out?" Sokobin knows he's being unfair. He doesn't give a damn. It's taking all his reserve not to grab the clerk by the collar and shake some sense into him.

"Sorry, sir, but I've only been here a few weeks. I just put the mail in the box. I'm not supposed to touch it once it goes in."

Sokobin takes up his briefcase and brushes by the young man, not bothering with the rest of the mail. He stands flustered in the corridor, his head full of ants and unsure which way to turn. His guest room is too far. He spies the men's room across the way and pushes open the door, bypassing a pair of clerks standing at the urinals on his way to the furthest stall. He puts his briefcase on the shelf over the toilet and pulls down the lid, staring at the envelope as he waits for the room to clear. Once again, he tries to make out the date beneath the censor's penned initials but can't.

At last, he hears a flush, the sink faucet, footsteps on tile, the thud of the door closing. Save for the hum of the water pipes, the room is silent, and he is alone. He works his thumb under the flap, ripping it slightly. Inside is a single sheet, folded in thirds, the paper the same pale blue as the envelope.

S:

Not much time to write—orders have finally come down. No more waiting. The guys are anxious to see action. To prove themselves. They are young, college boys mostly. I pray for them—they'll learn quick enough. I admit a part of me is hungry for it, too. I can't put the feeling, the rush of it, into words. I only know that when I'm up in the air, I'm who I was meant to be. Purer and closer to God, if that makes any sense.

Your letter reached me this morning. Good thing. Another day and it would have gotten waylaid with the move. So big brother is a Vice-Consul now. Not too shabby for an ugly kid from the old neighborhood. I can just hear ma kvelling about it to all her friends. Papa would be proud. So am I. Always have been. I still plan on coming out to China once this thing is all over, you know. Don't think you can get rid of me so easy. In the meantime, do your best to drum up some pretty girls for me. We're a little short on them here.

Sometimes it seems like this war has gone on forever. Time is funny that way. Whatever happens, know I chose it. Love always,
—E.

A smattering of tiny burn holes dots the bottom of the page; Sokobin runs his finger over them, feeling the burnt edges. He reaches into his jacket and lights a cigarette, watching the tip's orange glow. He wills the fiery plane and black waves away, refusing them entry. Instead he forces himself to remember what he's denied himself these past months: the last time he saw his brother, some seven and a half years ago on the Newark train platform. Ethan and their mother had come to the station to see him off on the train to Seattle. From there, Sokobin would catch the steamer to Hong Kong. He was twenty-six, Ethan twenty-one. As the train came into view, his brother's face twisted. *Don't*, Sokobin told him, as much for Ethan as for himself. He was leaving, the decision made. *It's not like it's forever.* The words had worked. Ethan's face had held firm as he helped Sokobin with his trunk. Sokobin climbed aboard, leaning against the open window. He remembers thinking how small his mother looked below, a tiny black bundle waving a lace handkerchief as she wept. The train jerked forward, and Ethan reached up to grasp Sokobin's hand. He'd held on even as the cars gathered speed, ignoring Sokobin's warnings to let go, running alongside and refusing to drop his grip until the last moment when the platform gave way.

The swing of the bathroom door startles him. He sucks in his breath, listening to the footsteps echo across the tile. They move closer, stopping in front of the next stall. Sokobin recognizes the flashy two-tone shoes. Welch.

The door hinges whine. He sees Theo's trousers drop beneath the partition, his belt buckle hitting the floor. Sokobin refolds the letter and slides the envelope inside his jacket.

"I heard you interviewed Meyer's boy."

It takes a moment for Sokobin to realize Theo is speaking to him. "How did you know it was me?"

"The unpolished shoes, the shitty cigarettes. Do yourself a favor, and don't become a spy. Smoking isn't allowed in here anymore, you know."

"What are you talking about?" Sokobin asks.

"New rules, by order of the Consul. The old man says he can't *abide* the smell. That's why there's a sign posted. Look up, pal."

Sokobin lifts his head. Indeed, the sign is there, plain as day, tacked to the back of the stall door. NO CIGARETTES OR CIGARS.

"I didn't realize," he says.

"Too bad. And here I was thinking you were committing an act of rebellion." Welch's fingers wiggle under the partition. "Be a good VC now and hand me over one, will you?"

"I thought you hated Chesterfields."

"Morbid curiosity."

Sokobin passes him a cigarette and his lighter.

"So, what's the official ruling?" Theo asks.

"On?"

"Meyer, obviously."

"Accident," Sokobin says. As soon as he says it, he knows it's what he'll write on the 192.

"Don't tell me you actually believe that."

Sokobin exhales. The stall traps in the smoke, surrounding him in a bitter cloud. He needs to close the Meyer file, finish it. He can keep digging until the end of time, but it won't change the outcome. Lin is right; not everything has a clear explanation. Sokobin wonders why this simplest of propositions has been so very difficult to accept, why every nerve and muscle in his body continues to fight against it. "That's what's going on my report," he tells Welch. "The service is tomorrow morning, in case you're interested."

"Didn't know him. Besides, I'm not much for funerals."

"You trying to steal my lighter?" Sokobin asks. He doesn't want to be here chattering with Welch a second longer. He needs to get back to his room, lock the door, shut the curtains. He wants to reread his brother's letter until he knows each word by heart.

Welch passes the lighter under the partition. "Christ, how do you smoke these?"

"Habit," Sokobin says. He takes a last drag, then lifts the lid and drops the butt inside. He pulls the flush. "How was your date the other night?"

"Pious."

"Not the one?"

"Are they ever? I take it we won't be going drinking before you head back."

"I've been ordered to take the express tomorrow."

"Tonight then."

"I have to write my reports." It's not entirely true. Sokobin expects to have his paperwork in by the end of business today.

"Ah, the duties of rank," Welch says.

Sokobin reaches for his case. "See you around, Theo."

AT A QUARTER TO SIX, SOKOBIN STANDS IN FRONT OF Miss Greene's station, the Meyer summary report in his hand— the result of transcribing his and Lin's notes into some readable form. He's already returned Meyer's photograph and papers to the basement and left the storage room key on Theo's desk. He'd waited until he knew Theo would be gone for the day. Whatever they once shared expired long ago.

Meanwhile the CG's secretary leans over her typewriter, her fingers working the keys with impressive speed. The resulting sound is not unlike the barrage of a machine gun. "Vice-Consul," she says, offering him the briefest of glances.

"The CG instructed that I give these to you. One is a report for David Fairchild . . ."

"No need to explain, Vice-Consul. I know what they are."

Behind her, the door to the CG's office is shut. Sokobin briefly considers knocking and letting him know the paperwork is in but decides against it. He's not a clerk anymore, in constant need of permission and oversight. Besides, he and the Consul have spoken enough to last both of them for quite some time. Aside from the service tomorrow, his work on Meyer—his first major file as vice-consul—is over. Sokobin never wanted the case in the first place, he reminds himself. Resisted and resented it. And yet now concluded, the moment feels bittersweet. Unfinished. Sokobin taps the form, suddenly reluctant to part with it.

"Where should I . . ."

"With all the rest," she says, nodding toward the heavy pile in her inbox. "Don't worry, I'll get to them as soon as I'm done with this." Her eyes dart back and forth between a short stack of handwritten notes at her side and the words emerging from the clacking keys.

Sokobin lowers the file into the wire basket—the past exhausting days reduced to the summary report and the single-sheet Form 192, which rests on top. His eyes travel to the bottom of the page. *Remarks: Mr. Meyer had been ill for quite some time and seemed depressed on the day he drowned.* He knows the CG won't like it, the potential implications. But this is Sokobin's case, his call. And it's as close to the truth as they'll ever get.

The office door swings open, and the Consul's gleaming silver hair pokes out. "I need the write-up for the exporters," he calls to his secretary. "I leave in twenty."

"Coming now, sir."

"What are you doing here?" the Consul asks, noticing Sokobin. His tone isn't particularly hostile, just harried.

"The vice-consul was just submitting the Meyer reports," Miss Greene says and pretends to shoo Sokobin away with her hand.

"Good," the Consul says with a nod. "And the driver for tonight?"

"Already out front," Miss Greene tells him.

Sokobin turns into the corridor and steps aside to let a pair of secretaries pass. Heading down the stairs, he pauses in the lobby where he takes out his pocket watch. He has a little over an hour before the shops close.

CHAPTER 23

Wednesday, June 11

SOKOBIN AND LIN PAUSE AT THE SPIKED IRON FENCE surrounding the Public Garden. Neither need read the sign posted on the pillared entrance to know the park is in fact not public. Despite its name, the garden is exclusively for Westerners; Lin may walk on its paths only as Sokobin's guest.

"Please," Sokobin says, gesturing him forward.

With Meyer's funeral over and another hour before the express departs, they find themselves with what they have not had these past days—a little time to kill. The small outcrop sits between the American and British sectors, at the convergence of Soochow Creek and Huangpu River. Trees line the garden's edge, their boughs weighted with green. A young girl dressed in summer whites rolls a hoop by them as her stiff-backed governess attempts to keep up. Otherwise, the park holds only a pair of suited men whose walking sticks stab the pebbled path with every step. Sokobin and Lin stroll the perimeter in near silence, save for the crunching of the gravel underfoot. Only a few days ago, Sokobin would have felt the need to fill the empty spaces, but no longer. Indeed, it comes as a relief to not be trotting out an approved repertoire of carefully measured phrases. Lin's reserve renders silence as potent, if not more so, than conversation.

Twice they stop to admire a rare blossom. No doubt Meyer would have been able to identify the flowers, perhaps even name where they originally grew wild. If there is anything they can do to honor the explorer's memory today, Sokobin thinks, it is simply this—to walk and see what beautiful things sprout from the dirt. Meyer's funeral proved exactly as the CG intended, a quiet perfunctory affair, with the hymn, "In the Garden," chosen especially for the explorer. Indeed the service's only remarkable moment came when Ting, who had otherwise stood still and silent, came forward to place a small statue on the coffin lid just before the ropes were lowered. Miraculously, the tiny idol held its spot until the bier reached its final ground, Sokobin's father's tallit and yarmulke with it, for all eternity. To his surprise, Sokobin was no longer angry about having given the precious things away. It didn't matter that Meyer wasn't a Jew. Sokobin's own faith remained. What he had felt while standing over the dead man's body upriver—reverence, compassion, even kinship—these had been real.

Sokobin and Lin leave the paths and make their way over the grass toward the shade of the empty bandstand. They stop at one of the benches overlooking the water. A small plaque mounted to the seat back warns that *amahs* caring for children are expressly prohibited from occupying the bench during performances. Sokobin never noticed the plaque before, or perhaps didn't care to. Now it just strikes him as petty and absurd.

They sit side by side. Lin pulls a small fan from his attaché and begins to cool himself. The faint wave of air brushes against Sokobin's damp neck. He considers rooting out his handkerchief but knows there is no point. It is hot; summer has arrived. There will be no relief from it for months.

He withdraws a fresh package of Chesterfields from his jacket and runs his nail under the flap. Through a veil of smoke, he watches as dozens of slim river sampans glide over the river's turbid currents. Across the way, a massive transatlantic steamer is docked along the British quay. Strings of bright, triangular flags snap between the red stacks. In only eight days, Meredith will board such a ship and sail for the States. He wonders when, if ever, Shanghai will cease to be a minefield of her memory. Perhaps after she is gone, he thinks. But not yet. He is still missing the feel of her skin, the intoxicating weight of her body against his.

"The little statue Mr. Ting put on Meyer's coffin," he says, in an attempt to distract himself.

Lin blinks. "Tin Hau, sir. Goddess of Heaven and the sea. Also of fisherman, sailors, wanderers, immigrants." He pauses his fan. "And actors and prostitutes."

Sokobin raises an eyebrow. "Interesting company."

"Yes," Lin says. "She watches over those with no fixed place in this world."

Sokobin taps his ashes; he suspects Lin would put him in that undefined category as well. "So not all falling leaves return to their roots."

"No, not all. Especially now."

Sokobin detects sadness in the interpreter's voice. Perhaps Lin is thinking of his brother in France. There are many, many questions Sokobin would like to ask the interpreter about his upbringing and time in England, but senses he hasn't yet earned the right to ask them. He and Lin are no longer strangers, but neither is Sokobin certain that the events of the last days, however intense, have made them friends. He would like to think so. Perhaps, he decides, this is what soldiers in the field feel for one another. Camaraderie, the connection not born of choice but necessity and experience.

"I could not have closed Meyer's file without your help," Sokobin offers.

"I don't think so either, sir."

Sokobin emits a small laugh, coughing on the air.

"It is not so good for you to smoke so many cigarettes, sir."

"I know. But for now, I feel I must." He holds up the package. "My brother's brand."

"The flyer."

"Yes." He taps his ashes into the grass, hesitating. "I found a letter from him in my mail slot yesterday."

"Here at the consulate?"

"Yes. It was just sitting there, stuffed in with a bunch of old papers. I'm guessing it arrived right after I transferred to Nanking. All these weeks and no one thought to forward it to me." The strain in his voice from yesterday is still there. Anger. "It almost went in the trash. If not for the Meyer case bringing me here, it would have."

"But you have it now."

"Yes." The blue envelope waits in the inside breast pocket of Sokobin's jacket. He can feel its edges through the thin lining, pressing against his beating chest. "And your own brother," Sokobin asks, attempting to steady his voice. "Do you think you'll be able to convince him to return home to China after the war?"

Lin shakes his head. His smile is brief, more resigned than content. "I have never been able to convince my brother of anything."

Sokobin nods. Ethan's last line sounds in his head. *Whatever happens, know I chose it.* "Even so, you write your brother every week, yes?"

"Yes. My mother has asked for this."

"You are a dutiful son, Mr. Lin."

"We should all be dutiful sons, Vice-Consul."

Sokobin thinks of his mother in the cramped row house in Newark, of all the letters he owes her. He's been avoiding them, so afraid that his doubt over Ethan would bleed through the words. But Lin, his unflappable dignity, makes Sokobin want to be a better son. A better man.

"I'm afraid I wasn't entirely honest with you when we spoke at the station house in Ti-Kang."

Lin stops his fan. "I don't understand, sir."

Sokobin exhales, keenly aware of the interpreter's stare but unable to meet it. "My brother was listed as missing in action three months ago. Three months and six days to be exact."

"Shot down in battle?"

"No, before. It was a night mission, I think. Reconnaissance in preparation for the fighting to come. I don't know the details. They don't tell you these things. I don't think they know. His plane was never found." He stops, trying to think of what he's left out of the story. It seems like the explanation should take longer, but there's nothing more to add. The sheer brevity of the facts is unbearable.

"I am deeply sorry, sir. Waiting like this, it must be very difficult."

"Yes." Sokobin feels himself wince. "I'm sorry I wasn't more forthcoming. I suppose I still don't know what to say, how to explain." He keeps his eyes fixed on the water, on the boats gliding downriver. The look on Lin's face, what he must be thinking—the only reasonable thing someone could conclude after so long—Sokobin would find it all intolerable.

"And what do you believe, sir?"

"I don't know anymore. I only know what I should believe, what a good brother *would* believe. Against all odds. Never give up. It's what we were taught as children. The problem is that holding out is so very exhausting." Sokobin inhales, containing the smoke. "All this time, I thought I'd somehow know, that I'd feel it if he were really gone. But that's absurd, nothing but superstition."

"A thing is only superstition, sir, if you do not believe in it."

Sokobin turns, meeting Lin's stare. His dark eyes blink from behind his spectacles.

"He was better than me, Mr. Lin. Braver." The words are out before Sokobin has even thought to say them. And yet, he needs to confess them, to relieve himself of their terrible truth. And if not to Mr. Lin, with his own brother in France, then to whom? "Do you understand?"

"Yes," Lin says quietly.

They sit for a moment, neither speaking. A breeze passes, scattering the smoke from Sokobin's cigarette.

"This letter, in your mail slot," Lin says, pausing his fan. "You said if you had not come to Shanghai, you would not have found it."

"That's right, only by chance of the Meyer file. It makes me furious to think it."

"Perhaps it was not chance, sir. Perhaps you were meant to come to Shanghai. Not only for Mr. Meyer's case but to find this letter. Perhaps it is a sign."

Sokobin's instinct is to disagree. Only a week ago, he surely would have, immediately dismissing any such notion. But given the events of the last days, he can't anymore.

"A sign of what?" he asks.

"That you still have reason to hope."

Sokobin closes his eyes. His throat tightens and for a moment, he must turn away. If Lin notices, he says nothing. Sokobin finds his handkerchief, pretending to dab at the sweat on his cheeks. How long they sit like this, Sokobin can't say. Eventually a faint metallic snap brings him to. Lin is checking his pocket watch.

"The station, sir." he says.

"Just give me a minute," Sokobin tells him.

He stares across the water, at the long curve of the bund, its buildings rising like temples toward the sky, and remembers the first time he ever saw Manhattan from a ferry on the Hudson. How infinite the city had seemed to him then, so full of promise and possibility. He'd felt the same rush when he'd arrived in Shanghai. They were magnificent cities, both of them. Charged and teeming. Electric. Each has shaped him; pushed him forward. And while he likes the idea that he might visit from time to time, he also knows that he doesn't belong in either place anymore.

"Sir?"

"You know you don't need to call me that, at least when there's no one else around," Sokobin says as he rises from the bench and returns his rumpled handkerchief to his pocket. "All the pretense and protocol, I don't go in for it." He holds out his hand. "Between us, Sam."

Lin hesitates, then stands and grasps Sokobin's fingers. "Bao. Between us."

Sokobin cocks his head. A short laugh escapes him. "Bao, as in dumpling?"

"That and also precious treasure."

Sokobin blinks. "Indeed." He drops his cigarette into the grass, crushing it with his shoe and resettles his hat against the glare. In his briefcase are two Chinese first-class tickets. "Enough then. Let's go."

CHAPTER 24

Thursday, June 12

MISS PETRIE IS THE FIRST OF HIS STAFF TO ARRIVE AT ten to nine.

"Good morning, sir," she says, peeking her head into his office. Sokobin is already at his desk, attending to all the correspondence he's let lapse. "I expect you'll be wanting a cool pot?"

"Yes, please."

Mr. Brundage soon follows. "Good to have you back, sir."

"Any attacks on foreigners in the last two days?"

"None reported, sir. But some cables came in yesterday that I think you should see."

Sokobin has the senior clerk pull up a chair next to his desk, and they discuss the latest communiqués—most pressingly, the ongoing National Assembly elections in Peking. Brundage deftly presents the latest intelligence; five provinces and counting, all Southern and under military control, are boycotting. After a week of thinking of Meyer, the news, however tricky, comes as a relief. Sokobin feels a slight charge of the like he used to in Shanghai when the office was abuzz with some sudden development. Politics and diplomacy. His first loves. He'd almost forgotten them.

The bell sounds over the front door. A grin spreads across Mr. Brundage's face, and he gives a slight nod with his chin. Sokobin turns in his seat, lowering the stack of cables. It takes a moment to recognize the young man at the threshold. "Is that you, Mr. Windham?"

"Hard to know, sir, when we've never seen his face," Mr. Brundage teases.

Windham laughs, shoving his hands into his pockets, and for once, his hair doesn't fall into his eyes. His strawberry locks have been cropped and cleanly parted to the side, revealing a wide brow dotted with freckles. The strands gleam with oil. The effect would be distinguished if the young man weren't as red as a beet.

Sokobin finishes up with Mr. Brundage. Windham soon follows with the mail.

"For you, sir," he says, handing over the stack. "Also, this came yesterday afternoon." He lays down a small parcel tied with string. Sokobin glances at the return address. Chase.

"I imagine you were happy to see Shanghai again, aside from the business with Meyer, of course," Windham says. "I only know it to pass through myself, but Mr. Brundage says a fellow can get himself into trouble there pretty fast."

"Plenty do, Mr. Windham," Sokobin says, thinking of Welch. He looks up from sorting the envelopes—one pile for himself, the other for Mr. Brundage. "I hope you're not looking for trouble?"

Windham shakes his head. "Oh no, sir. I just meant you must miss it."

"Sometimes." Among the envelopes Sokobin finds yet another invitation from the college. Lin's alma mater. He drops it into his pile. "Though to be fair, I'm not sure I've given Nanking much of a chance to work her charms."

"Right. Before I sailed, my mother told me that home was where we make it. I try to keep it in mind, sir, whenever it feels like things get too far away." Windham's fingers trace the scrimshaw at the edge of the desk. "Handsome piece," he says, tapping the paperweight.

"My old college professor gave me that when I was your age. A graduation gift."

"Sentimental then."

Sokobin has never been one to consider himself sentimental, but of course, there's no other explanation for having carried the scrimshaw across an ocean. He holds out a stack of envelopes. "For Mr. Brundage, if you would—and one other thing. The list of approved interpreters. From now on, Mr. Lin is to be the office's first choice."

"Will do, sir," the clerk says and tucks the letters under his arm.

Sokobin senses the clerk lingering, just as he himself used to do after Everton's lectures, waiting his turn to ask a question in the hopes of gaining a spot of the old man's attention.

"I thought a lot about what you said, about serving my country here. It did make me feel better." The clerk's lips spread into a knowing smile.

"What is so funny, Mr. Windham?"

"I'm just trying to imagine it, sir."

"What?"

"You my age, sir."

Sokobin gives him a wave. "Off with you."

Sokobin takes a pair of scissors from the slim drawer of his desk and snips the string on the package from Chase. Beneath the brown parcel paper is a small black velvet box and a hand-written card.

Soko-
I know you said you didn't want one, but I choose not to
believe you. Like it or not, you'll need to get used to looking
the part, Vice-Consul. No company goods here either, but from
the best on offer in Wuhu. Forgive the monogramming; you
know I can't help myself.
Your pal,
-Arthur

Sokobin opens the box. Tucked inside is a gleaming silver cigarette case with his initials engraved across the front. He lifts the cover and reads the inscription inside:

Shield and shelter us
beneath the shadow of Your wings.
—In gratitude & friendship, AWC

He and Ethan used to whisper the words each night before going to sleep. How Arthur has come to know the prayer, Sokobin can't say, only that the effort deeply touches him. He takes the Chesterfields from his pocket, running his fingers over the package's waterproofed coating, then transfers the cigarettes, neatly lining them behind the bands. The case closes with a satisfying snap. He holds the warm metal in his palm and decides he rather likes the weight of it after all, its solidity and heft. And the design—striking but simple with nothing to detract from the lines. Arthur knows his tastes well.

Miss Petrie appears with her tray and sets it on his desk. She pours him out a cup.

"There's a matter I'm hoping you might help me with," Sokobin tells her.

"Typing?"

"No, nothing like that." He sips. "I was thinking it's time I moved out of my rooms and into something more," he pauses, "permanent."

"You mean a house, sir?"

"Exactly. Since you're a local, I thought you might know of something."

"What sort of house?"

He hesitates. He only settled on the idea while riding the express with Lin. The only house he's ever lived in was his parents'; since then, it's all been rented rooms. Even if it could be found, he doesn't want anything as sleek and new as Chase's villa. He'd rather something old enough to have earned its cracks. Someplace that's withstood storm and flood and come out the other side.

"Nothing fancy. Or too large," he tells her. "With a study, if possible. And a little garden." He eyes the cigarette case from Arthur. "And a spare bedroom for guests. Is that all too much?"

"No, sir. As I matter of fact, I do know of such a place—a cottage for let near the university. I was friends with the family that used to rent it. They've returned to the States now, and it's sat empty a while. Of course, the furnishings are still there. Quite charming, if you can look past the dust cloths. I could arrange for you to see it, if you'd like."

"I would, very much so."

"There's only one thing about the house, sir."

"Please don't tell me it's haunted."

She smiles. "No, sir. It's just that it's owned by the college. So, if you took it, you'd need to attend a lecture or tea talk every once in a while. Just for the sake of keeping up appearances. It might do you good to mingle, Vice-Consul. You never know who you might meet."

She only means to be encouraging, he knows, but the words pinch his heart and remind him of who he won't be meeting there. Meredith. The self-doubt, the questions of what might have been. The certainty of his mistake. He suspects they'll remain with him a very long time.

"Thank you, Miss Petrie."

She takes up the tray, tucking it under her arm like a file. It's then that he notices the small brass pin on her lapel. A circle of stamped blue stars surrounds the words *Votes for Women*. That Miss Petrie, of all people, should be wearing it, takes Sokobin by surprise. The personnel manual expressly forbids such displays—a rule he's certain the secretary knows from her years of service.

"Miss Petrie, you are wearing a political pin."

She turns back, her jaw tight. "Yes, sir, I am."

"I assume you're aware of the regulations against wearing this kind of thing."

"I am, sir. With all due respect, if they were just, I wouldn't need to break them."

There is no fear or defensiveness in her voice, only certainty. And truth, Sokobin thinks. If the CG were here, he'd insist she remove the pin at once, likely even write her up for it. But then the CG isn't here. And Nanking isn't the Consul's office. It's Sokobin's, and it's high time he owned that fact.

"Very well, then. Perhaps we can sort out the details about the cottage tomorrow, once I'm caught up?"

"Of course, sir." She continues to hold his stare. "You're not going to write me up?"

"Not unless you'd like me to."

"In that case, I'd rather you not." Her knotted hair quivers as she taps across the floorboards. She pauses at the door, reaching for the knob. "Closed, sir?"

Sokobin sees Mr. Windham rooting about in the file cabinet in the front room, Mr. Brundage penning letters at his desk. "Open for now," he says. "Better to get the air crossing through."

Her lips broaden, and for an odd moment, Sokobin would swear they'd known one another for years. "Very good, Vice-Consul. I forgot to say it before, but welcome home."

THAT EVENING, AFTER THE OTHERS HAVE LEFT, HE takes the blue envelope from his jacket pocket and places it atop the others in the bottom drawer of his desk. His fingers linger, not wanting to let go, still very much aware of how close he'd come to not finding the fourth letter at all. Lin could be right, and Sokobin was meant to find it as a sign. Or maybe God above saw fit to reward a good work after all. What is certain is that if Meyer's file hadn't landed on Sokobin's desk, Ethan's letter wouldn't have reached it either. But it had and now the letter was here, within Sokobin's reach—exactly where his brother had intended it to be.

He shuts the drawer. Turning from his desk, he splits the curtains and lifts the window, letting in the damp air. He opens the new silver case from Arthur and lights a Chesterfield. Sampans jostle on the currents as the lantern men come down the bund, lifting their poles and hanging lamps against the coming night. He senses the fiery plane and dark sea waiting. He knows they won't fade away; his mind can't release them, not until he knows, one way or another. Perhaps not even then. The plane and sea have become a part of him—the very ghosts Everton warned of and Meyer's many-headed beasts. Sokobin doesn't know how to live with or without them, only that he must. The chances, he reminds himself for the ten thousandth time. To hell with the chances. He refuses to give his brother up to the dead. Ethan may still be out there, breathing and alive. In Sokobin's heart, he is.

Sunset slants through the open window, making rippled waves of the smoke from his cigarette. He could easily sit here for hours as he's done these past months, watching the river and lapsing into oblivion. He's wasted more time at this than he'd care to admit. No more.

He pockets the case from Arthur and shuts the window. From his briefcase, he removes his brother's photograph, now sheathed in glass and a handsome lacquered frame purchased the evening before in Shanghai. He sets the picture next to the scrimshaw paperweight. Fear, uncertainty, regret, Sokobin thinks as he takes in his brother's figure, those are the rub. Not letting them wear you down, not surrendering to doubt. Sokobin sees none of them in his brother's eyes. The major had asked for volunteers, and Ethan had raised his hand, unhesitant and understanding the risks. *Whatever happens, know I chose it.* Sokobin doesn't know why seeing those words in his brother's hand should bring a measure of relief. Or why they now bolster him. But they do. Perhaps superstition is just another word for faith, he thinks. Faith for hope. Hope for love.

He lifts his jacket from the chair and slips the silver case into the pocket, then reaches for his attaché. It's late and he's hungry.

AFTERWORD

I will become famous. Just wait a century or two.
—Frank Meyer in a letter to his family, 1906

I BECAME ENTRANCED WITH FRANK MEYER YEARS AGO, after coming across some of his expedition photographs. I wondered, then obsessed—for much longer than I should have—over what sort of person would permanently uproot himself to sail over oceans, thrusting himself into difficult and, at times, outright hostile territory and forsaking all stable relationships, familial and romantic, in the pursuit of plants and human progress. No doubt, the aspiring writer in me wished for some of this unwavering dedication to my own creative work.

Gradually I came to see Meyer's passion for exploration not as a matter of desire or even vocation, but a thorny, insatiable compulsion and means of self-survival against chronic bouts of depression. No matter how hard I tried, however, I could not make those first attempts at a novel work. Meyer's expeditions were too monumental, his tasks too unrelenting in their details. I also realized a fatal flaw that should have been obvious early on: Meyer did indeed go missing from a ferry on the Yangtze River and was found dead nine days later.

This novel draws heavily from the report written in June 1918 by the actual American vice-consul Samuel Sokobin, then stationed in Nanking and who was dispatched upriver to find the missing man. The real Sokobin never actually spoke with Meyer but felt he could reasonably identify the remains as he'd seen the explorer at a consulate event. Sokobin's colleagues in

Shanghai did, in fact, lead him to initially believe that Meyer was Jewish.

The details chronicled in Sokobin's report formed the basis for this novel's timeline, the facts around Meyer's disappearance, and its subsequent investigation. A few dates and days of the week have been fudged for narrative purposes, but the essentials of the original case are largely unaltered here. Vice-Consul Sokobin did indeed travel upriver to Wuhu with an interpreter (name lost to history), where they stayed at the house of a Standard Oil executive. While there, Sokobin's interpreter did interview the servants, thereby uncovering critical information about a white man's body having been towed to shore by a fisherman. Without this clue, it is doubtful Meyer's remains would have ever been found farther upriver in the town of Ti-Kang, where they had been buried in an unmarked grave on a hill. Likewise, the fisherman who brought the body ashore and who had been given Meyer's suspenders and shoes as part of his compensation was interviewed in the station house, with the items Sokobin requisitioned as necessary for additional confirmation of the body's identity.

As with the major aspects of Sokobin's investigation, the novel remains largely true to the factual details of Meyer's life, including those about his childhood, values and beliefs, assistants and colleagues, and expeditions. That said, I am a fiction writer, not a historian, nor can Sokobin's original investigative summary substitute for a novel. This book is a work of imagination and as such, I have invented freely, most notably in the fictionalized character of Samuel Sokobin—who I suspect bears little, if any, resemblance to the man who actually lived. Sokobin's relationship to his interpreter, including the character of Mr. Lin himself, as well all those in Sokobin's personal life— brother, parents, friends, and romantic interest—are wholly invented, as is Sokobin's strained relationship to his own faith.

While some details of the American consulate building and the city of Shanghai are drawn from photographs of the era, every character in the Nanking and Shanghai consulate offices hails entirely from my own head.

No doubt some readers will curse my name for not offering a definitive answer as to how Meyer met his end. Nevertheless I felt it important to remain true to the historical facts, including this ambiguity, and one that came to define this narrative. While this novel found its start in the investigation of the explorer's fate, its heart grew to lie elsewhere—in the fragile, imperfect yet resilient spirit prompted by the mystery's ongoing uncertainty. In modern psychology, this lack of clarity or closure is known as *ambiguous loss*, a term I came to deeply appreciate during the writing of this book. What began as an historically-inspired account of a real-life missing man gradually became the invented story of its investigator, Samuel Sokobin—his self-reckoning of past choices and faith, his thorny relationships, his unexpected connection to his interpreter Mr. Lin, and above all, his unyielding, unresolved grief about his missing younger brother, a fighter pilot in the war.

As humans, each with our own stories, millions of us live, even thrive, despite such ambiguous losses every day. "Much of life's challenges are not problems that we solve," the brilliant psychotherapist Esther Perel recently noted. "They are paradoxes that we manage." The notion that in the face of not receiving explanations to the questions we most desperately want answered, we must find a way to cultivate acceptance and continue to grow is ultimately what inspired me to complete *Foreign Seed*.

Allison Alsup

New Orleans, October 2023

ACKNOWLEDGMENTS

THIS NOVEL WOULD NEVER HAVE COME TO BE WITHOUT the diligent research efforts of the late writer and historian Isabel Shipley Cunningham. Her biography *Frank N. Meyer: Plant Hunter In Asia* (Iowa State University Press, 1984) formed the basis of my understanding of Meyer's exceptional character and his four expeditions to China. Cunningham's detailed notes regarding her sources led me to experience firsthand many primary documents concerning Meyer at the National Archives, including photographs, letters, Meyer's "resignation" envelopes, as well as the original Form 192 signed by Vice-Consul Samuel Sokobin and the summary of his search for Meyer, which provided the structure for this novel's timeline and investigative developments.

Other key material about Meyer's work at Foreign Seed and Plant Introduction can be found at the National Agricultural Library in Beltsville, Maryland. Among the library's online collections are photographs taken by Meyer during his final expedition to China as well as letters between the explorer and his supervisor David Fairchild. Additional expedition photographs by Meyer can be found via Harvard's Arnold Arboretum online library; photo archives from the National Oceanic and Atmospheric Administration provided much needed images of pre-Communist China. Mark O'Neill's *The Chinese Labour Corps* served as my primary reference for

China's unsung contribution to the Allied victory in World War One.

The very first lines that would eventually become this novel were written in the snowy Wyoming wilds while on a generous artist residency awarded by the Jentel Foundation. I remain obliged to the spirited Jentel staff and to the five exceptional women who shared that month with me and whose dedication to their craft spurred my own: Lynette Lombard, Molly Sawyer, Nancy E. Floyd, Katerie Gladdys, and Melissa Burch. Thanks also to Adrienne Brodeur whose early enthusiasm many years ago for a budding story about a botanical explorer in China encouraged me to see value in the project, and to the Aspen Writers' Foundation's awarding of a residency during which I developed material about Meyer; short fiction inspired by the explorer's life later appeared in *Alaska Quarterly Review* and *The Potomac Review*. Supreme gratitude to my agent Gordon Warnock of Fuse Literary for his patient determination in finding a home for a debut novel during the trying pandemic publishing market, and to Amanda Chiu Krohn and the editorial and marketing staff at Turner Publishing for embracing a historical *almost* mystery, and for the tremendous effort required to bring a manuscript to publication.

First novels often appear many years after endeavoring to become decent at one's craft; as a result, the line of folks who helped a writer on her way often stretches around the block. I am both overwhelmed and humbled at recognizing the scores who, in one way or another, helped me reach this point, and I will no doubt leave out many who belong on this list. Gratitude to my business partner and anchor, the gifted poet Jessica Kinnison and all those associated with the New Orleans Writers Workshop—students, clients, writers, and friends all at once—who in sharing their stories, vastly improved my own, including Priya Sathyanarayan, Brenda Horrigan, Christine Junge, Jordan Fos, Kayla Min

Andrews, Michelle Dumont, and Nora Wetzel as well as cherished family friends and writers Laura Snyder and Joe Garrett. I am indebted to Danny and Sharon Cupit for the generous use of their lovely lake house—a writer's dream—where I edited many times. Special thanks to Louis Gertler who, in addition to being a superlative human being, kindly offered invaluable input about Jewish observances (any oversights are mine alone) and to Alan Brickman who, after I broke my wrist and could not type edits to the accepted manuscript, spent many hours alongside me as I dictated changes. Elisa Speranza, your talents, drive and generosity are as long as the mighty Mississippi—thank you.

Heartfelt gratitude to the Key West Literary Seminar for awarding me a scholarship to attend Richard Russo's fiction workshop, a week that proved pivotal for this novel. To my fellow workshop members there: Gerald Goldin, Julie Reiser, Diane Hinton Perry, Nancy Freund Fraser, Claire Lombardo, Andy Brilliant, Zach Halpern, Michael Hamlin, Judy Mandel, Meg "Leigh" Shaffer, Claire Gélinas—several of whom have gone on to publish books, your support of my first chapter could not have come at a more critical time. Julie, special thanks for your continued friendship and wicked humor, and above all, thanks to Rick Russo himself.

The writing life affords many, many chances to quit. The continued nudges of family and friends—too numerous to entirely name here but always keenly felt—were essential that I did not. Tina Boudreaux, Elizabeth Pearce, Lee Domingue, Andrew Tully, David Dunham, Drea DelliGatti, Robin Horton, Nicole Eiden, Jon "Angus" Deal, Joe Mistrot and Diana Vaughan-Nielsen—thank you for seeing me through tough times with encouragement, wisdom, and as necessary, stiff cocktails. Rose Tomey, friend *par excellence*, you are unparalleled. To my parents, Aunt Maggie and Uncle Don, my brother John and his wife Emily, cousin Leah—your longtime support of my writing, even when a questionable endeavor, has meant more than you know. And lastly to my tiny beloved Frieda, who showed up for the work day after day, and whose quiet presence under the corner chair made the solitary task of writing feel less so, you are missed.

ABOUT THE AUTHOR

ALLISON ALSUP'S WRITING HAS WON MULTIPLE CON-
tests and recognitions, including the *2014 O. Henry Prize Stories*,
Best Food Writing 2015, and the UK's 2018 Manchester Fiction
Prize shortlist. She is the co-founder of the non-profit New Orleans Writers Workshop, where, in addition to teaching, Allison
mentors fellow writers one on one to develop their stories.

Foreign Seed is her first novel.